SHANGHAI SCARLET

Also by Margaret Blair: *Gudao, Lone Islet, The War Years in Shanghai, a childhood memoir*

SHANGHAI
SCARLET

All good wishes

Margaret Blair

MARGARET BLAIR

Order this book online at www.trafford.com
or email orders@trafford.com

Most Trafford titles are also available at major online book retailers.

Cover design by Margaret Blair, photograph from Sea Bird Publishing, Japanese military images
Maps and Photographs by Gary Moon

1. Old Shanghai   2. 1930s   3. adventure, romance, suspense   4. Chinese Holocaust
5. Rape of Nanking   6. Japan   7. China

Printed in the United States of America.

ISBN: 978-1-4669-1470-4 (sc)
ISBN: 978-1-4669-1471-1 (hc)
ISBN: 978-1-4669-1472-8 (e)

Library of Congress Control Number: 2012902711

Trafford rev. 02/23/2012

Trafford
PUBLISHING®   www.trafford.com

North America & international
toll-free: 1 888 232 4444 (USA & Canada)
phone: 250 383 6864 ♦ fax: 812 355 4082

For RSB
and
In Memory of China's Modernist Authors:
their Talent and Achievement, their Dreams and their Sorrows

Praise for *Shanghai Scarlet*

. . . a moving and significant historical novel, with an effective ending. It is written in a style that fits well into the mood and feel of 1930s and 1940s Shanghai.

Poshek Fu, professor of history, University of Illinois

Margaret Blair's impressive research brings pre-revolutionary Shanghai to life. After reading *Shanghai Scarlet,* I felt that I knew Mu Shiying and Qiu Peipei, and had a real sense of the now-vanished Shanghai in which they had once lived.

Meg Taylor, Editor

What a leap Margaret Blair has taken from her staggering memoir of her young life as a prisoner of the Japanese to the dazzling novel, *Shanghai Scarlet* . . . . the poignant love story stayed in my mind long after I had turned the last page.

Betty Jane Wylie, **CM,** award-winning author and past chair of the Writers' Union of Canada

Contents

N.B. There are two narrators, Mu Shiying and Qiu Peipei. Mu's voice is modeled on translations into English of his work. To indicate where Mu begins, there is a rosebud. Each of his narrations ends with an asterisk.

Author's Note

Most historical fiction is based on real people who have caught the imagination of the author. With few exceptions, namely the original and later families of Qiu Peipei, and the population of the Alleyway of Prosperity and Benevolence, the characters in *Shanghai Scarlet*, have the names of real people whose actions are restricted by what actually happened.

In the literature, Qiu Peipei is always referred to as merely a dance hall hostess. However, I cannot imagine her being an unsophisticated woman and so have portrayed her as something more.

The historians I read have not chronicled Qiu Peipei's life and death beyond her name, occupation, birthplace and return to Hong Kong. I have had a blank slate to fill. Perhaps because she is so elusive, Qiu Peipei has fired my imagination to the point where she has become a major presence in this story, and its main narrator.

Set in China's roaring 1920s and turbulent 1930s, *Shanghai Scarlet* provides a cameo of what has happened, and still happens generally, to creative intellectuals and their families in times of political turbulence. Mu's fervent desire to be free to write as he pleased was part of a universal longing for freedom. The expression of this desire is prominent in the world today (2012).

Notes

1. "The Japanese Sandman" (tune)—is available on Youtube in several recordings, including one made in 1920 by Nora Bayes (very clear words) and the Paul Whiteman one mentioned in this book. Also, try Amazon.com. I found the tune on a CD by *Mandy Patinkin Kidults* by Nonesuch Records, 2001, a Warner Music Group Company.

2. Alexander Vertinsky—for further information on the great Russian entertainer, and to hear "Matrosi" and other songs sung by Alexander Vertinsky himself, go to: www.crocodile.org/vertinsky.html. A CD of his singing is occasionally on sale on the internet.

3. For songs of the 1920s and 1930s, at a reasonable price, see Ella Fitzgerald CDs as follows: *The Very Best of the Song Books* which contains the song: "Where or When", and *Ella Fitzgerald Sings Irving Berlin*, which contains the songs, "Always" and "How Deep Is The Ocean? (How High is The Sky?)" An excellent source of pipa music is the CD, *Chinese Traditional Pipa Music*, interpreted by Liu Fang and available on Amazon.

4. For atmosphere and sounds of Shanghai in the 1920s and 1930s see the following DVDs: *The White Countess,* (the last Merchant Ivory film) and *Lust, Caution,* made from a story by the quintessential Shanghai writer, Eileen Chang (X rated).

The nostalgic contemporary music and portrayal of noisy street scenes and contemporary people such as Alexander Vertinsky (Vertinsky is depicted in *The White Countess*) are worth the effort of obtaining these DVDs.

5. Shanghai had its own way of doing things and even its own way of writing things down. Instead of rue, a French Concession address was capitalized as Rue, and instead of *jai alai*, Shanghai used *hai alai*. Extraterritoriality (or extrality) gave expatriates (or expats) the right to live in Shanghai under the laws of their own country. This not only protected foreigners, but also conformed to the Chinese habit of delegating responsibility, in this case for foreign groups, to their own country.

6. For poetry of Yu Hsuan-chi see: David Hinton, trans., and ed., *Classical Chinese Poetry, An Anthology,* Farrar, Strauss and Giroux, New York

7. Names used are a mix of Cantonese and Wade-Giles used at the time.

8. See Wikipedia listing of Mu Shiying for his photo.

Foreword

This work is composed from the notes made by Mu Shiying and Qiu Peipei for an autobiography Mu Shiying would write at the end of a long and successful literary career. I have not presumed to edit them. To indicate where Mu begins, there is a rosebud. Each of his narrations ends with an asterisk.

In the treatment of written materials at my disposal, I trust I have shown the love and respect I truly feel for the people named and indeed all the people in Shanghai and in other places in China during the current dark and extraordinary period in our history.
A.V.
Shanghai, China 1942

SHANGHAI
January 1934

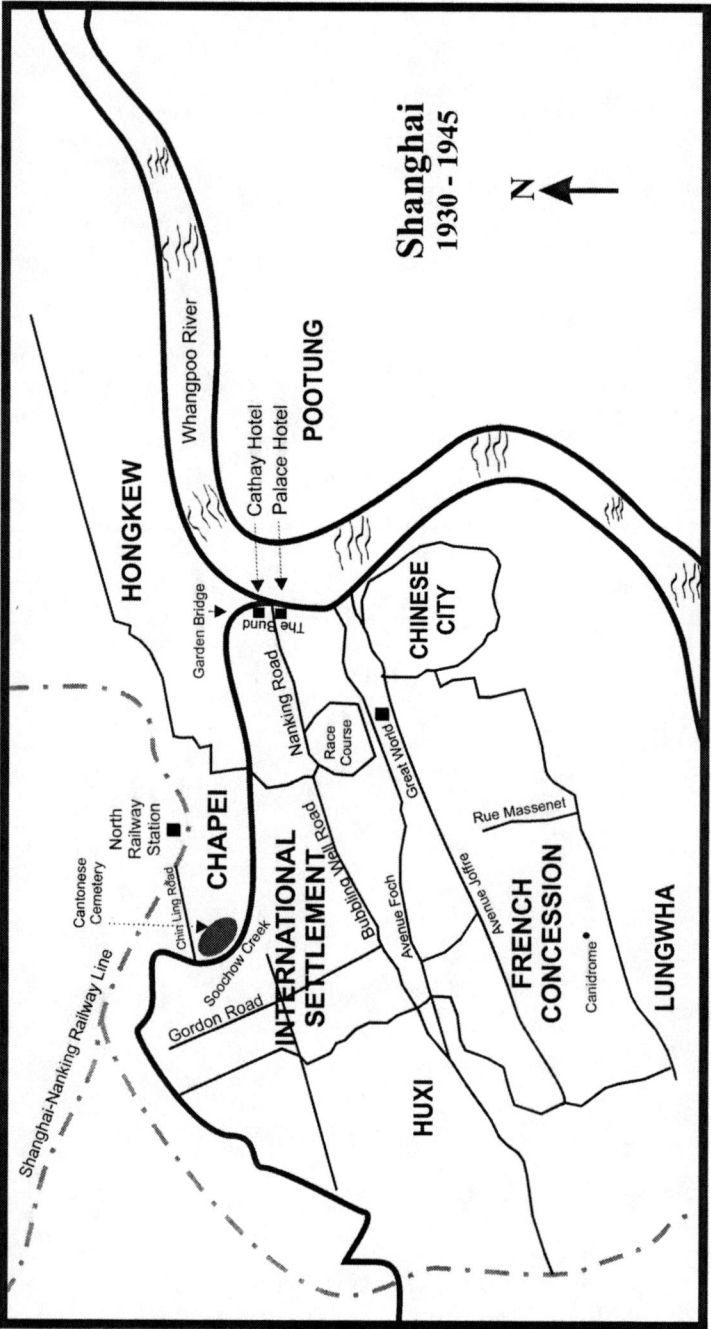

Shanghai
1930 - 1945

N

Whangpoo River

HONGKEW

Cathay Hotel
Palace Hotel

POOTUNG

Garden Bridge

The Bund

Nanking Road

CHINESE CITY

North Railway Station

Cantonese Cemetery

CHAPEI

Chin Ling Road

Soochow Creek

Gordon Road

INTERNATIONAL SETTLEMENT

Bubbling Well Road

Race Course

Great World

Rue Massenet

Avenue Foch

Avenue Joffre

FRENCH CONCESSION

Canidrome

HUXI

LUNGWHA

Shanghai-Nanking Railway Line

1 (January 1934)

The Girl. Tonight I was at the Zengs' salon and met the most wonderful, marvellous, sophisticated, modern young woman, and she was so *sympathique,* so young, speaking such perfect French. (I'm running out of adjectives.) At last! I had found the perfect *modeng* girl, embodying that quintessential modernity found only in Shanghai, expressed by *modeng,* the word we had invented to describe it. That's what was missing from my research: the last piece of the jigsaw puzzle. I was so bemused I didn't go on as usual to dance the night away at Moon Palace. I *had* to go back to my room to savour the experience, to write about it, to think and think and think . . . about it . . . about *her.* Like a fool I didn't remember to ask her where she lived, to ask her *anything* about herself.

After our meeting, I staggered out of the Zengs', shrugged on my padded jacket and entered Rue Massenet, crossing through Rue Molière, past Number 29 where Sun Yat-sen had lived, to Rue Père Robert. On this part of the walk home, I was still in my French "bubble". However, turning left on Avenue Joffre, I entered Russia: saw and waved to my friend the doorman of the Renaissance Café, a huge Cossack in full regalia with medals. He was standing outside the café, opening the door. On a wave of the warm aroma of cabbage soup and beef stroganoff, the doorman let out a blast of plink plink balalaika music with loud, lingual Russian conversation and hearty singing fuelled by vodka and kvass. My Cossack waved back and gave me a big smile.

"No girls tonight?" he said. "No, thank goodness. But I've just met *the* one," and I did my famous foxtrot on the road, pretending I was holding her.

Since *Les Contemporains* had published my photo, the Cossack doorman had often rescued me from female admirers who tried to tear pieces off my clothing, even kiss me, saying how beautiful I was, the idiots! I knew that *she* would never behave like that.

I continued north to reach Guanghua University where I had lodgings. Usually on that walk I had the thrilling feeling that I had, in effect, returned home to China across two continents and oceans as well as a sea, that this was the life I wanted! But not that night: *that* night I was in a total, Eureka-discovery daze. I couldn't sleep for thinking of her, conjuring her up again in my mind, like the most beautiful painting I'd ever seen. Peipei, Peipei, over and over like music, like the best story I had ever written: Qiu Peipei! I felt like going out into the darkened streets and shouting it, shouting it down the echoing caverns of Shanghai's business district where the expatriate Swiss yodelers did their thing, hearing it echo and echo, as it did in my brain all night.

Once I came to, I decided to find out where Qiu Peipei lived. At least I knew her name. However, first there was the little matter of finishing my story for *Les Contemporains, the* literary magazine in Shanghai, responsible for launching the careers and reputations of many modernist writers, not just me. I had worked so hard to get published in the first place, that I couldn't afford to let slip any opportunity to continue my writing career. I must *never* stop working hard at that.

But I had barely passed the piece to the desk of editor Du Heng, when it happened again! To loosen up after the high of creating a story, I went to Moon Palace, and there she was with a friend. I couldn't believe my good luck.

I shall always remember, every split second of it, the first time that perfect girl took my hand and walked out with me as the band in their immaculate dinner suits started playing, and held me, in public, on the dance floor of the Moon Palace. We circled the space to a slow tune: "Always." This was nothing like the calculated plays of the dandy and man about town that I had by then become. There was nothing calculated about it at all. During that dance I reached certainty: I had found the perfect *modeng* girl to act, with the city of Shanghai, as my writing muse—and so young! I could inspire myself with her for months . . . even years, until she lost her youthful bloom, when I'd have to look for someone else. But where would I find her equal? And why hadn't I met someone like her before in my researches into Shanghai? But then Qiu Peipei certainly wasn't like other dance hall hostesses. She was a cut above them and I wondered how that had happened.

*

After I came to Shanghai in 1931 at the age of fifteen, I continued with the French language studies I had begun in Canton, where I was born. I regularly attended the salon of the writer and publisher Mr Zeng, at 115 Rue Massenet, and contributed to discussions of French literature in the impeccable French I had acquired at the girls' school in Canton.

At the salon above the True, Beautiful and Good (Zhen, Mei, Shan) publishing house and bookstore, we could come and go informally as we pleased, often staying quite late in the evening. In an eclectic assortment of comfortable chairs and couches, we sat around and talked. There were some low, antique tables for plates of snacks. They reminded me of home. Latecomers were welcome to sit on cushions on the floor. Some cushions, made of embroidered silk, were very like the ones in my Auntie Lo's drawing room.

As people were arriving for the salon, the son, Zeng Xubai, played French music softly on the piano. That was different from the pipa music I played myself, but the gentle strains had the same, calming effect.

Although I am female, and the others attending were mainly men and older than I was, they understood my motive of continuing with French studies, and took an interest in me and in my education. Mr Zeng was an expert on Victor Hugo and from him I learned much about that author.

During another salon, at a break for tea, I was talking to Mr Zeng: "Yesterday my friend Xuan and I went round the film sets of Zhang Shankun's Xinhua, New China Pictures Company. I was amazed at how elaborate, how real the sets are, at such a thriving movie industry right here in Shanghai." Mr Zeng mentioned that here we also had a lively and modern literary community, that I really should obtain some pieces by Mu Shiying, a wonderful writer, even better than Liu Na'ou. Like Liu, Mu set his stories in scenes, with the written words panning round from person to person, just like the camera in movies. They were friends, and Liu wrote film scripts as well.

"Miss Qiu," he said, "If you want to find out what's going on right now among our young writers, you should get hold of some back issues of magazines such as *Trackless Train, La Nouvelle Littérature* and *Les Contemporains*. Here," and he picked up a few magazines from a side table, "You can start with these." Mr Zeng paused and frowned a little, "But things are getting very political. Writers have to be careful what they publish . . . so as not to offend any political party."

Later that week, dressed in the blue and white robe I had brought with me from Canton, I sat in the little garden of our house and read the stunning first line of *Shanghai Foxtrot* that had been published two years before, in 1932: "Shanghai, a Heaven built on Hell!" After that the images followed fast: the Shanghai Express rushing by belching steam like a dragon, the da, da, da, sound of its wheels, "dancing to the beat of a foxtrot," Shanghai's neon signs promising utopia. I had been instructed in classical literature. However, this was something entirely different: faster paced, more vivid.

At his next salon, when I told Mr Zeng about my reaction to *Shanghai Foxtrot*, he said, "As he's busy with his writing, we haven't seen Mu for some time. I'll call and invite him along to our next salon. You'll be there, won't you?"

And so I met Shiying. Taller than the average, and impeccably dressed in a Western suit with a pink rosebud in his lapel, Mu's entrance had an electrifying effect. Conversation stopped and time stood still. Seated a little apart from the others, we discussed *Shanghai Foxtrot*. With a self-deprecating smile on his long narrow face with the straight nose, Mu said it was a fragment of a book he intended to write. The title would be *China 1931*. He signed the front of my copy of *Shanghai Foxtrot*, and then whisked out of the room.

I looked down for the signature and there, lying across it, was a pink rosebud.

"Ah, he's going to Moon Palace to dance," said Mr Zeng, "Mu loves Western style popular music and dancing."

I knew my friend Xuan loved that same style of music and dancing as much as I did, and therefore I explained the situation to her, and we decided to go to Moon Palace and sign on as dance hostesses. The money we made was much less than what we could command at our principal occupation, but then it was enjoyable, as was the whole of the French Concession where the Moon Palace dance hall was located. The area was so relaxed, full of Western people other than the French, such as the Russians who had fled the Russian Revolution and, often penniless, had to work at whatever they could: taking jobs as riding instructors, and shop assistants, especially in the Russian dress shops that sprang up in the Concession.

It was at Moon Palace that I again met Mu Shiying. I shall always remember, every split second of it, the first time he took my hand and walked out with me, as the band in their immaculate dinner suits started playing, and held me, in public, on the dance floor of Moon Palace. We circled the space to a slow tune: "Always." This was nothing like the calculated plays towards men I had learned. There was nothing calculated about it at all. During that dance I fell truly and utterly in love with Mu Shiying.

From that first moment in his arms, I knew that this was the man I wanted to stay with, to be my lover and companion for the rest of my life. But how could I persuade someone like that to ask me to marry him? Even in the permissive culture of Shanghai, a respectable man would not actually marry a courtesan. Instead, he took the woman as his second wife, as the concubine.

On my way home, I mused that by this time, the profession of courtesan was a thing of the past, especially in the fast-paced, *modeng* life of Shanghai. Who had the time for the leisurely role-playing, conversation, music and entertaining of the courtesans' approach to loving? And was it real love? After all, there was a great deal of money involved. Who had the wealth? And yet in rich Shanghai, some people had the time, money, and also good taste, for something special: the courtesan's way. I decided I wanted nothing less than marriage from Mu Shiying, who was still single, after all. However, I would have to have a steely resolve and nerve to achieve it.

Over and over I asked myself: *Will he want to see me again? What shall I say about my real occupation? When shall I tell him? Will the truth repel Shiying? How had I managed to trap myself in such a predicament and how could I escape in the way I wished?* Thinking back to my reading in our school library, I remembered the famous quotation from Leo Tolstoy: "The two most powerful warriors are Patience and Time." I vowed that Time and Patience would be my weapons. By now I had been forced to develop an endurance and resilience far beyond what one would normally find in a person of my eighteen years.

CANTON, NINGPO AND SHANGHAI
(1920-December 1937)

East China

Peking

Yellow Sea

Yangtze River

Nanking

Soochow

Hangchow

Shanghai

Ningpo

Canton

Tung Shan Park

Pearl River

Shameen

China Sea

Formosa (Taiwan)

Canton

Hong Kong

2 (Early 1930)

That morning when my life changed, the maid had pulled back the blinds, and I woke up to see the sunlight streaming in on a tranquil two-thousand-year-old statue of Kwan Ying, lovely goddess of Compassion and Mercy, sitting in the lotus position and cupping in her hands a plum flower. The statue had been there for as long as I could remember. In a way it seemed like the spirit of my mother, who had died during my birth, watching over me.

My mother's widowed sister Auntie Lo and Father, were sleeping in as usual after the Western style meal we always had on Fridays, using the unusual eating tools, so much heavier than chopsticks. Father followed this with a short nap before the arrival of his colleagues and rivals for their weekly game of Mah Jong. As we left the table, my father always said, "Peipei, during my nap you can prepare the Mah Jong table."

I enjoyed that task. From the leather case in which they were carefully kept, I was allowed to take out the one hundred and thirty six pieces, made from panels of wood and ivory back to back. I loved the colourful appearance and smooth feel of them from the three principal suits: Dots, Bamboos and Characters. I preferred the Bamboos.

Like my father, whose name was Xinren, the colleagues were owners of large grocery stores in Canton. However, this was no ordinary Mah Jong tournament. The stake was not directly money: the outcome would decide whose would be, for the next week, the only store to stock certain popular groceries such as lentils. Rising from the dining room, the clicking sound of the ivory tiles continued well into the early morning hours.

That morning, I poured water from the ewer left by the maid and carefully washed my hands and face. In front of the long mirror in my room I brushed my hair and quietly put on my dressing gown, stopping to make sure it was tidily wrapped around me. Then I padded in bare feet through the house, with its austere furniture of antiques (another business of Xinren's) into the welcoming sunlit kitchen to have breakfast with dear Ah Ling. She had been my mother's amah and now helped our cook. Father never spoke of Mother, and it was left to Ah Ling to tell me about her. Sitting beside her at the kitchen table as Ah Ling chopped vegetables, or sometimes on her ample, cushiony lap, from an early age I heard that my mother had the fine bones and beauty of the women of her family.

With a faraway look in her eyes, Ah Lling once said that as a child Mother was never noisy or dirtying herself. "You know, your mother, dear Lingyu, played the pipa beautifully. Ah, if only you could have heard her . . ." And Ah Ling's eyes had clouded over with tears. "But then you are learning to play so well," she had continued, in a more businesslike tone.

The calm voice and comforting scent of Ah Ling, the scent of mint and cinnamon when she was in the cosy kitchen of our family house, gave me a sense of being mothered that I never had from my mother's childless sister, Auntie Lo, who ran the household.

One afternoon Ah Ling was continuing the story of my mother, saying she was so gentle, and what a fine musician, and how Lingyu loved to take personal care of my now recently married sister, Ailing. With her own hands Mother embroidered all my baby clothes in advance. She was so looking forward to holding the new baby in her arms. Ah Ling was in the middle of telling me one of those stories of hers when Auntie Lo came into the kitchen, and the old lady abruptly changed the subject. "Look at the way we make chopped vegetables to put in dumplings, Peipei," she said, pointing to the pile of vegetables mounting up in a bowl.

This morning, Ah Ling took me on her knee (at fourteen I was still not too big for that) and fed me delicious fried bread and savoury pancakes, with pieces of dim sum. We had just finished eating, and Ah Ling was telling me another tale about Mother, when the maid who had gone to waken Father screamed. She ran to Auntie Lo's room, then came downstairs, "The Master, he is awake but cannot move," she said.

Soon, Doctor MacDonald came. As usual, Mr. Wei also arrived. In our panic we had forgotten about him. Auntie Lo said: "While Doctor MacDonald and I decide what to do for Xinren, you will take your regular lessons in calligraphy and poetry from Mr Wei." I was distraught: Father had his eyes open, but as the maid said, he neither moved nor said anything. Auntie Lo took the teacher aside and explained the situation to him.

Mr Wei was always impeccably dressed following the old Chinese way, in a black long garment with frog closings and the black silk domed hat worn by elderly gentlemen. With him, Mr Wei always brought a little singer to entertain me as I worked. It was his pet cricket. As with everything else relating to my teacher, the insect's cage was beautiful, intricately woven in thin polished bamboo. I found Mr. Wei rather intimidating—goodness knows why, as he was very gentle, and I knew he preferred me to my sister Ailing whose work had been so slapdash. I think it was his seemingly great age and fragility that created the awe I felt.

As usual, we sat at a big table in Father's study. First, Mr Wei took out some flash cards, pictographs for memorisation. They were stylish characters, beautifully drawn with the long-fingered and elegant hands of the teacher. He sat very upright and patiently explained how each one resembled a stylised version of what it said, for instance a bridge or a bird. "If you remember what it looks like, what it means, then it will be easier for you to read *and* write it."

Next I normally took out pig bristle brushes, and ink, (prepared ahead by Mr Wei's assistant), and tried to copy the fine calligraphy of the master. This was pure memory work, and I felt it would take a long time to learn to read and write in Chinese. I far preferred the ease and flexibility of the European alphabet of only twenty-six letters from which you could form thousands of words in the different languages (French, English, Greek and Latin) that I learned at the weekday school for girls run by teachers from Great Britain.

This Saturday, Mr. Wei was not strict with me about how I was to position myself and hold the brush, held vertically in my fingers, the palm also held vertically. He decided on an easier lesson than usual. Mr Wei told me that the primitive Chinese Autumn "Qiu" words (like our family name) are in the shape of a cricket, and he drew some, bringing forward his own cricket in its cage and pointing out their resemblance to it. Nevertheless, it was a struggle to avoid thinking too much about my father.

Today, Mr Wei quickly turned from calligraphy to the classical Chinese poetry he also taught me, and to the ninth century female poet, Yu Hsuan-chi. "From what we know of her life, she was a very well-educated, independent young woman who decided for herself what she would do in her life." *Exactly the modern kind of woman Father wants for me as a role model*, I thought.

"'In Yu Hsuan-chi's time though, to make enough money to determine her own life's direction, Yu Hsuan-chi had to become first a concubine of a wealthy official, Adept-Serene, and then a courtesan." By then I knew that a courtesan was very well educated and provided entertainment at private social events. Yu Hsuan-chi also occasionally gave sexual favours, but only as she wished.

I read the poem Yu Hsuan-chi sent Adept-Serene, titled *Gazing out in Grief,* with its melancholy images of autumn and evening, and her verbal picture of the never-ending longing she felt for Adept-Serene. I wondered how, after receiving such a poem, he could continue to abandon Yu Hsuan-chi. (Although there were still concubines and courtesans in Canton, I knew that such things had not happened to my married sister Ailing, and would not happen to me: this was the twentieth century, and our wealthy father had other plans for us.)

Mr Wei told me that as well as her artistic and social skills, Yu Hsuan-chi's beauty was legendary in her own time. I thought it amazing, but also right, that she was still remembered eleven hundred years later. As he left Mr Wei said kindly, "You may keep the book of poems."

After a light lunch, Auntie Lo still kept me away from my father and told me to take my afternoon nap. I lay on the bed in my room with Yu Hsuan-chi's poems, and read her sad songs. On reading the poem written while visiting Ancestral-Truth monastery's south tower, where the new graduates had their names inscribed on a wall, I could *feel* Yu Hsuan-chi's rage at not having her own achievements formally recognized, not having *her* name inscribed on a wall because she was a woman.

I myself vowed to work even harder at my studies and become an independent young woman capable of choosing my own husband, as Father had promised my sister Ailing and me. Already I was receiving high praise for my work in school and also read widely beyond what my teachers required, borrowing freely from the excellent school library, which had many translations into English of works by major European writers.

In the afternoons on Saturdays I usually sat in the garden and played my pipa, savouring the views through the moon gates. Auntie Lo was delighted when instead of the piano Ailing was practicing I asked to learn how to play that ancient stringed instrument. I liked the idea of creating each note myself, and the nuances involved in playing on strings, requiring more meticulous attention to detail than the piano, where all you did was to hit a predetermined note.

The pipa appealed to Auntie's traditional tastes, but what she did not know was that I knew it was the instrument played by my mother. Like our father, Auntie Lo never spoke of Mother: the loss of that beloved person seemed a subject they both still could not bear to talk about. The nearest she came to telling me about my mother was one afternoon when Auntie Lo came out to the garden where I was playing the pipa. "You are a real lady. You take after our side of the family," then with a quick nod of approval she was gone.

For my part, I liked to imagine myself in the garden shown on the blue and white Ming vases in Father's display cabinet.

He had promised that sometime they would be mine. I even bought a long, blue and white dress to wear while playing the pipa. Lounging on a comfortable seat and looking at the scraggly, holey rock and little trees and flowers planted so prettily by the gardener, I thought: *Such happiness, and it will continue for my whole life*. I knew I was highly privileged and felt grateful for it.

However this particular Saturday, it was more appropriate to stay out of the way and read my poetry, do homework for the coming school week, and spend time with dear, comforting Ah Ling. When I was in the kitchen, there was a great deal of banging going on upstairs. This was the moving of Father's antique wedding bed out of his room and its ordinary, modern replacement being installed from one of the other bedrooms.

Father's carved wood bed was over two hundred years old. Surrounding three sides it had a wood canopy with a dragon and phoenix silhouetted across the bed's top. Once Auntie Lo had said rather vaguely, "They're the Yang and Yin . . . about the balance in the marriage. . . . But you'll find out . . ." Since his marriage to our mother, Father had slept in no other bed, but Doctor MacDonald said it was too awkward for nurses to manage in their round-the-clock care of him. I grieved for poor Father, who may not be able to say anything. However, I knew he would feel sad about the move.

On Sunday, things were again disoriented. Ailing and her husband, Bobby, came. As a member of the group of modern young people in our city, Bobby had chosen for himself a European name. He also loved the modern way of dressing in Western style suits and smoking cigarettes. Bobby Ch'en's family was related to the powerful man who ruled Canton in those days. The huge, ornately carved Ancient Temple of the Ch'en Family in Canton symbolised its power.

We had a family conference round the dining room table. Although the servants had aired it out after the Friday night Mah Jong session, the dining room still smelled slightly of opium. I thought I also caught a whiff of the tiger wine which I found so disgusting (tiger bones left to disintegrate in rice wine??!)

that Father served to his colleagues, supposedly to add to their strength.

Father subscribed to the Canton saying that: "One who indulges in brothel-going and gambling is a smart chap; and an addict of (expensive) imported opium is a first class (i.e. wealthy) fellow." For someone in good health, opium smoking in reasonable amounts was not regarded among our acquaintances as being dangerous. In fact it was supposed to aid one's concentration in business negotiations.

In the stale atmosphere of the dining room Bobby Ch'en, taking the position at the head of the table, led the discussion in his business-like way. "Qiu Xinren has often been seen on Ho-nan Island, which is run by General Li Fu-lin. Gambling is the main occupation there."

Ailing and I exchanged glances. All the people we knew enjoyed gambling and even children regarded it as innocent fun. Gambling was part of our constant seeking for luck to come our way. Ailing and I used to sit in the kitchen with Ah Ling, and ask for two oranges to eat. "I suppose you'll each want a bowl, to put the pips in it and count them," she said indulging us. Ailing might ask what today's prize was for having the most pips. The reward was set at a small amount of money or a toy the winner wanted that the other person had.

There was another saying among us that supported gambling as a way of giving hope, the hope of having money for those who were poor and probably couldn't get it any other way: "An ordinary man can never get rich without a windfall, as a horse can never grow healthy without feeding on wild vegetation."

This last saying didn't apply to our father who was obviously very rich from his business activities. However, he did love to play Mah Jong and go to the fan tan dens for a game of complete chance, and place money on the pigeon lotteries.

Bobby arranged his pen and pad in front of him on the table and said: "It is well known in the city that Qiu Xinren has been spending above his means, has not been paying suppliers for groceries, and has been selling off personal antiques. Only yesterday I saw the pair of Ming ducks in Doctor MacDonald's house."

Ailing and I again looked at each other. Even before Ailing's marriage we had noticed the disappearance of favourite, valuable antiques such as a complete tobacco leaf dinner service for twelve, the adorable pair of turquoise Ming ducks, about six inches high, very rare as a pair, with orange feet (promised to me when I was older) and some exquisite pieces of furniture. *So that is what had happened to them: sold to pay gambling debts.*

Ailing and I sat silent. Auntie Lo and Bobby decided to summon our father's brother from Shanghai. He would determine our financial position and help decide what to do next.

While Auntie Lo and Bobby were coping with the details, Ailing and I went to my room where Ailing hugged me and said she had something to tell me: "I wanted you to be the first to know that I'm expecting a baby. Doctor MacDonald thinks it may even be two babies, twins." We hugged again and I said I'd be embroidering some clothes: two baby coats in case of twins, "My sewing has improved enormously."

We had an excited discussion about the coming event and reminisced about the incident in Ailing's wedding when our little relatives were encouraged to jump around on the wedding bed and chase after fruit and nuts that were thrown on it. This was supposed to aid in producing children for the bride and groom. One of Bobby's small cousins jumped so high that he landed right out of the bed on to the lap of Ailing who was seated nearby. This caused much petting and consoling and more sweetmeats for the frightened child. However, everyone was delighted and said it was a good omen for Ailing's future fertility. "It certainly worked," I said smiling.

We remembered times with our dear, indulgent father. "Do you remember that evening he came in from work really annoyed?" This was unlike our father's usual good nature. Father said he'd just found out about the local government's ban on Western dancing in public. Father gave his opinion that this was a half-baked political ploy to appear patriotic. So for a while in 1929 they banned Western dancing. (When that ban was lifted, there was a five-day, twenty-four hour a day dance held in the large Sports Hall.)

However, the Western dancing was allowed in private. As our father believed we young people were too madly in love with all forms of such music and dancing to stop, he decreed that we had to hold our own celebrations in the living room. Father watched our delighted reaction, and smiled his golden smile.

Therefore, during the period of the ban, sometimes Ailing and Auntie Lo hosted a *thé dansant* at our house, and from a bend in the staircase I was allowed to watch. My sister and her friends, the girls dressed in flapper attire and the boys in Western style suits, danced to tunes from the films they had recently seen. I watched Ailing and her then boyfriend Bobby Ch'en dancing together to such tunes as "Smoke Gets in Your Eyes" and "Love is the Sweetest Thing" and later, "Cheek to Cheek" from the Ginger Rogers and Fred Astaire film *Top Hat*. My favourite tune was the fast-paced and happy song called "The Japanese Sandman."

Sometimes, I even thought I heard the cheerful words of that lively American song in my dreams. In these, I saw the Japanese Sandman as a benign, slight little figure at a distance, standing in a sunlit garden under a blossoming cherry tree. Dressed in a black cotton peasant's top with trousers, he was holding a beige sun umbrella patterned in red peonies. This Japanese Sandman conformed to the words of the American song to which my older sister Ailing and her friends danced.

Our father was the kind of person who embraced life with both arms and wanted Ailing and me to do the same. Ailing ressembles him and always enjoys life the way he did. Father looked the part, as when he was enjoying himself, his broad, expressive face lit up with pleasure, and his many gold teeth shone. Whenever he saw us he'd put out his arms offering an embrace. Auntie Lo frowned upon his spontaneity.

"You must not throw yourselves into your father's arms. Indeed you must not throw ourselves around at all, but should try to maintain a ladylike demeanour." But then I would see her rather austere and narrow face bursting into a smile at our father's jokes and easy going good humour. I possessed the longer face, fine bones and small stature of our mother's family. Ah Ling said I was growing to look more and more like my mother. In the poignant look my father gave me sometimes, I could see that even though he never mentioned her, I reminded Father of Lingyu.

At that older, (teen) age, I wondered about the effect that my mother's death giving birth to me must have had on my father's attitude towards me. Many men would have blamed the child as the cause of their wife's death. But I never had any feeling of being loved less than Ailing by our father. In some ways I was his favourite, following in his footsteps almost like a son. Then there was my growing resemblance to Lingyu. So far as I could make out, this seemed to make Father love me more, not less, than before.

"Hasn't our life been wonderful?" I asked Ailing.

"It was so joyful, and I didn't feel kept down as a girl in any way."

My sister and I had a varied life, between school and parties and taking part in the local events like the June Dragon Boat Festival. Father always took us to see the races on the Pearl River. He usually smiled his golden smile and said, "Only for fun, I'll bet a few dollars for you on whatever boat you choose." So we would choose a boat and cheer it on to win.

I could hardly wait for all the exciting things that would take place when I was older. Some of them came sooner than I had thought. When I was thirteen I began to accompany Auntie Lo when she was chaperoning the bright young things of Ailing's age. My favourite place was the Sun Company Building. The sight of the four elevators, and all the luxury foreign goods on sale, was exciting. The first time we went, I ran up the circular staircase to the third floor. The building was very different from what I had so far experienced in the sheltered life I led. Up twelve storeys, at the rooftop amusement park, we attended the latest Hollywood films and had afternoon tea in the restaurant. As this was Canton's highest building, from the restaurant we could look across the whole city.

Remembering our past life together, Ailing and I almost forgot about the trouble in our family.

3 (Early 1930 continued)

The next week passed in a miserable grey blur. Auntie Lo decided I should attend school as usual, and the only event I remember from that sad time was a class outing to the sandbar on the Pearl River called the Shameen. That is where the foreigners lived and had their banks and clubs. Our people were not allowed to stay there.

To reach the Bund, which led to the bridge over to the Shameen, we went in rickshaws through Canton's quite narrow main streets. Passing by in our rickshaws after that morning's showers, we could see people avoiding splashes by sheltering in the arcaded walkways with their decorated ceilings. The arcades looked exactly like the photographs of parts of Paris in my geography book.

Travelling along the broad street of our Bund I could see a city of floating sampans lined up in orderly "streets" with life going on very much as it did in the narrow alleyways behind the city's actual main streets on land. The girls commented: "Those sampan people are so poor that as their kitchen god, Tsao Wang, all they have is a piece of red paper with the god's name on it."

As we passed the watery street where the Flower boats were that morning, we saw beautiful young girls combing their hair and hanging out their washing. Someone in my rickshaw said (not so loud that the teacher could hear), "The Flower boat girls are prostitutes. They sleep in the same bed as the businessmen they entertain, without even knowing them before." This provoked a gale of giggles. "That's not what we'll be doing." More laughter followed.

In our pink cotton summer uniforms with panama hats, with the red and gold school crest on the hatband, we trooped across the spotlessly clean, white stone bridge with three arches. From the Shameen we could look back and see the crowded Canton waterfront opposite. Dirty two storey shacks of the poor leaned crazily over the dividing channel.

The contrast with white buildings, immaculate lawns and tidy grass boulevards on the other side of the bridge was extraordinary. However, I felt too empty to enjoy the trees, bushes, silence, fresh air, the scented flowers and grassy streets where bicycles were the only traffic. After all, it was not too different from the upscale Tung-shan where we lived. While the others strolled around, I was allowed to sit shivering on a bench with a teacher. (Despite the cardigan we'd all brought against the river breeze, I felt cold.) My teacher reached over and draped her own jacket round me.

I thought of Father (he was all I could think about); when I was eleven or twelve, my father called for a car and took his gold and money to the Shameen in suitcases, walking across the bridge to deposit it in the foreign bank and save his wealth from the "compulsory lending" extorted by the Kuo Min Tang (KMT). Father also took his more valuable antiques. At the time my father said to me: "I have to leave something, the less valuable antiques, for the KMT troops to loot, otherwise our safety will be in doubt, even in Tung-shan."

My father told me that at least Chiang Kai-shek was now leader after Sun Yat-sen, and was fighting the Japanese together with the Communists. But then the Shanghai financial interests persuaded Chiang to turn against the Communists, leading to the White Terror bloodbath and purge of them in China.

At the dinner table one evening, Father told us, "Sun Yat-sen often complained that although the Manchus were gone, he had inherited a Chinese nation that was like a loose heap of sand, needing cement to make it a cohesive and strong nation."

His voice echoed in my head, but it seemed I would never again actually hear it.

On Friday evening Uncle Donghua arrived from where he lived in Shanghai to evaluate the businesses. Over dinner he barely acknowledged me, speaking mainly to Auntie Lo. A thin and rather humourless, shrewd-looking man we hadn't seen much before, Uncle Donghua stayed for a week. First he spent the whole weekend looking through the financial and other records of Father's businesses and talking to the general staff. Later, Uncle invited the senior managers into Father's office at home. In my room upstairs, I could hear the men's voices talking far into the night.

On Sunday evening Uncle Donghua held a meeting with Auntie Lo and me. We sat in stiff formality in Auntie Lo's room of antiques. "Why isn't Ailing here? She is always present at family conferences."

Uncle Donghua exchanged a glance with Auntie Lo that was difficult to interpret. He seemed to be warning her not to speak. Uncle then did the talking, and said first that Ailing was now part of her husband's family, and not someone with whom to discuss our own family affairs. In his dry, whispery voice, Uncle Donghua continued: "I have studied the financial records for all your father's business enterprises, and am very concerned at what I have found out." Here the Uncle paused, wiped his face with a handkerchief, and asked Auntie Lo to order tea.

Once that service was taken care of, Uncle Donghua asked the servant to leave, as he recommenced to explain that both the import/export and antiques businesses were burdened by heavy debts. There was even a sum owed to suppliers for the grocery store, hardly a maker of big profits. Embarrassed at what he was going to say next, Uncle coughed into his handkerchief, "It seems that your father has been borrowing to gamble and lost more than he made." Auntie Lo preserved her silence.

Donghua then said, "There are not many of the remaining antiques that can be sold. I understand your father has been training you to succeed him, and has no second-in-command to step into his place." As not only in the antique trade, but also in detecting fakes, the main asset was Father himself and his expertise, the antique business could not be sold for a large sum as a going concern. The conclusion was that I was definitely too young and didn't yet have the training needed to take over, in that or in the other businesses. Auntie busied herself with pouring more tea and offering cakes, and there was a pause before Uncle Donghua delivered his final verdict.

"The sale of what assets are left will provide some immediate cash and then a lump sum to be conservatively invested to provide a very small regular income." Perhaps the sale of the grocery store could be accomplished as a going concern to bring in some money. However the grocery business was very competitive, with low profit margins. I nodded, for thanks to Father's training I fully understood his meaning. Uncle concluded, "For its own support and Xinren's care, the family needs more. I cannot provide for an invalid in my establishment in Shanghai. We are considering how best to arrange things so that *you* can provide for your family." *How can I possibly do that?* For guidance I looked across at Auntie Lo, who did not meet my eyes. With a wave of his hand, Uncle Donghua indicated that I was dismissed.

I left in distress. *How on earth can I suddenly become a wage earner? My sewing is improving. What good are my studies in classical Chinese literature and foreign languages? Perhaps I could take lessons in typing and become one of those secretaries who translate letters into foreign languages for clients abroad, But how could that bring in enough to support all of us and Father's medical needs?* I gave up thinking along these lines, and spent a miserable night worrying.

On Monday morning I would normally go to school, but was told by the maid to wear my home clothes and go to our family sitting room after breakfast. There, I met an imposing, well-groomed lady I had never seen before and to whom I was not introduced. Regarding me all the time through her western *pince nez,* she asked me to walk across the room and sit down. Then she said, "Good, you are a graceful walker. Please stand in the centre of the room and turn around slowly. And what are your skills in literature and playing the pipa?" I asked her if she was interviewing me for a job.

"Do you mean to say your aunt has not told you who I am?" she said, raising her finely plucked eyebrows, and then swept out of the room. In the hallway outside, I could hear an irate conversation between her and my Auntie Lo. Then the lady left our house.

That afternoon Uncle Donghua and Auntie Lo again summoned me to a conference in Auntie's living room, where we again sat stiffly round the low antique table, on the embroidered cushions. I glanced at Uncle's impassive face. He said: "You are the only hope for a decent future for all of your family. The lady who just left the house was Madam Zhu who trains courtesans. She has assessed you favourably, and a courtesan is what you must become. You are of the right age, appearance and education. It is the only way for the family."

"I know about courtesans, and I will not be sold to the highest bidder to sleep in his bed for a little while, and then become a prostitute and do the same for other strange men. Is that what you want for me, your niece?"

"Really Peipei," said Auntie Lo embarrassed, and omitting a reply to the first part of the comment, "Don't be vulgar. It's not like that at all. There will be very little of that sort of thing."

"What has Ailing to say? What about Bobby and his family? Won't *they* help us?" In his dry, whispery voice Uncle Donghua said that Bobby was expecting to provide for an expanding family, and his relatives were not prepared to look after a man who had disgraced himself with gambling debts.

"A courtesan is not like a common prostitute. You'll choose who, if anyone, you go with," continued Uncle Donghua, without missing a beat and also ignoring the initial comment, "And if you play your cards the right way, you will make so much money that you'll not only be able to support your family, but will have a fortune left over for yourself."

"Besides," said Auntie Lo, "After the training, you'll be a courtesan for only five years and then you'll be too old. You can marry whom you please and settle down, have children."

"You mean be a concubine. No one will marry an ex-courtesan."

"Do not answer me back! I have always thought Xinren was over-indulgent with you and Ailing."

"Don't you *dare* criticise dear Father!"

Neither of my relatives answered. Uncle Donghua again waved his hand in dismissal. I went to my room. I had now learned to be submissive to those more powerful, an important first lesson for the new life.

And so it was settled. Later, Uncle Donghua came to my room and standing in the doorway said, "Your training is to begin immediately and will be completed after a year when you are fifteen. You can pack some things, say goodbye to your father and then leave." I thought back to what Auntie Lo had said. *Five years, that's forever!* And that's what five years felt like to my fourteen-year-old self.

That afternoon, as I packed the clothes I wore for the evenings and weekends, and some books (not the school ones), including the poetry book as well as my pipa, I thought back to Ailing's wedding only a few months ago. During the celebrations, I could hear the whispered comments of the old women about how beautiful I was becoming, and what a good match I would make. *What a nuisance, I'd rather dance the days away to "The Japanese Sandman" than bother with marriage and children,* I had thought. *Anyway, I'm far too young yet to choose a husband, and don't have to face all that "stupid stuff" for a while.*

Now I thought: *Maybe I can run away to Ailing. She will help me. But then what will happen to dear Father and Ah Ailing, the maid, even Auntie Lo who as the widow of a not very wealthy man, was totally dependent on my father? I felt a twinge of sympathy for her: she was as helpless as I was, had run our household for fourteen years . . . This really was the only solution.*

As I left my room with my belongings in a suitcase, Ah Ling came and enveloped me in a huge hug. Into my free hand she pressed a cloth bag.

Then I went to bid farewell to my dear parent. Father had caused all this to happen, but I loved him still. I sat beside the bleak new bed and poured out my grief. "Dearest Father, to take care of the financial necessities of our family, I am now to become a courtesan . . . I don't love you any less than I did before. Thank you for the fine life and education and love you have given me. I promise I will never resent what I now must do." Explaining to Father my new poet Yu Hsuan-chi and her life, I told him I was resolved to emulate Yu Hsuan-chi: be brave, continue with my studies, be submissive, follow the instructions for becoming a good courtesan and make an excellent living as she did.

Looking at his expressionless face, I wondered whether my father understood what I was telling him. However, as I turned away, something was glistening, tears were pouring down his beloved face. Father wept; we wept together. Then Uncle Donghua came.

Something I realised that day about my future position was that I would never again see my family. Attitudes in Canton were very strict: neither my own family nor the prestigious Ch'ens could be seen to have such a person as a courtesan among their relatives.

That afternoon I made the bitter vow that I would become old enough, and above all rich enough, never again to be in such a powerless situation, always to decide my own path in life. I would face life like Yu Hsuan-chi.

As I walked to the waiting car with Uncle Donghua, I still had Ah Ling's bag in my hand. From it came the comforting scent of mint and cinnamon.

4 (Early 1930 continued-End 1930)

I was surprised at the establishment (that is how I thought of it: an establishment) to which I now came. Here Madam Deng, another lady from the one I had seen before, welcomed me. She was a small, plump and bubbly older person, very chatty, pretty and extremely well groomed. "Welcome," she said, holding out her hands to take mine. I could see that the house itself was comfortably furnished in the Western manner with many windows bringing in light.

My days passed quickly in determined work at studies in languages, music (playing the pipa and singing) deportment, social skills such as conversation and acting as a companion at different types of social occasions (always set in private rooms), the care of my skin and application of make-up and study of hair styles, how to evaluate jewels through a jeweller's magnifying glass . . . all I needed to know from Madam Zhu and Madam Deng.

I found the social skills I was learning the most difficult. All my life, I had conducted myself for the approval of my indulgent father. He was the only man I really knew well. Now, I must learn to please other people, notably men, of whom I had little experience. I did not think these new men would indulge me as had Father. I found it demeaning. But then wasn't the whole idea of being a courtesan distasteful to a decent girl? I remembered my classmates' laughter at the Flower Boat girls.

"The other matters you will learn in Hong Kong," said Madam Zhu one day. *What "other matters"?* I wondered. But then I thought again, and knew. These other matters were about sharing the same bed as the men who would buy that privilege, and I shivered at this thought: the fundamental demeaning of myself, my whole body, my whole view of myself, my soul . . . my ultimate humiliation. (How my classmates must have giggled together when they found out. By now, they would know.)

Madam Zhu and Madam Deng had been in this profession themselves, and said I could be one of the outstanding courtesans, "Provided you take the next stage of your training seriously," said Madam Zhu in her severe way.

Madam Zhu rarely chatted, unlike Madam Deng, who used to talk to me. One day Madam Deng said, "You should know that courtesans don't by any means always end up as concubines. There are many exceptions such as the famous Ling Ling who married an American widowed diplomat and resides in great comfort in Berkeley, California. She sometimes returns to visit her well-off former colleagues, who are also principal wives, and even holds large banquets for them."

Later, Madam Deng quoted what she said was the well-known Cantonese saying: "Laugh at a penniless man, but not at a prostitute." I had never heard it but was duly cheered and felt more in control of my destiny. And after all, a courtesan did have a great deal of influence over who she allowed to "make love" to her. A skilled courtesan could bring in so much money from her entertaining skills, that she need never have intercourse with any of her suitors.

That I came from a good business family and in particular that I was a cooperative and quick learner, made Madam Zhu and especially Madam Deng treat me with kindness. This was not the case with the other trainee, Miss Jiang. They beat her when she refused to apply herself. For the first time in my life I was afraid. I did what I was told because of fear, not affection as before with Father. At this house we, the courtesans-in-training, were not encouraged to make friends with each other. Our life was all work, work and more work.

What I didn't know but would discover, was that just as when I'd lost my mother at my birth I had been lucky to be in a wonderful family, so now in losing that family I would be lucky in finding another good family: unusually skilled trainers of courtesans, madams as they were called, who treated me as their relative.

I was so busy that it seemed no time at all before I had graduated from my Canton academy and was ready for further training in all the courtesan arts, especially the sexual ones, in Hong Kong where all the area's better courtesans resided. Madam Zhu accompanied me by boat. As we were boarding, I said to Madam Zhu, "I'm really looking forward to seeing the Pearl River and Hong Kong. I've never been out of Canton before."

"Oh no, no, on this boat you must stay in seclusion."

On our arrival in Hong Kong, I was hustled into a covered conveyance and then to a high-class bordello there. This house had spacious and beautifully furnished public rooms. However, behind the walls was a veritable warren of passageways with peepholes through which the madams (and courtesans-in-training) could view courtesans at their entertaining and sexual work.

There I was left in the charge of Madam Shen, a strict person. She was always extremely well dressed. Madam Shen extended my training to acting: how to twist my face and body to express emotions. She explained that this was a very important aspect for creating the erotic fantasy world that clients expected. They liked to be taken out of their rather stressful business worlds to come into a pretend universe where they were imagining themselves in the role of the young lover of a beautiful young girl. Often the love story was never to be consummated: the young lover taken away to marry another woman. This situation was typical for the courtesan relationship anyway, where the "lover/client" was usually already married.

These acting lessons were good training for suppressing the emotions as well as expressing them. They helped me to conceal the fear and revulsion I felt towards the physical act with an unknown man that I would be forced to perform. Madam Shen explained I would take another, professional, name under which the man would court and make love to me. I realised that this was all a game after all, the creation of an illusion. I decided to pretend it was happening to someone else, the person with the other name, not to me, surely not to *me*.

One day Madam Shen said, "I know your father was a seller and collector of antiques. He helped me with my collection of antique fans. There is not one fake. Perhaps you would like to see some of them," and she ushered me into an inner sanctum, where displayed in glass cases in dim lighting to preserve their colours, was the most amazing array of ancient fans.

I examined them with care, "But these are painted by the very best artists of their dynasty, and decorated with genuine ivory and silver or gold. . . . The materials, workmanship and art . . . they are almost beyond price in their value."

Madam Shen gave a slight smile, "I see you have inherited your father's talent." From then on she somewhat unbent towards me.

The next day, Madam Shen asked me to come and see her and lost no time in letting me know that while on the one hand my sexual duties as a courtesan would be light, they must be performed to the highest possible standards. Whereas later I could choose, there must be no nonsense of refusing at my defloration that was soon to be discreetly arranged in Canton by informing the wealthier men there about me, and by negotiating for the highest bid. Madam Shen informed me that now my training was complete, I would have to think about choosing another name, to play to the fantasy world I was to create. Of course, I didn't have to think long about it and chose Hsuan-chi, the name of my poetess heroine, who had also been forced to become a courtesan.

Soon, a servant ushered me in to a beautifully lit room where photographers took a succession of "bridal" portraits of me. My deflowering was to be treated like a wedding, with the man staying with me for as long as two weeks.

The session took up the whole day and part of another. With the help of a maid, and overseen by Madam Shen, I changed behind a screen into the most luxurious garments the bordello could provide. The dresses had many layers. Several portraits involved taking my photograph reflected in a mirror, sometimes in a window frame looking out, with curtains drawn back framing me. This type of picture emphasizes the erotic fantasy world aspect of the profession.

In the meantime I mixed freely with the resident courtesans who welcomed me with open arms. "You are our little sister," one said.

"Come here and we will tell you about dress, grooming, manners," said another.

A third courtesan offered me her personal tips on how to interest a man, "You must keep him at a distance but enchanted enough to give you expensive gifts." They instructed me on pleasing him sexually. These kind courtesans emphasized the pleasure, for both male and female, of the sexual act. I really couldn't believe them—not with a man who did not love me, whom I did not love in return. This could never reflect the romantic dreams of the young girl that I still in essence was.

Looking back on this time, I think I worked so hard in order to prevent myself from thinking of that dreaded return. In my innermost self, I still could not accept that for my first sexual experience I would have no choice but to have it with an unknown man who had paid the most for this encounter. However, the welfare of my dearest father was at stake, and that of Ah Ling and the whole of the household I had left behind. I *must* do well at this profession.

The timing of my departure was excellent, because during my year of training rebel soldiers split away from Chiang Kai-shek and took control of Canton. From the news we had, we learned that Communist forces led by Mao Tse-tung were also threatening Chiang. In addition, there was devastating flooding from the Yangtze, and the world economy worsened. I received an urgent letter from Auntie Lo, "Peipei, as the money we have for living and for the care of your father is fast running out, it is of the utmost importance that you apply yourself to your studies." Auntie signed it: "Your affectionate Auntie."

By the time I returned to Canton, the political situation there had settled down and I learned that my family, being relatively poor and with an ill person in residence, had not suffered too much from the plundering that troops, even our own, habitually visited on places they occupied. The main concern for China came late the next year. (It was the invasion of Manchuria by Japan in December of 1931.) By that time I was a fully-fledged courtesan and had left for Shanghai.

However much I put off thinking about it, the time came anyway, and accompanied by Madam Shen, I was on my way back to the house of Madam Zhu and Madam Deng. The other courtesans came to see me off: "Make sure he doesn't take away with him any of the jewels and money he gave as wedding presents," said one. "And find some time to really look at the jewels to see that they're not fake," said another. (This courtesan had advised me to always carry a jeweller's glass in my handbag.) Then followed by a chorus of goodbye, goodbye, and good luck, I boarded the boat with Madam Shen, and as it turned in the direction of the Pearl River, I waved farewell over the side, thinking how I would miss the other courtesans and their bright chatter.

During the journey Madam Shen kept me strictly in my cabin, but was kind and gentle for a change, bolstering my self-confidence. "Everything will be fine, you'll see." However, all too soon we disembarked at Canton. Here I was again kept in seclusion. Waiting for us was a sedan chair with the openings covered, in which we travelled back to my previous house. I knew that there I was to hear the name of the man I was to "marry" in that establishment.

The next morning my Uncle was waiting in the formal living room. He bowed and addressed me stiffly in his dry-sounding voice, "You are contracted to Cheng Ziyao, who is a friend and rival of your father's . . . a major successful businessman in this city." I tried to think who this was, and then remembered. I had seen him before: Cheng Ziyao had an upright, athletic appearance (being versed in the martial arts) and a forthright, joking manner with younger people. I had heard the young men of Ling's crowd say that they could trust him with their confidences, and obtain good business advice from Mr Cheng.

"How did you choose this man for me? Did Mr Cheng offer the most money?" Uncle agreed that it was partly that he did offer much more than the others. However, there was the added inducement that my father was deeply in debt to Mr Cheng who had agreed to forgo repayment. This made the price (Uncle did not tell me what it was) even more lucrative: much higher than any of the others. *So*, I thought *I have been sold like cattle to the very highest bidder.*

"How is dearest Father?"

"He has shown no sign of a change for the better. Indeed, your father seems weaker than he was when you left. But the doctors are doing all they can, and we are looking after Xinren well, keeping him very comfortable." I suspected that Uncle Donghua was trying to put forward the best scenario about the care of my father so that I would keep up the agreed payments to the family. *Am I already, at the age of fifteen, becoming cynical about life?* I thought, and asked Uncle please not to let dear Father know who had won me, or about the financial details. Uncle nodded his assent.

It happened then, that not so long after Ailing's, I faced my own, shameful wedding. I had already decided to go through with the experience, in my mind, as the ninth century courtesan Hsuan-chi.

But the good luck I had tended to have so far in my life continued. This "marriage" did not turn out to be as awful or generally frightening as I had feared. The pre-nuptial feast was by no means the disgraceful, drunken brawl with louche jokes that such affairs so often became. In public and in private, Cheng Ziyao treated me with great respect. He provided many beautiful clothes, in both the Chinese and Western styles, and a truly magnificent banquet to which Cheng Ziyao invited a limited number of his friends. I was not to be made into a spectacle for my father's business colleagues in our home city of Canton.

Cheng Ziyao and I sat at a head table. The china settings were gorgeous and the food came in many courses. He conducted the evening in a respectable way. At the start of the feast, Cheng Ziyao leaned over to serve me with some initial sweetmeats and said quietly, "Out of respect for my friendship with your father and my high regard for him, I bid highly for you," and he let me know the staggering amount. He continued that I had nothing to fear from him and should relax. I should enjoy the festivities. "After all, you are the bride," he said with a kind smile, kissing my hand respectfully. I felt reassured and ate the food put before me. I found I actually had an appetite for it.

Later, when we had said goodbye to all the guests, Cheng Ziyao treated me with great delicacy and stayed beside me for three weeks, which was longer than usual, during which time he became my friend and mentor. Cheng Ziyao told me he had put only a small part of my dowry into the hands of my family, the rest to be held back until he had proof of my virginity.

For our first business meeting, and that was how he described it, Cheng Ziyao met with me at a large table in the dining room. "I have set up an account in your name at the Ningpo Commercial Bank, and into it have deposited the balance due of the money and jewellery which you have seen." He then gave me a lesson in financial record keeping. It was not my first, as Father had taught me as well.

"This is the final amount you should give your family each month. Working with your Uncle and Auntie Lo, I have divided my calculations up into house expenses, personal expenses for your Auntie Lo, and expenses for the care of your father. You will need to arrange for the Bank to send this total amount to your family, regularly each month, and this is how you do so . . ."

After that, Cheng Ziyao rang a bell for some light food to be served, and we talked about Canton and my friends there, especially about Ailing and her family. "She now has two children, twins, a boy and a girl." I couldn't help contrasting our different fates. However there was nothing to be gained in feeling sorry for myself. *Be like Yu Hsuan-chi*, I thought, straightening my back.

When we had finished our meal, my mentor spent time continuing with his advice on how to keep strict accounts, save, and look after my financial affairs. "Any currency you receive must be in American gold dollars, and should be deposited in the bank as such. It is the only currency that will hold its value." My madams had already informed me about the kind of vocabulary they would use with clients in asking for payment for services, but Cheng Ziyao gave me other counselling from the viewpoint of himself as a client. The extra week my mentor spent with me was to be invaluable for the rest of my life.

On our last day Cheng Ziyao said, "I have advised your Uncle to take you to Shanghai where, although courtesans are now somewhat going out of fashion, you will undoubtedly be more than able to hold your own in that very competitive environment. Although you have learned well the lesson of submission, nevertheless, I sense in you a great need for freedom, for self-expression. In Shanghai, courtesans have a different milieu from anywhere else in China. They have the richest clients. Unlike in other places, they are not expected to keep themselves in seclusion, but can move freely in public and are more confident, because they are regarded as excellent businesswomen. In the past, Shanghai courtesans have been celebrities in that city."

Cheng Ziyao was sitting with me in a private sitting room and having tea. He took another sip and ate a little cake before he explained that the higher social status of Shanghai's courtesans made them more likely to actually be married. Given the sound policing from the Shanghai Municipal Council force, there was virtually no preying upon the courtesans by organised crime. This was not the situation in other parts of China. In Shanghai, we kept all the money we made.

"Also there is in Shanghai, across the Soochow Creek from the Settlement, a group from Canton. You will be able to mix with colleagues from your own city, will feel more at home than if you were going to a city where everyone is a complete stranger, with no memories in common with yours." I realized anew that my mentor had thought of everything to smooth my transition, and thanked him again

During that afternoon, he had more to tell me: "You should become accustomed as quickly as possible to what I know will be your future high status. In that regard, I have paid for your first class passage with your Uncle, on a ship to Shanghai. With the greatest respect, I ask that you will accept me as one of your regular admirers, and will receive and entertain me when I am in Shanghai."

Cheng Ziyao had one further request for Madam Zhu. It was to be my first client, in Canton. For this, he would have to go through an initial introduction from another client and take me through this whole next experience himself.

Therefore, a current client at the bordello formally introduced my mentor, who came in mid-afternoon to take tea and fruit with Madam Zhu and me. This timing was to allow for the late rising of the courtesan and the preparation of her hair. He had formerly asked to be my client, and after some conversation, as a token of my acceptance, I personally served Cheng Ziyao with tea. This phase was short, to allow for me to make myself ready for the evening's entertaining duties. I felt I had been properly launched, and confident in my new career.

A few days later, the next stage of Cheng Ziyao becoming a client took place and was quite wonderful. He first gave Madam Zhu a large sum to be handed to me and used to buy any more new clothes needed, and also furniture for my room in the new Shanghai abode. My mentor gave the madams a further sum, which would have been their share of the original. Then, to gain even more face, he gave not one but three expensive dinners for successive groups of his friends, one after the other on the same evening. It was past midnight before we could retire alone to the fantasy-themed room prepared for us. Here, we entered a beautiful garden of real and not so real flowers and trees, some painted on the walls. Here, Cheng Ziyao courted me as my young lover, a man of letters, not a businessman. Here, I again pretended to be Yu Hsuan-chi, the poetess. Our bed was in the midst of a woodland scene. And there we made love until we were exhausted in the early morning.

Before Cheng Ziyao ended this second time with me, we had a final meeting in the elegant living room of the madams' house. My mentor bowed, looked at me kindly, and taking my hand said that given my extreme youth he did not want to be crude in what he was about to tell me: that I not only possessed the external skills and appearance of a high class courtesan but also, in providing sexual services, I was truly wonderful. Cheng Ziyao kissed my hand, and his last words were: "You will most certainly become the brightest star in the firmament of courtesans."

5 (Early 1931-January 1934)

With Uncle Donghua I took a riverboat to Hong Kong where we joined the P&O liner S.S.Orient and travelled to Shanghai, a journey of several days. For the whole trip Uncle stayed in our stateroom and said I should do the same. However, for this voyage I refused to be kept in seclusion. I wanted to look at the ocean's sights, and so in the early evenings I went to the boat deck to look over the side and see whales in the distance and schools of dolphins swimming with our ship. Another person who was on the boat deck told me about the huge jellyfish you could see on your way across to Japan: "Like a tabletop, so big," he said, holding wide his arms. "They move about by squeezing themselves into a tight ball and then letting go to expand. The motion propels them." I tried to imagine it. I decided to go to Japan some time and see these wonderful jellyfish for myself.

All too soon we were steaming up the Whangpoo to Shanghai to see the Bund Father had described so often (for when I would be accompanying him on business trips when I was older). With my uncle I stood at the railing of the ship. The grand sweep of the Shanghai Bund was certainly a new version of the one in Canton and the buildings were definitely more regal. But despite my father's photos, and all his stories, the first impression was a surprise: *It's so like the photos of England. Why haven't I noticed that before?*

Slowly we passed the big Victorian pile of the British Consulate near the Garden Bridge spanning Soochow Creek, which my father had said was part of the ancient Grand Canal system for moving trade between Peking and the south. (Donghua didn't have the curiosity, and with it knowledge, of his brother.) Soon the ship drew opposite the neo-classical Customs House with its commanding clock tower. The clock, called locally Big Ching, struck the quarter hours in the same way as Big Ben in London. I was thrilled to see the statue of Father's hero, Sir Robert Hart, whose major work in establishing sound customs regulations and standard time in China my father greatly admired. There it was, clearly visible in front of the Customs House.

We passed all the impressive major foreign banks, the Oriental Bank, the Agra Bank, the Mercantile and the Chartered Bank, and the Comptoir d'Escompte de Paris. But I was looking for my own, special financial institution, the Hongkong and Shanghai Bank, topped by the magnificent dome Father had described. As we passed it, I was enchanted to see some of my countrymen touching for luck the feet of the famous bronze lions on either side of the initial flight of steps. Father had told me the touching polished these feet, making them shine like the gold that people desire. At this point, I felt in my handbag for the bankbook and information I would need to set up a local account.

When the ship reached the end of the mile-long foreign avenue as we called the Bund, my uncle pointed out the imposing Victorian building, the Shanghai Club at No. 2, the Bund, and told me it had the longest bar in the world at 110 feet. (He didn't realise that Father had already told me this fact.) There the ship anchored and we disembarked.

As we looked over the side of the boat when it docked, I saw ships flying the colourful flags of many nations, and also the familiar sight of a second city floating out on the river beyond the Bund. (It was much bigger and less orderly than the one at Canton.) There, thousands lived their whole lives on small boats, cooking their meals at charcoal braziers on the stern, selling meat and vegetables (bought wholesale at the Hongkew market) to each other, and doing their washing in the river, the children being looked after, as usual, by the family grandmother.

We hired a motor launch to take us to shore. Most others were making the crossing by sampan, but we could not risk the large trunks of expensive clothes and jewellery on such a small boat. On the way to the wharf, from the lower perspective of our launch I looked up at the high wooden junks, with a huge evil eye to deter devils painted on their prows, expertly weaving between the tiny sampans and Butterfield & Swires freighters. I was amazed at the many other ships flying flags from all over the world. We were tossed about in the wakes of the larger boats.

Dressed impeccably in white, Fok, the male servant from the courtesans' house, met us at the bottom of the wooden gangplank with some coolies to carry baggage up it. "Are my bags safe going up that gangplank?" (It had only open rails for sides.) He said smiling that they would be very careful, and they were. However, I was relieved when everything was safely on land, and vowed to put the valuables in a strong box at the Hongkong and Shanghai Bank as soon as possible.

"But what about the famous Cathay Hotel. I didn't see that?"

"It's behind the Bund at the corner of Nanking Road. You'll see it from the rickshaw when you go to your house in the Cantonese area across the Creek."

Standing for the first time on the edge of the Bund, the edge of Shanghai as my father had described it, I shall never forget the first thrilling experience of the frenetic atmosphere, the smell—stench more like it—and the sheer noise of Shanghai, which they called *jenao*. Beggars and coolies wanting money or something to carry pulled at our clothes and shouted their singsong rhyming pleas. I am accustomed to it now, but then it was all so new. No description could really explain the feeling of energy, noise and excitement projected by this huge, modern and vibrant city.

While I stood there entranced, Fok loaded the luggage onto a taxi. Before going on ahead in the car, the house servant shepherded us to one of the many rickshaws, which thrust forward, looking for custom. There Uncle Donghua said goodbye, and without letting me know how to get in touch with his Shanghai address, disappeared into the crowd. Plainly, he did not want anything more to do with me, his courtesan niece.

Feeling alone but excited, I travelled to what was to be my new home, back along the Bund, past the main Western thoroughfare, Nanking Road, and a glimpse of the outside of the Cathay Hotel on the north corner of the Bund and Nanking Road. Because of Father's teaching, these were all familiar names. To me, they spoke of a magical new place, where my life would be so different.

I watched the amazing parade of traffic: girls in high heels dodging in and out among the trams, wheelbarrows piled high with sacks of rice, furniture or even bars of silver, and people balancing long poles carrying crabs, vegetables and cages of live chickens on either end. All these were being honked at by cars, which were trying to travel along what would normally be their exclusive thoroughfare. In the Settlement there was the exotic foreign background of Art Deco buildings reaching high into the sky.

After reaching the British Consulate at the end of the Bund, the rickshaw puller did not take the usual Garden Bridge route across Soochow Creek, but turned north along Soochow Road, crossing the Creek at North Tibet Road and swinging through the maze of streets to reach Chin Ling Road near the Cantonese cemetery, south of the Nanking-Shanghai Railway line. Here he left me in front of a two-storey, single bay newly built house belonging to Madam Wong, and with an alleyway entrance proclaiming itself to be that of Huile Li (Alley of Joint Pleasure). The round banners and lights outside some houses advertised the name and profession of the courtesans inside. My name was not yet registered and would go up in a few days.

Our house was smaller than the older, *shikumen* neighbourhood houses across Soochow Creek in the International Settlement, or the Settlement as I came to call it like everyone else. But unlike the older alleyway houses, ours had electricity and running water, with appliances, what the foreigners refer to as all mod.cons. (modern conveniences). The people of Shanghai called these smaller houses the Japanese ones—after the small stature of the Japanese, of course. Different from the *lilong* houses nearby, our house was wider, being detached, not joined together with several others in a row.

Here, there were only two of us courtesans, the other one being Xuan, who was also from Canton. We had a pleasant time comparing our backgrounds, which turned out to be quite similar. We actually knew some of the same people. I updated Xuan on the latest Canton news or, more like it, gossip. We compared clothes, even agreed to lend some to each other, and tried out new hairstyles and makeup together. So I now, as it were, had a piece of Canton with me. Something else that accompanied me from Canton was the Japanese Sandman. In Shanghai, he continued to be a pleasant presence in my dreams.

There was yet more training to go through: Madam Wong informed me I would have to learn to speak in the pretty Soochow accent, regarded as necessary by most Shanghai clients. She said Xuan would help me. Also I had lessons from a lady actually from Soochow.

I had yet another task: that of choosing a working name. Madam Wong explained that the name Hsuan-chi would not do for Shanghai whose Chinese clients were still charmed by the classic story *Dream of the Red Chamber*, about a wonderful garden and its twelve main female inhabitants, with only one young man there. She said they wished to re-enact the fantasies with courtesans named after its characters. Madam Wong suggested I read the book and choose my character, usually from some aspect of my own life—or as I envisioned myself. She was not surprised when I chose Lin Daiyu, whose appearance and abilities closely matched my own. But in that first conversation I probed further:

"Chinese clients? Are there any other?"

"Oh yes, here you must entertain those from other countries."

This was a difficulty I had not foreseen. Now I understood why my studies in French and English were so important to Madam Wong. I found the idea of closeness to a man of a different race distasteful, but knew I had to overcome that feeling. After all, the welfare of others was at stake, as well as my

own future ability to decide matters for myself. I must continue
to discipline myself toward that end.

The initial duty I found enormous fun: the furnishing of
my entertaining room. As Cheng Ziyao had provided ample
funds for this project, unlike most beginner courtesans I did not
have to borrow from Madam Wong. In Shanghai the furniture
had to be a mix of antique and Art Deco designs. I thought
the rather austere black laquer of the antiques I bought blended
well with the black and white straight lines of the modern style.
With Xuan's help I decorated the walls with a blend of antique
scroll pictures drawn from episodes of *Dream of the Red Chamber*,
and modern art and framed photographs of film stars such as
Greta Garbo and Ginger Rogers, also Fred Astaire. One unusual
piece was a framed copy of the first cover of the *New Yorker*
with its image of the dandy Eustace Tilley. In keeping with the
Art Deco background, I learned to sing the latest tunes from
America. Foreign clients were charmed by my interpretation of
"Embraceable You" and "Three Little Words."

Xuan and I worked hard. "I am glad you are so well trained,"
said Madam Wong one morning as she delightedly counted
the money from the previous night's entertaining. "You bring
in much business in entertaining men and giving them dinners.
During the day they are using our house more often as a place to
hold business meetings. Here is your share," and Madam Wong
handed me a sizeable amount in American dollars. "Mind you
put it in the bank this morning. I don't want the same thing to
happen to you as happened to Madam Chen's daughter last week.
Did you know that she spent all her money on fripperies at Wing
On's, and forgot about the banking of it?"

Our Madam looked after Xuan and me well. In being small
and rounded, kind and gossipy, she resembled the Cantonese
Madam Deng but with a Shanghai style and polish not to be
seen elsewhere. She had set up a small shrine for us in the house
so that we could worship daily the God of Wealth. With other

Cantonese courtesans, we also attended the (Buddhist) Hong Temple.

After I arrived in the City, there were many distractions. With Xuan as my guide and companion, I explored Shanghai along the showcase areas of Western culture: Nanking Road and the Bund. I found that, like our own areas, they teemed with life and traffic day and night, but there was a difference.

"Look at the advertising. I've never seen anything like it," I said to Xuan, pointing to the neon lights outlining the main department stores, and blinking invitations to buy, buy, buy (Whiskey, superior cigarettes that do not hurt the throat, hats, perfumes, shoes) that lit up the night. There was even a dwarf or two, in evening clothes and a top hat, importuning the passing throng to spend, spend, spend.

When we went to the Big Four department stores Xuan said, "Get your money out." I asked why I needed money so soon. "It's an entrance fee: we have to pay for a ticket to go to each of the shops." I found these stores amazing, like nothing in Canton or in sleepy, colonial Hong Kong. Imagine their effect on me as they featured so many more Western goods than I had ever seen before, and exhibits of calligraphy, or paintings. There was also the opportunity to see and hear a radio broadcast during transmission (you could see the performers through a glass screen) and also the occasional opportunity to relax and have the wonderful afternoon tea. This pastime was only occasional because we must remain slim.

In this new life I soon became the "savvy" Shanghai resident, knowing where to shop, an important skill for me as a courtesan. For instance Chekiang Road was the best place for shoes. I could tell who the newcomers were as they were gawking at foreigners and at the wide range of goods in store windows, and also looking way up at high-rise buildings in the Art Deco style.

Luckily for us, the 1932 Japanese bombings of most of the Chinese area of Shanghai did not reach our little enclave near the Cantonese cemetery. However, they affected my dream of the Japanese Sandman, or rather that's what I thought was the reason at the time. Now, in my dream, the dear little figure was coming closer. He seemed to be changing, growing larger. *Did his attire look more practical than before? Was he in overalls?*

Every now and then we took some time to attend Western, especially American, movies in the International Settlement. The first time I attended one, the usher handed me a thick program, like the ones at a theatre. Leafing through it, I could see there were several pages of print there. "What is all this?"

"These are the summaries for the film in several different languages," and she found the different sections for me. "This must be your first time at a movie theatre in Shanghai, They all provide this type of program," and smiling, the usher turned to another customer.

When I first arrived, Fred Astaire and Ginger Rogers were the most popular musical stars. I thought their flapper and evening dress style fitted in with the Art Deco image of the Western sector of the City.

Although I found my first years in Shanghai so pleasant, during this time something happened that upset me deeply. This was the death in 1933 of my father. Uncle said it was better that I stay in Shanghai and not attend the funeral. So I had to mourn him by myself without the proper rituals. I knew what was behind the request. It was that they were ashamed of me. This was a bitter pill to swallow. I couldn't have loved dear Father more. However, I did burn joss sticks and pray for him.

At that time, Cheng Ziyao wrote me a letter that was completely unlike the bleak communication from Uncle Donghua, and also the rather tentative, anxious little note from Auntie Lo to which I replied with my assurance that I would continue to support the household in Canton. I have my mentor's letter still and have read it many times:

> Dearest Peipei, Please do accept my sincere condolences on the death of your father. I know how much you loved him and would wish to have been at his side when he died. But that was not possible as his

death was very sudden, and peaceful. As you would no doubt have wished, your father died in the arms of Ah Ling.

Knowing how much you loved him, I understand how you must feel, being excluded from the funeral rites. But you must always remember that you were the light of your father's life. Had he lived longer, you were to succeed him in managing his businesses. I knew your mother, and you are the image of her, in appearance and spirit. Your mother was so looking forward to your birth, and to actually holding you in her arms. She spent much time preparing baby clothes for you. Both yor parents will be watching over you for the rest of your life.

Qiu Xinren was a fine person, one who had my greatest respect. He was always a good comrade and adviser to me, and I have tried to return that wonderful friendship

However, there was a more practical side to this message, as he advised me to change the monthly amount of support to my family. My mentor again knew exactly what my father's care had cost, and advised me to reduce my cheque by that amount. Thanks to Cheng Ziyao, I was able to start further increasing my by now considerable savings.

This letter brought back memories . . .

I walked along in front of the huge glass-enclosed display cabinet in my father's study, and counted the complete set for twelve of tobacco leaf dinnerware, and rows of Ming Dynasty artefacts that Father had said were anything from four hundred to seven hundred years old. Then there was a pair of vases in blue and white with large blue leaves aligned up the long necks of the vases, which were decorated with garden scenes of willows, flowers and a boy playing a pipa. Despite the great age of the vases, against the straight neck and rounded outline of its body, the four strings of the instrument were still perfectly clear. Looking at the vases, I imagined myself actually in the garden they portrayed, lounging beside the woven bamboo fence, eating sweetmeats and listening to the music, and wishing that my mother would magically appear and play the pipa with me.

When I reached the age of ten, I started to accompany Father to his storehouses to evaluate the latest shipment of antiques, or of grocery products. The first time you do something is often the one you later remember, and I still remember the first time I went with my father to his businesses. The storehouses themselves looked so wonderful, decorated in ornate carving and bright red and yellow banners inside and out with characters on them. With difficulty I could see that the characters were giving protection from thieves and natural disasters, and also granting good luck. I decided to improve my attention to the lessons with Mr Wei.

When I entered I sniffed the air and said what a wonderful scent the groceries had. There were different aromas, of tea, and coffee, spices: mint, turmeric and cinnamon.

"What else?"

"There's the slightly dusty taste in the air of rice and lentils."

"Correct," my father was obviously pleased.

"You know what kind of feeling these scents give me? They provide a feeling I'm sure I'll never forget of security and comfort. It's like Ah Ling and her scent . . . the spices she rubs on her hands and face against the smell of the garlic she uses in cooking."

Father smiled, "She mothers you, doesn't she?" I nodded. "I'm glad."

Outside his office high up in the antiques storehouse, I walked out onto a carved and painted wood balcony that looked out over the goods laid out below. From my viewpoint, I imagined what was in the packing cases in rows on shelves: antiques from all over China, spices from all over the world.

"We trade with almost everyone on the Far- and Middle-East, and even the whole world. That's amazing."

Father laughed, "I suppose for you, being young, it is more of a thrill than it is for me having done this trading for so long that I've become used to the whole thing . . . regard them merely as trade goods, like rice or soap. To see your reaction lifts my spirits," and he picked me up and swung me round.

Afterwards, we'd have one of our helpers unpack a few items. "How much do you think this cost to buy and transport here? And how much should we sell it for to make a decent profit? Remember the overheads, mind. But first, what do you think is a decent profit, as a percentage of all that cost? You don't have to give me the answers right now," smiled Father, looking at my puzzled frown, "But these are the kinds of questions we'll be discussing as part of your training. We have to discuss all these types of business considerations and good record keeping as well. But I don't want to confuse you with too much at once."

On one of our business discussions I asked Father why Ailing never came with us to see his businesses. It was such fun. But Father shook his head and said she didn't have a talent for either business or antiques. "You will take over from me when I grow too old for it."

Giving myself a little shake, I put away Cheng Ziyao's letter and thought that while things hadn't turned out as Father intended, I was now, at the age of seventeen, considerably wealthy and independent. By the time I met Mu Shiying, I had achieved poise, self-discipline and reached the goal of financial control over my own destiny.

But how was I to surmount this next difficulty, that of not only marrying a respectable man, almost possible for a courtesan in the permissive culture of Shanghai, but of joining myself with a charming, fabulously handsome, literary celebrity?

6 (1920-Mid 1928)

It all began with the shrike's larder.

Turn west when you leave the Ningpo railway station, keep on right and turn off at the sign to the suburb of Cixi, and you will reach where we lived. The Mu family home was an old, large, rambling place with many rooms. One day, having stumbled on a sudden step down along a corridor, I asked our house manager Ah Shi-Yuan, "Why the hell does our house go up and down? No one else here has a house like this."

"It's older than the other houses in this area. It was someone's house for his country estate. Added parts have caused changes of level—and mind what you say!" *Always mind what you say, how you speak. When I grow up I'll speak as I bloody well please!*

Round our house was an exquisite formal garden ringed by high, uncultivated weeds. Needless to say it was in those weeds that my brothers and I preferred to play.

On a warm afternoon, Shiyan and I were exploring the deep greenery. We crawled silently along, pretending we were in a jungle's undergrowth, stalking lions and tigers. Our breaths went uhhh . . . huhhh . . . uhhh . . . huhhh, as we slowly savoured the mingled scents of the grass and wildflowers.

Slinking through the deep undergrowth, we came upon a briar, and saw the less beautiful side of Nature. There, impaled on thorns, was the food of a shrike, a bird whose harsh cry had often broken the afternoon silence. There were moths, butterflies and baby field mice, bumblebees and grasshoppers, some with their limbs still moving. That really gave me the creeps. It was disgusting! In the summer heat, above the silence of the afternoon and adding to my feeling of horror, all around, rising and falling again, came the high, metallic, zing zing singing of the cicadas.

I ran into the kitchen, and pulling off a length of wrapping paper started to write.

"What are you doing?" asked Ah Shi-Yuan, "Why aren't you drawing as usual?"

"But I am: I'm drawing what I *feel* about what I saw, only with *words* instead of lines." And that is how I started to write. That is also when I started to work really hard at learning the Chinese characters, because I found that without such knowledge, I had a rather limited palette with which to "paint" my stories.

I didn't have the right family background for a writer. My Parents. Well, in relation to our friends' fathers, ours was tall, an impressive man. He was a banker, senior in the Ningpo Commercial Bank. When Mu Guanglin went to the office he was always impeccably dressed in Western business suits and blindingly white shirts with ties. My father had smooth dark hair that was going bald on top. I always knew when Father arrived home in the evening, by the tinkling of the gold watch chain on his waistcoat as he took off his jacket. Then he always gave a big sigh, "It's so *wonderful* to be home again with you," he said to our mother.

As was usual for married women of her class and generation, our beautiful, slim mother, Cheng-mei, stayed most of the time at home where she dressed in traditional Chinese garments. With the help of Ah Shi-Yuan, she ran the house like clockwork.

One night, when I was six, I was in bed about to go to sleep, when my parents came in to say goodnight before going out for the evening. I suddenly noticed that my mother had on different clothes, the same kind as I'd seen on foreign ladies in rickshaws, only in a darker colour.

"Mother, why are you dressed in clothes like those of the godawful foreign ladies?"

"I change to European clothes when we go out to a social occasion with Chinese and foreign business people and their wives. You've probably noticed that Father wears European suits to work at the bank—and watch what you say!" *Watch what you say, watch how you express yourself, blah blah, nag nag.*

Like many of their middle class friends, my parents had a rather ambiguous attitude to foreigners. They adopted the clothes and to a certain extent the culture. However, I had the impression that they did not like the Japanese, and often expressed dislike of the Western foreign presence in Ningpo and China generally. One evening at dinner, Father complained: "We are too much pushed around in our trading by the unequal treaties with other countries like France. They are interfering in our politics far too much, backing the Kuo-Min-Tang (KMT) versus the Chinese Communist Party (CCP). We need a united political system. The influence of Japan is dangerous to Chinese sovereignty."

Education. I and my younger brothers, Shiyan and Shijie, and later sister Lijuan, who was born after we went to live in Shanghai, learned to read and write in Chinese, but also in Western languages: English and French. We had to write essays in the new languages. I thought English was terrific. I have always preferred it above all others. Given its many words, in English one can be exact, choosing one word only for what you mean to say. In French, I find myself involved in a rather clumsy concocting of a phrase to say what I want. Not that anyone has ever asked, but English has my vote every time.

One day, as I struggled with a mountain of homework after school I asked my father, "Why are we learning all these languages? For Pete's sake, we live in China, not France or Great Britain."

Father paused before he answered. He always spoke in the measured way of most accountants, "It is to prepare you for the future. You may well need them. In my job I use all three languages. It is much easier to learn these when you are young than later. For one thing, you have the spare time—and mind how you express yourself. Remember your position as the eldest son. You must set a good example for your brothers and sister! Your mother and I think you should stop using slang,"

"Spare time, *what* spare time? I do nothing but work, work, Work. And would you want me to speak like one of my teachers, or those banker friends of yours?"

"Yes. You have much to learn about good manners, and you *will* learn."

Food. Generally, we ate like everyone else. However, one day a week we dined in the Western style. Father said it would be an important skill in our later business lives. I remember thinking, *Those later business lives, I'm not looking forward to mine: working at a desk, minding my ps and qs (another phrase I mustn't say) and behaving, behaving, behaving.* I would rather write, perhaps for a newspaper.

As I reached my teens, the atmosphere at home became more restricted. Because of Father's ill health, we couldn't make a noise, have our friends in to visit and discuss our views. This was not at all favourable to expanding myself, and writing.

Father's Health. It deteriorated until he became too ill to work. The doctors Mother brought in could find no particular physical cause for what was a steady decline. The Chinese doctors tried herbal remedies and dried body parts of animals, but nothing worked. The foreign doctors said it was all in the mind, but it was also very much affecting our father's body.

During his illness, I often went to the sick room to talk with Father. The puff puff, of my father's laboured breathing formed a depressing background to our times together. The conversations were full of Father's disappointment, not with *me* in lacking a business orientation, but with *himself* in yielding to the temptation to leave the previous steady path in life to try something different on the side. My father told me he'd been gambling on the stock market and in gold. With his regular job, it was too much of a strain. Father partly blamed his actions on the more exhilarating, permissive atmosphere of Shanghai where he had transferred to a position in the Ningpo Commercial Bank there.

Father Discussed Life's Crises. My father said that the desire for variety, to set and achieve new goals, or have new experiences: curiosity about the path not taken, but for which there may still be time, *this crisis*, visits many men in their later middle age.

"Some men deal with it by taking a young concubine but," and Father shook his head, "I could never do that to your mother. And anyway my crisis has been about not kicking over the traces, not sowing my wild oats, in the sense of my *occupation*, rather than in the sense of my personal life. I could never regret my early and steady devotion to your mother, and hers to me." At that time, I felt cramped by the gloomy atmosphere in a house where we all had to keep quiet. I was getting keen to sow some wild oats of my own!

An aspect that bothered my father was that his own distress paralleled the (more unconscious) turmoil that often takes place in the teenage years—something I must currently be experiencing. *He could say that again: I was thoroughly fed up! I needed to meet some different girls.*

Girls. My whole life my mother had concentrated on making sure that I met girls, ho-hum respectable girls, girls that were no fun. I couldn't start finding out about the female body from them because these were virtuous girls. They filed in to my birthday parties, their eyes respectfully cast down, their voices never raised, daughters of the bankers we knew through our father. The same young ladies came to all my other parties. I attended their similar events. I bowed and asked them to dance, holding the girl at a respectable distance. By the time I reached fifteen, I realized: *All this is for my future marriage to one of the respectable girls and for the breeding of ho-hum, respectable, banker types of children. Not if I can help it!* (By now I knew enough not to even *think* in terms of *not bloody likely!*) My hormones were going wild!

Father apologized, "I am so sorry that I'm not being of more support to you. Try not to allow your confusion to take over your life and studies. Have your regular studies form the secure basis of your life. Make yourself into the best person you can be."

The sad atmosphere at home weighed me down: the stuffy smell of my father's decay, the taste in the air of medical concoctions. What use were apologies to me? Nothing was going to change.

When I went in to see Father it was always to hear: "Would you please draw the blinds and curtains more tightly over the windows? Are they properly tight across the next room's windows as well?" I would go and see if everything in and around the sick room was as dark as it could be made during the day. These shadowy surroundings were in contrast to the light, modern furniture throughout our house, which reflected our former lighter mood. So as not to disturb, everyone moved about quietly. Over the stillness rose the khu khu sound of his darned annoying cough.

University. Well, feeling rather guilty about it, I longed to get away from the dark hole where I lived with my parents. When the University's prospectus came, I ran to Father with it, excitedly tearing open the big envelope it came in, "Look, Father, it's on shiny paper with photos of the grounds and lecture rooms." I turned it over in my hands. "It's pretty fancy, but too wordy. It goes on blah blah Blah about the newness of the place; a few years ago, in 1925, some faculty and over five hundred students left the American Anglican St. John's University and set up there. Who cares?"

My father frowned, "That was a serious matter. The exit from St. John's was to protest the shooting of several Chinese students by the International Settlement police on May 30th. They had been demonstrating against the exploitation of Chinese workers in some Japanese cotton mills in north Shanghai, also complaining about the shooting of the workers' leader, who was trying for better conditions. People *died*." *But what on earth had all this to do with me—now? This was old history from three or four years ago when I was twelve or thirteen. Let's lighten up here: at sixteen I wanted to look forward, not back.*

Father saw my expression and frowned again. "You must start taking an interest in current affairs, start bothering about what is going on around you, Shiying." But I persisted in my views. So what if the university I attended was essentially founded to protest foreign domination in China. I had other things to bother about, like getting away from home, and having a much better time.

University or any other old place would do. Anyone, anything would be okay to come and save me. I wanted to work out different ways of doing stories. I felt I could really spread myself out in the Big City of central Shanghai, discover a wider range of subjects for my stories than the ones of my childhood, find a broader canvas to paint with my words. I arrived in September of 1928, at the age of sixteen, to begin studies in Chinese literature at the Guanghua Chinese University.

From then on, I didn't take anything very seriously except my own enjoyment, and above all those writing goals.

7 (September 1928-End 1928)

Shanghai's International Settlement. My arrival to stay in student lodgings at university in central Shanghai was a mind-blowing occasion for *me*, but not for the city, that went about its own life in the usual frenzied and self-centred way. Wherever I went I couldn't escape the blaring, blah blah hot din, what they called the *jenao,* which went on in the streets almost around the clock. But then I didn't *want* to escape. I loved it all: trams and cyclists clanging their bells, car horns honking, rickshaw pullers and others shouting their wares, people doing business deals in the middle of the street, pedestrians talking to companions in voices raised above the surrounding racket—this whole jingle jangle orchestra, raggedly conducted by Sikh policemen on traffic islands, played exhilarating music to my ears. That city held an all-day party celebration, and I was part of it.

World Travel. There were so many different nations represented in Shanghai, (some said everyone but Eskimos), and so many different neighbourhoods where people from abroad settled down together, like the Parsee section full of stores with bright silks, and Little Vienna for the German Jewish people, that Shanghai seemed to be the whole world in microcosm. I soon found out that, within this background, you could have the sensation of travelling. For someone like me, from the quiet backwaters of both Ningpo and Shanghai, and with my own background in the respectable, terminally boooring banking community, central Shanghai afforded a mind-blowing change. I'd really be able to live it up!

My world expanded and my potential grew: on the Settlement's flat landscape and straight streets I could see for miles.

Wandering around in the first few months as a student, other parts of the world burst in on me, such as the waltz of the French Concession, slow-voiced French chanteuses, uniformed Russian generals and even princes in the Renaissance and other cafés of the serene, tree-lined, very French streets and buildings; then, as if moving to the rhythm of a rackety jazz tune, the Art Deco high rises, modern goods and music, flashy cars and hurrying, clackclack, dada steps of the people of Nanking Road in the British and American International Settlement, danced by.

I plunged into this crowd from different nations, even from other parts of China that I'd never visited, and immediately felt with it, part of the modern scene. Armed with a notebook, I set out to learn the writer's trade, and wrote down snatches of overheard conversations: "C'est la Vie." "I can't live without her." "Name your price." "At the formative stages of the advertising, the imprinting of consumers is huge" and "It's not yet carved in stone."

Most of the dozen or so student clubs I joined at Guanghua University had no connection with my stated subject of study, Chinese Literature—but then, who cared? Like all young students, we spent our lives earnestly discussing philosophy, religion . . . the whole world. Some of the overheard fragments I jotted down in my notebook at that time were: "Alcohol and religion are not a good way to solve problems." Someone near me came up with the comment: "Plato said that the unexamined life is not worth living."

"Oh rubbish! That may have been all right for four hundred B.C. but I think you can examine your life far too much, and from so doing, make it not worth living. The main thing is to get out there and *live* your time on earth, *enjoy* it. That's my philosophy, and you can quote me on it: Mu Shiying, almost two thousand A.D."

Then I returned to my note taking of fragments of conversation: "Thinking logically about ourselves puts us less at the mercy of others." "It's not how long you live, but what you *do* with the time." the puzzling: "How can we get to that same, visceral, connective level?" and the even more puzzling comment by the astrophysicist Sir Arthur Eddington that a student quoted: "Something unknown is doing we don't know what."

Air Travel. Its future was the subject of one of our debates and some of the notes I took were: "It's far too expensive." "Now, but what about twenty years from now?", "Yes, look at railways, and also cars. They were all too expensive for most people at the start." and the philosophical: "Ah, but will future air passengers have the same type of experience as Lindbergh?"

Of course the debate was sparked by Charles Lindbergh's solo flight across the Atlantic in the previous year (1927). I was so captivated by the subject that I read up on it in the university's library. One comment by Harold Anderson in the *New York Sun*, written before the flight, caught my attention, "Alone? Is he alone at whose right side rides Courage, with Skill within the cockpit and Faith upon the left?" Boy, would this be a good subject for later writing! I vowed to take a trip in a 'plane—when I had the money. In the meantime, I wrote an article on the future of air travel for the student magazine—perhaps I should aim at newspaper writing.

Neitzsche's Religion of Comfortableness. A philosophical debate we had on this subject at university affected my aims in life. Here are some more of my jottings: "Neitzsche says that the religion of comfortableness is one of small, mean people who hide in the forest like shy deer. But isn't it better to be cautious and comfortable, and not take too many risks?" "No, he also says that for true fulfillment, we must abandon comfort and face difficulties." "Yes, any worthwhile achievement is born of constant struggle and hard work, and a lot of practice." "As he says, we must learn to respond well to suffering. It is also our patriotic duty as students to . . ."

These discussions confirmed me in my desire to work very hard at my chosen career. In these wonderful days of freedom I tended to stray from the Chinese literature of the past that was supposed to be the focus of my studies, and thought hard about what my own writing should be like in the present. It was high time to get away from the stories about family and friends I had written for the amusement of my brothers and sister. Should I study philosophy, and with the insights I obtained help others in their lives?

Well no, I decided to continue portraying the world as it was, but in a deeper way that would show the reader what the Japanese referred to as *mono no aware*, (*lacrimae rerum* in my school Latin classes) or the pathos of things. I wanted to demonstrate the poignancy behind modern life, and move readers. But as Neitzsche would have said, first must come the hard slog—or something like that.

I became rather flippant about my studies, exhibiting a lack of seriousness that I now understand possibly came, partly anyway, as a reaction to my young years spent with the sadness at home over my father's ill health. I specialized in leaving essays and studying for exams until the last minute, staying up half the night to finish, and then publicly exulting when my results surpassed those of my duller, more plodding fellows. One morning when I dashed in to class, late as usual, having stayed up all night to complete the assignment in my hand, the instructor said, "Here comes our brilliant Mu, seeking attention as usual. He's our limelight case." There were other comments I overheard: "I saw Shiying with his head in the air, gawking at the high buildings on Nanking Road. One of these days he'll get himself run over." and "I can't believe his countrified clothes."

Yes, I did like the limelight. Yes, I had the large ego that one of my later mentors informed me was present in all authors, however modest and quiet some seemed to be. And yes, I did need to develop more of the polish of central Shanghai.

One of the clubs I joined within Guanghua University was one for political debates. There I took part in heated, fascinating discussions on Marxist theory and practice. During one debate, another student actually accused me: "*You* should understand what *bourgeois* means, Shiying, you are from that middle class stratum of society yourself."

Another stood up and turned to me. "Yes," he said, "Your father is always sending you money, you don't work as hard as we do on your studies. It's *your* class that has persecuted the helpless masses, and lived off the fruits of their labour."

I thought back in a puzzled way to our house manager, Ah Shi-Yuan. *Were we persecuting him and living off his labour? Perhaps.*

An ardent Communist I saw at these debates, was a quiet, gentle person, called Rou Shi, who used to drop in to take part. We became great friends: the attraction of opposites, no doubt. He was ten years older than me, but did not hesitate to spend time explaining the Communist philosophy. We used to wander round Yu Yuan garden for ages, sitting on the benches having snacks and discussing not only Communism, but also the art of writing. It was partly due to Rou's mentoring that I achieved my first published short story. He had been the Education Bureau Director for his birthplace, Ninghai. Rou Shi's austere hairstyle with his hair drawn tightly back from his face and also the round glasses he always wore, added to the overall impression Rou gave of being a genuine intellectual.

He was very much part of Shanghai's writing scene and in two years published the much admired love story *February*, which was made into a movie, and the serious and sad *My Slave Mother*. This was a story about a situation, so common among the very poor, where a young mother was loaned for three years to an older scholar, to have another child by him. When she returned, her own first son didn't know her. He looked ill cared for. This was a typical story for the Communist propaganda.

Over the next two years, partly because of his busy involvement in publishing with the famous Communist sympathizer and fervent nationalist Lu Xun who had returned from Japan, and also because of my own other activities, I rather lost track of my friend. However I had learned a great deal from him. Rou Shi had a definite effect on my thinking, on my later growing sympathy toward the common man, as I matured as a man and a writer. Above all, my conversations with Rou Shi affected my writing about this subject. Both in my initial publications and even later

I criticised the rampant capitalism of Shanghai. The first line of *Shanghai Foxtrot*, published in 1932, says it all: "Shanghai, a Heaven built on Hell."

From my fellow Marxists, (for that was what I decided to become), I learned that this was the way forward: I was to live *and* write my Marxism. To achieve that aim, I decided I must have some experience frequenting the seamier streets of the city, and develop an ear for dialect and language, to imitate the speech and manners of the "lumpen proletariat", the lowest of the low. Through this writing I vowed to further the cause of the masses. Conversely, I also needed to become more like others in the centre of Shanghai, less of a clueless, suburban import.

Shanghai type of *Flâneur*. During my initial period as a student, I began to see myself as a *flâneur*, a sophisticated, leisurely observer of the city scene. But I soon realized that this French type of person, typically found in Paris, could not be transplanted to our Chinese (albeit at the same time international) city without some modification. Walking around as an observer in Shanghai required a rather different type of person. Due to the fast pace of the city, confusion of sound, light, colour—and dangers especially after dark—such an individual would have to be in a state of tense alertness all the time, keep a level head. He would have to learn to filter out the honkhonk, flashflash and dada of the surroundings, to focus, to notice what was really going on, to get the flashes of dialogue that were so revealing.

At this stage, it was the voice of the ordinary people that I was looking for, but other dialogue infiltrated my consciousness and invaded my more mature writing, like the conversation of three young men about Daisy Huang from my story, *Five in a Nightclub:* They said she was regarded as "quite a dish" before, but now she was not good looking. One youngster said it was a pity—and amazing, what havoc a few years could do to a woman's appearance.

In student life there were classes to attend, essays to write and time-consuming but valuable participations in discussions about politics and philosophy. The lodgings and food were Spartan. The expectation of us was to work endlessly as a patriotic duty. In addition, for me, came the constant walking around on foot watching, learning and taking notes on a different vocabulary in the seedier parts of this new city. Here one night, I was going past a narrow side street when a young streetwalker propositioned me. "I'll do it for no money at all—only food for my mother and me. We haven't eaten anything for two days," she said. *Shanghai was truly a Heaven built on Hell.*

Becoming a Shanghai Native. Soon, I seemed to be staying up all day and all night. I couldn't get enough of the City. Soon, my ear for vocabulary and turns of phrase, and my unerring eye for clothes, had me fitting in with the seasoned residents. I blended to the point that I even learned the local slang, for instance, referring to Sikh members of the Settlement's Shanghai Municipal Police force as redheaded flies, after the red turbans these extra-tall men wore with their blue, brass-buttoned uniforms. Standing on raised concrete platforms they directed traffic, with the help of the city's ultra-*modeng* traffic lights no less—but with no great success: in Shanghai, traffic had a mind of its own.

Modeng: what a word! Everything here was so leading edge, even the vocabulary. "Modeng modeng Modeng," I shouted, staggering as I looked up at the wild flashing colours of neon signs, and no one even noticed, no one so much as blinked.

Girls. Let's not forget about them! Girls in Guanghua University were different from those in Xiuneng Institute, the school I had attended. I figuratively and literally embraced them with all my new enthusiasm for life. At first anyway, they seemed to personify the real, sophisticated city woman of my imagination. I was entranced. They knew about make-up, shoes and how to dress. They would even discuss these with me: "With a dress this colour, you wouldn't wear dark red lipstick, or blue eye shadow, you'd put on . . ." and "The higher the heel, the more fun life is at night."

At last I was enjoying my life. That's what life is for after all: a glass of fine wine, to be emptied to the last drop. With this new set of girls, I went to all the best dance halls (these young women certainly knew about dancing). I thought of myself as learning to dance in the *modeng* Western way.

Research in the Dance Halls. Soon after coming to the Settlement, I started frequenting the dance halls to take notes on the modern men and women I saw there, observe the human fauna of the city. I was putting aside the early interest in Nature developed during a Ningpo childhood, but using essentially the same observational techniques. Out came my notebook. These human fauna were to be much different from the more naïve ones I saw at university.

My foxtrot. It became quite spectacular. The daa daa da da daaa rhythm formed a bubble of sound in which I moved around the dance floor. Every time I was at Moon Palace a ring of dancers formed, "Go on, Shiying, let's see your foxtrot," they said, clapping in time to the music. Indeed, my foxtrot quickly became the main attraction when I took the floor, entranced by the dance. Other dancers always drew to one side to watch. The saxophone's wooo wooo held me in its spell. With the girls from university I danced all night and we ran from one nightclub to another until someone said: "Let's crash at Wong's place," and we collapsed to sleep in each other's arms in someone's lodgings, wherever we were when we were too tired to continue. It was the foxtrot that gave me the title for my famous piece, *Shanghai Foxtrot*. (I do know I've mentioned it already.) In it I painted a picture of 1930s Shanghai, imagining a saxaphone as having a mouth to give out its whooowhooo music to which women in their slit skirts and high heels danced.

Ningpo. I thought back to my days there when I first started my observations, and realized that in a few years, and in particular the past few months, I had come a long way.

In my solitary wanderings, (my student friends did not like visiting tough places), I visited the worst parts of the city. I saw people existing in makeshift shelters by the side of open creeks. They used the brackish, filthy water, oozing up from the Whangpoo sea-river. I saw them depositing their sewage in it, bathing in it and drinking it. Such water made them ill. The women often turned to selling their bodies.

Going out into real life at night in the City, without the lifebelt of other students around me, I was increasing the fun, but also increasing the risk. However, taking risks is what life is all about. I worked at acquiring the language of these poorer people. I soon understood the nuances of appearance and the power imbalance between rich and poor: In one of my early writings, "Black Whirlwind", I pointed out that whereas the rich had face cream, and a special product called Stacomb for their hair, the faces of the poor were smeared in dirt and they used gasoline to dress *their* hair.

Walking through the city, I experienced this intoxicating blend on the roads of bicycles, coolies carrying loads balanced on both ends of long poles, rickshaws, pedicabs, wheelbarrows loaded with people or goods, and as if incidentally, *cars*, their beep beep, honk honk complaint reflecting the frustration of the drivers. I adored adored Adored this hybrid mix that passed for traffic in Shanghai: the bicycles almost pushed off the road by trams, the blinking colours of the traffic lights and the onrush of people and traffic when they changed. All these featured in my later writing.

As the Guanghua administrators had followed the example of their parent, St. John's University, in providing student magazines and many other activities, there was scope within the university for my writing. For the student magazines I wrote stories and articles about what was going on in the university, but wished for greater fame and glory. An outside world, *real* magazine run by established writers was my goal. I *was* laying down the groundwork. However, now I had to decide how to meet with real writers, published writers, find out how to become a published writer myself.

So far during my university career, I had been beset by the stories racing around in my head, that had to be beaten back for the, albeit occasional, pursuit of my studies. Behind my writing chair thronged a multitude of phantom characters, jostling for attention, crowding my humble student's room. "Take me, No me, Make *me* come alive," they begged. Now, I ceased resisting them.

8 (1929)

At this point I need to slow down. Slow down, but how can I do that when the very air of Shanghai says "Hurry, hurry, Hurry?" Nevertheless I must let you know how I met my mentors and took my first step as a writer, published my first short story. Even this beginning was not without struggle, for as in other human endeavours, so in writing, practice makes for improvement, if not for that perfection which is largely unattainable, but that I decided to strive for all my life. My writing was one thing I worked hard at. It became the focus of my whole life.

In Shanghai there were the endless gift boxes provided by the foreign concessions, all asking to be opened: new sights and sounds, new subjects for stories. One evening, another student from the university's French Club, Ji, saw me in the cafeteria and came up, "Why don't you come along to the Zengs' bookstore at their publishing house on Rue Massenet. They're holding a salon tonight, discussing French literature. It'll improve your French."

What an experience that was! It was to be the high point of my first year of study. All conversation was about French authors and was *de rigueur* conducted in the French language. Wide-ranging discussions swooped quickly back and forth in time. I listened as the others examined the philosophical ideas of the contemporary poet and man of letters, Paul Valéry, (from my notebook): "Of course he shares Goethe's fascination with science," and, "His conservative and skeptical outlook verges on cynicism about human nature."

Then also nineteenth century authors became the subject of conversation, such as Honoré de Balzac and his cycle of novels on *The Human Comedy*, and Gustave Flaubert whose *Madame*

Bovary had initially been banned (from my notebook): "Of course he was banned because he started something new, that is the painstaking and true depicting of real life," and, "Isn't that why some of our own writers are being banned right now?"

On that first visit, I learned that, given the tightening grip of political groups, the question of banning literature was becoming one of immediate interest to Shanghai's writing community. The main political factions named were the Kuo Min Tang (KMT) and Communists (CCP). Having at first made a united front against the Japanese with them, Chiang Kai-shek had started in 1927 with sweeping arrests and massacres of Communists throughout China. In Shanghai there were the notorious killing grounds at Lunghua airfield, near the temple. Thank goodness the White Terror had not yet focused on the works of the non-political writers. So there was nothing to worry about yet, and everything to enjoy. Enjoying life, that was the main thing.

At first I was on my best behaviour, but soon relaxed as the talk was informal, and people came in and out as they pleased. However, the discussions of literature were all in the past. I wanted to know what was new *now*. At the Zengs' salon I was thrilled to meet well-known Shanghai authors; the first one was their good friend and prominent Shanghai literary figure, Zhang Ruogu. Among his many works was "Café Forum" in which he rightly depicted coffee houses as a key element of modernity, with an enormous effect on modern literature worldwide: across Europe, Shanghai and Tokyo, and providing the stimulus of coffee, a social network for authors and the charming presence of waitresses. This was the good life. I was talking with other authors. It was all so exciting!

It was on a later visit to the Zengs' salon that I first heard of Shi Zhecun, the prominent literary figure who was to take on the role of one of my mentors. At first the discussion was about the French author, Charles Baudelaire, and the darkness of his works. I'd had enough of darkness at home. Give me some relief! It then focused, briefly thank goodness, on Baudelaire's translations of the equally dark tales of mystery and the macabre by Edgar Allan

Poe, and the effect of these on the writing of Shi Zhecun. Shi experimented in the supernatural sphere of writing, "But no one could say that he is decadent in the way that Baudelaire was," said Shi's friend, the literary editor Du Heng.

"Some say this type of writing specializes in turning the ordinary, cozy situation into the supernatural one," came a deep voice from the back of the salon. "Yes, think of Shi Zhecun's *Traveller's Inn* in which a traveller from the city complains about the poor conditions in a country inn, only to find himself in the midst of ghosts and demons." "Or his *Demonic Way:* the three appearances of the old woman in black, presaging the death of the protagonist's little daughter. Both these have overtones of Edgar Allan Poe and his tendency to make the ordinary change into the . . ."

But then, (and here's the good part) I heard: "Shi has started some successful literary magazines; they last a few months, which isn't bad these days, and he may be starting another one." Now we were getting somewhere; this was good information for my own interest in writing stories.

During these long debates, with their constantly shifting population of debaters, I realized I was even *thinking* in French, as my language tutor had suggested I would, if exposed to the language for long enough. I soon found myself knowing more about French literature than about my own, which was supposed to be the subject on which I concentrated my studies. But I was expanding myself, and that was the main thing. At the end of a session at the Zeng salon, I was often by myself without Ji, a very quiet person who had stopped coming out with me, given the late nights and raucous company I loved.

The Writing Community. During the day I frequented the cafés to meet other writers. (*Other writers?* you say, *What impudence!* But I just knew I was one of them, and I *knew* that like them I would be published.) The Zengs' salon, father Zeng Pu and son Zeng Xubai, had introduced me to a wide spectrum of books and also to some of the literary set in Shanghai such as Shi and Dai Wangshu, from whom I learned which places to attend, such as the Balkan Milk Store. Entering, I could hear the rhubarb rhubarb rhubarb sound from the conversations of poor writers (writers are seldom rich) attracted by the reduced prices for coffee and cakes that prevailed in the less busy afternoons between lunch and teatime. Zeng told me that he and other Shanghai writers felt like the French ones who congregated to talk in the Paris cafés, such as Les Deux Magots.

My walks took me past bookstores selling second-hand publications in English. I loved the musty smell of the books. Soon, through their books, I was also speaking to contemporary writers such as Ernest Hemingway and F.Scott Fitzgerald, John Dos Passos and also the French Paul Morand whose movie-like descriptive techniques my later friend and publisher, Liu Na'ou, and I followed. We put in our own interpretation, our own Chinese background and, may I say without again being potentially told off for being conceited, our own talent. But I'm rushing ahead of myself as usual.

Café Society. As I've mentioned before, as far as possible, I made a point of spending the afternoons in cafés frequented by the literary crowd, such as Rio Rita, which had a garden section that was ideal in better weather. I also frequented the Renaissance in the French Concession (a favourite of mine with its exotic mix of different people and music) or DD's on the Settlement's Bubbling Well Road. The leftist writer, Mao Dun: why did we have to describe a writer from the point of view of his politics? Because, due to the actions of political factions, his safety was at stake. Mao Dun made Rio Rita famous by his description of it in his book *Midnight, A Romance of China in 1930*. And later, there I was, sitting in places like Rio Rita, actually in the centre of our new Chinese literature, of the stories I read, at the source of everything important in literary life that was happening in China.

One afternoon, early in my first year at university, I was at DD's, yak-yak-yakking as usual, when along came this stocky, pleasant looking man, with a round face and wearing Western clothes. I'd never seen him before. The man spoke rapidly to everyone and they seemed to know him, but I couldn't understand a word he was saying. *Is he speaking Japanese?* I asked myself. And then, *But he doesn't look Japanese. He's also of medium height, doesn't suffer from the lack of stature (not like the Japanese dwarfs). Yet some words sound vaguely familiar.* I smiled and addressed him politely, "Excuse me, are you speaking Japanese, or Chinese?"

Liu Na'ou, for that's who it was, laughed in a good-natured way. In slow and distinct speech he said, "I'm speaking Chinese with a Japanese accent. I've not long returned from a two-year visit to my family in Japan."

A Profitable Friendship. I quickly adapted to Liu Na'ou's way of speaking and was soon spending much of my time in his company. The first time I went to see Liu at his Frontline bookstore in the Chinese sector of Shanghai, Liu clapped me on the shoulder and said, "Just the man I need, with strong young arms to help me unpack the crates of books I've brought from Japan."

I admired, and decided to emulate, his perfect personal grooming, well-kept clothes and self-assured manner. Liu had money and the ingrained confidence that came with it. He was able to finance a bookstore, and later, magazines. One time, as I was unpacking books, I started to read out the titles and suggest where they should go.

"Heavens!" said Liu, "I didn't know you could speak all these languages. . . . You should have said so before," and he handed me a volume he was shelving. "Here, you take over and I'll look at the finances," he said, departing to his office at the back. So then, with minimum instruction from Liu, I was able to help in shelving the amazing range and number (thousands) of Japanese, Chinese and European books brought from Japan.

Addictions. There was another benefit, that of being paid for my help. It was money that went immediately to feed my obsessions with dancing and gambling. It was at this stage of my life that I started to have the occasional flutter on the racing dogs at the French Concession's Canidrome, and on its *hai alai* courts. There they paid no attention whatsoever to the KMT's edict against gambling, but publicly went ahead with it. I admired their independent attitude. What we all needed was more freedom to do as *we* wished to do, and not as others dictated. If people wanted to enjoy themselves gambling, why shouldn't they?

It was also at this point in my life that I took up the habit of smoking. I smoked only the expensive brand smoked by Shanghai sophisticates, Craven A, which became part of the image I was at that time consciously developing for myself. Craven A even gave me the title and name of the main character (a sophisticated, *modeng* woman) of one of my later stories. I saw myself as a bit like the ultra smart Fred Astaire, lighting up a cigarette and looking at Ginger Rogers through the smoke, which I carefully blew to one side so as not to be a nuisance to her.

Movies and the Cinemas. With the new set of girls, I haunted the cinemas and watched movies from America. There was a wide range of types of story and we all enjoyed the musicals. Fred Astaire and Ginger Rogers, in gorgeous modern clothes and with their slick backchat and perfect dancing, fitted the image I was developing of Shanghai as the quintessential *modeng* city.

To finance my interests, I needed some other source of income and my attendance at movies gave me the idea of going to the theatre proprietors and offered to write the plot *précis*.

The first manager I approached, at the Odeon, looked doubtfully at me. "You seem rather young," he said. *I felt like punching the paunchy old idiot.* But remembering my family's training, smiled and produced a free sample of my version of a summary they already had. The manager read it and compared it to their summary, a copy of which I produced with mine. "Hmmm," he said drumming on his desk thrum, thrum, Thrum (exactly like my father), "This is good . . . more enjoyable and easy to understand, than what we already have. We'll give you a try, young man. Come to the theatre on Monday, our day off, and view next week's movies. You can write the summaries in French, English and Chinese. I'll expect them by Wednesday." *Bliss: I make an income on the summaries and have free pre-viewing of the films. What could be better?*

Soon, I had gone through very much the same interviewing process with other theatre managers, but this time with previous experience, and was receiving more writing assignments that involved following one of my favourite pastimes. From there, it was one short step to writing reviews, and occasionally having them featured in local newspapers.

Despite this infusion of cash, and the generous allowance from my father, I didn't have any money in my pockets, not for long anyway. My initially rather mixed attitude (of guilt and pleasure) to the losses on my other, and newer, enthusiasm congealed into a regular way of thinking: *I'll keep gambling only long enough to gain back my losses, and then I'll stop,* I assured myself, feeling I was being sensible and virtuous too, careful about money.

But the odds were always more against than for me, and my lucky streaks never paid enough to cover all the losses. At the end of the week my pockets were as empty as before. As well, attendance at the Canidrome dance floor was much more expensive than the afternoons and evenings I spent at my favourite nightclub and dance hall Moon Palace. But then at the Canidrome I was mixing with the smart set in Shanghai. At Moon Palace, I was enjoying myself and observing the *modeng,* rather risqué type of woman for my stories.

At that time, I would rather dance than eat, gamble than buy a drink of soymilk. Soon, the puppy fat that I had put on under my mother's careful feeding melted away. I had always had an above average height, but now became slim, and elegant in the wardrobe of *modeng* clothes I had purchased: always down to my last cent and always trying to get my story writing improved and published.

At the end of the whole day's activities, there was that of staying up into the early hours of the morning writing in my new proletarian vocabulary about my new subjects. This was to further my overall aim of becoming a published writer.

After a few months I drew my pieces to Liu Na'ou's attention by literally throwing them onto his desk saying, "Why haven't you asked to see my stories? You know I'm writing them."

Good-natured as always, he smiled, read them and said the stories showed promise but that they simply didn't ring true. "Practice, practice, practice," he said, "And immerse yourself totally in the background you want to write about." However, Liu Na'ou did further help me financially by commissioning some translations into Chinese of short stories originally written in French or English.

I join the coterie. The leaders in Shanghai's literary scene regularly dropped in to Liu's Frontline bookstore. The most frequent were Liu Na'ou's former classmates at Aurora University, run by French Jesuits. Like Liu, Shi Zhecun, (the leading writer discussed at the Zengs' salons), and Dai Wangshu, known as the foremost modernist poet in China, had all come from the university's French language program. Another regular visitor to the store was Liu's friend, the prominent writer and editor Du Heng. These four were the coterie I joined. With them I discussed questions of literary techniques and one's philosophy of life and writing.

"You have to have plenty of action," said Liu, "And lots of conversation too. Otherwise the reader will put the story down and not read it to the end."

"Another thing," came the knowledgeable voice of Du Heng, "is to vary the subject you're writing about, don't stay too long on one aspect, jump about."

"Talking of jumping about," came Liu's voice, "I like the idea of imitating the film camera, panning from one person to another. My aim is to have a visual effect to my writing."

We hotly debated the statement by John Dos Passos that Hollywood was a "bargain sale of five and ten cent lusts and dreams." "I cannot accept that. Our Chinese films are not so oriented to simply making money. Is that what John Dos Passos means? . . . that the bottom line is all that matters. What about Art?" Hour after hour we talked.

"The whole aim is to keep improving and developing your mastery of the craft. Although absolute perfection is not possible, you have to keep reaching for it. Never lose faith in yourself," chimed in Shi again.

So we sat around together reading old issues of our favourite American magazines, *Vanity Fair*, the *New Yorker* and *Harper's*, all of which we read in the original English. As with Na'ou, the writers of this group were older than I was by seven years, and in the case of Na'ou twelve years. Yet the age gap didn't seem to matter. These new friends of mine understood that, given some time to develop, I would be like them. Mentally, I hugged myself with satisfaction and thought: *What a great step forward: to find my cohort.*

9 (1930)

Within a year or two, I came to be known in the busy literary community of Shanghai. One morning I was walking along Nanking Road and heard someone say, "There's Mu Shiying, he's a real literary up-and-comer." But *still* I had not been published as a writer of stories. I was dying to feature in a literary magazine Liu started, called *Trackless Train*. These delays were a total pain. Why wouldn't Liu publish me? I felt like screaming at him. But by now I had learned not to do that sort of thing, courtesy of my parents.

"Why are you calling the magazine *Trackless Train?*"

"In China the new writing is entwined with speed, power . . . the architecture and machinery of modern life. That's why I've called it after one of our icons, the train. The title also makes you think of one of the ultra modern trackless trams that provide transport in Shanghai. Anything very modern becomes one of our symbols."

Another time when I was moping about his bookstore, and glowering about the latest rejection notice, I lashed out childishly: "It's all right for you, you can publish your own work. You don't like mine because you're rich, and my stories are about treating everyone equally, rich or poor, about treating the workers fairly."

Liu looked at me earnestly and said: "I understand your desire to write in the proletarian mode. Others are doing the same and are getting published, especially those who, like you, are committed to Marxism. As your friend and being also a publisher, I should give you a chance, but not yet." Liu pointed out that he had his own reputation and standards to think about. Although what I wrote about was different from the subjects he himself chose, it was not the subject matter that was the problem: "It's that, while you're improving and getting the type of speech well, your writing is simply not yet good enough for me to feature it in *Trackless Train*: not the subject matter that's the problem, but your writing. You're still in your teens, have patience*" There it is again,* I thought, *I'm too young.* But I resolved to keep trying.

Although I wasn't published in it, helping with proofreading the magazine, short-lived though it was before the KMT banned it after six issues, was a useful experience. It gave me valuable access to the ideas and writing of China's foremost writers, and also to translations from their colleagues in Europe. It showed me the basic work involved in putting out a publication. This helped me visualize the appearance of my work when it later came up for presentation to Shanghai's literary public.

A background to the trials and tribulations involved in my literary aspirations was a fact that, technically on moral grounds but really for ideological reasons, the KMT were banning publications. This was not a good time to be starting out as a writer committed to his own development. However, you have to start sometime, and if not now, when?

Exposure to Liu's fast, free style of writing planted the seed of my own experiments in modernistic style. In the first issue of *Trackless Train* I read Liu Na'ou's story "Games" that focused on the modern woman. This was not the modern woman as seen among the female students with whom I went about, but the more sophisticated woman, her clothes, hair: "her short hair waves in the wind," and especially her body: "protruding breasts, and a body soft and smooth like an eel," also the erotic description of her love of fast cars, describing a 1929 Viper as: "really beautiful, its body entirely in green, and harmonizes nicely with the suburban pastures in early summer," and so on. After reading this story, my personal notes of Shanghai's sights, made while walking around in the city, took on a sharper quality. I needed to have more experience, develop my first-hand knowledge of the female body.

Paul Morand Visits China. When we heard that the famous writer and intellectual would be visiting us in Shanghai, Liu said to me, "Paul Morand is coming here to the bookstore, would you like to meet him?" *Would I? The whole literary world, inside China and elsewhere, wanted to meet him.*

There are many words I can use to describe Paul Morand: impeccable appearance, bow tie, diplomat, lightly witty, charming. Although I kept in the background, this was indeed a heady experience that made me feel part of the whole world's literary society and its current trend, and I was still not yet eighteen! As we all sat around the editing and proofreading table one afternoon, Liu announced: "In honour of his visit, we're going to devote the October 1928 (fourth) issue of *Trackless Train* entirely to Morand." We all heartily nodded our agreement. "There'll be a long article about the writer, translated by me," he said smiling, "in which I myself am characterized as the Chinese Morand, and in which the favourite techniques of the modernists, such as ellipsis, the film technique of panning round a scene, and irony, are spelled out." Two stories by Paul Morand, translated by the poet Dai Wangshu, rounded out the issue. I was still oriented to the Marxist way, and no one in the coterie tried to influence me on that.

During enjoyable discussions with one of the magazine's writers, Feng Xuefeng, about an article he'd written, the self-confidence that had been eroding with each rejection notice did increase. Feng was becoming a convinced Communist, (those damned politicos), but not yet an inflexible ideologue. I felt that in pushing my views about freedom of expression and choice of subjects for all writers, I had helped crystallize his thinking.

As expressed in Feng's writing, these thoughts became very influential in the early 1930s when writers were still trying to write in the way that they found best suited them. At this time, China's writers still thought they could escape the increasingly inflexible edicts of the country's opposing political groups.

Basically what Feng said was clear: that there were three types of writer in China at the moment: first, the socialist who renounces the middle classes and second, the middle-of-the-road writer who embraces both the leftist ideas in his writing, the idea of the need for a revolution, as well as accepting the urban, privileged world.

"I feel I can work with this second type of writer," Feng said to me, "In fact I believe that these are people who are in transition to becoming socialists. At this point, therefore, I have no hesitation in involving myself closely with the *Trackless Train* magazine." But then, in Feng's article appeared what later became known famously as the Third Category writer who wrote in all styles: rural proletarian, consumerist urban sophisticate and styles embracing the modernist movement that was sweeping not only China, but virtually the whole literary world.

One afternoon our thoughts turned to other, non-literary, matters. Liu and I were dusting and shelving a new consignment of books from Japan, when he asked, "Have you noticed that we're being watched?" For weeks now I *had* seen men hanging about across the road, leaning against the lamppost or looking out from the doorways of the grocery and printing shops opposite the bookstore. Some were dressed in shabby Western suits and others in shabby Chinese-style clothing. When I went out to the back door to throw out garbage, there they were again. All appeared aimless and were reading newspapers and then walking around a bit before returning to their posts.

"I had wondered who these men were, idly hanging about, but thought nothing much of it."

"Nowadays in Shanghai, you have to notice everything, and wonder what it means."

"But why?"

"The political bosses are closing in on those of us who write or sell written materials."

"Political, political" I burst out, "Is there no escape from these politicos?"

"Well, they see us as possibly subversive to their causes," said Liu reasonably, "The pen really *is* mightier than the sword.

Some of the books in my store, and the content of *Trackless Train,* could be construed as left wing. Conversely, others could be perceived as anti-imperialist or anti-foreign."

"What idiots, spoiling our development of our literary talents. We should be able to do as we please—and anyway, who *are* these people who are watching us?"

Liu thought they came from the KMT, and also the Settlement police. It was shortly after this conversation that the KMT ordered Frontline bookstore to be closed. While they were considering the matter of Liu Na'ou's bookstore, the KMT also banned his magazine, *Trackless Train.* The reason given was that it encouraged working people to think they could be equal, an idea that could lead to trouble. This gave us a foretaste of what was to come. The KMT didn't want any ideas in print but their own, and in particular not those of the Communists.

This meant packing up all the books and vacating the store.

"Thank goodness I kept all the packing cases," and we went to the storeroom to pull them out to where the books were.

"It's going to take a while, but not *too* long I hope, we only have a few days left to get out." *That's news to me,* I thought, "But we'll ask the others to pitch in," and soon Liu's former classmates from Aurora University, Shi and Dai and Du Heng, came to help. Two days later, the books were all off the shelves, and we sat on the last packing cases with our sleeves still rolled up, drinking a nice cool beer and waiting for the van to come and move us to our new premises.

We were not daunted, for we writers still thought ourselves free to pursue our careers and writing ideas, free to join the world modernist movement that was taking place in the more open, Western societies. Liu had decided to move to new premises in the Japanese district on North Szechuen Road. He said that at least the Japanese police who patrolled that area were not going to bother about Chinese nationalism, either in its KMT or CCP form.

"You could be wrong about that. The Japanese seem to be out to destroy ideas of pursuing our own destiny."

"Oh, no, no, no," replied Liu, smiling easily, "I know the Japanese inside out. They want what's the best for *all* Asian people *together.*"

Huh, fat chance, from what I hear, I thought, but pursuing my new approach said nothing.

The concept of nationalism was a puzzle for those of us who tried to make our way through the complicated maze of ideologies. In a colony such as India, where the colonial rulers were on one side, there was an easily understandable feeling of Indian nationalism on the other. Shanghai, only part of which was given up to the foreign concessions, was a Treaty Port. The city as a whole was not regarded as being colonial. The country as a whole was not under foreign rule.

However, there *was* political and economic interference from the European powers and Japan, and a looming Japanese military threat to China. In addition there were two Chinese parties claiming to be struggling for the Chinese nation, each tending to evolve in their ideas, thus providing a moving target for those writers who wanted to identify with either of them. Add to this that to please one side was immediately to be regarded as an enemy by the other, and we could suspect that logically the situation was fast becoming untenable, in particular for those of us who simply wished to develop our writing talents as we pleased.

At the moment, we weren't bothering too much about all that, at least *I* certainly wasn't, and Liu Na'ou chose a new, light-hearted name for the store, Froth. Here he financed, and produced with his friends and former classmates at Aurora University, a new magazine. The poet Dai Wangshu and writer/editor Shi Zhecun moved in with Liu to live above the store. Du Heng, who like the others became my loyal friend, joined them in the work of editing. This coterie was incredibly hardworking and prolific. They not only published their work in their own magazines, but also gained publication in others such as the popular *The Young Companions* (*Liangyou*) periodical.

As well as a different name for his new store, Froth, Liu chose a name for the new magazine, *La Nouvelle Littérature* and it was there, when I was eighteen, that I published my first piece, written in the proletarian style, titled "Our World".

10 (1931)

After I started publishing, I somehow managed to graduate from Guanghua University and found a day job teaching in a village outside, but not too far away from, Shanghai. There I had the usual initial problem with discipline that many beginner teachers have. That solved itself, given some very hard work on my part in always being well-prepared with my lessons and my then insistence on being given the opportunity to communicate them to the young people in my charge.

In the country, I became a reformed character: playing basketball, riding horses, frequenting teahouses and taking walks in the countryside.

"Don't you understand the importance of your studies?" I harangued the pupils, "Do try to think ahead to your future jobs, even to passing this year with your friends. It's no fun being left behind to repeat classes surrounded by a new set of students." *Was I beginning to sound like my father?*

I was determined to make my own living, not bother my ill father for money any more. I also wanted to live near Shanghai where the action was in my chosen profession as a writer. On Friday afternoons I eagerly ran to the bus to go and spend the weekend where it was all happening, in the city that so enchanted me. I crashed at the weekends and holidays with Liu and his group of friends of which I had become a part. We fitted somehow into the apartment above his bookstore. In fact, proximity helped us to work together on our next magazine *La Nouvelle Littérature*.

This was a wonderful, expansive period beginning in 1930 with my first publication of a short story. During this time I could do no wrong. I lived as I liked, wrote as I wanted, enjoyed my life as it should be enjoyed. After all, what's the point of living if you don't have fun and do as you please? I was free, free, Free . . .

I had written a series of stories in the proletarian style, and the powers that be in Shanghai's literary world couldn't wait to publish them. These tales brought enormous praise from the newly formed League of Left Wing Writers. They said this was Marxism in practice, a writer living his ideology. I simply could not stop writing, and my first stories were gathered together in a collection titled *Poles Apart*.

Soon we writers were discussing aspects of writing and what one should write about, for instance the city's teeming life. I found myself lapping up ideas other than the Marxist ones I had been following.

"There are other ways than Marxism or Communism for helping our poor people," said Liu, "You should be thinking of how to get equality through prosperity, through an Asian prosperity sphere where we could all share in our own wealth instead of handing it over to foreigners." *Yeah, handing it over to Asian 'foreigners', like the KMT and Japanese,* I thought, but by now had learned not to say, courtesy of my parents.

I listened, but for the meantime anyway, continued with the Marxist approach in writing. (I had put too much work and emotion into Marxism and believed I must make my mark at that kind of composition.) The fascinating city of the concessions was so *bourgeois,* so much the antithesis of my current political stripe. I wondered where more contact with Liu Na'ou would lead.

Liu and I had become fast friends, but I still couldn't understand how he came to have such an accent. Over coffee and snacks at the cafés I questioned Liu further about this.

"How can you, a Chinese person, possibly speak the language with such a strong Japanese accent?" I asked, "Are you really Chinese?"

Liu laughed in his usual, easy-going manner, "Yes, I really am Chinese. I was born in Formosa, and both my parents are

Chinese. But my father's business interests took him permanently to Japan."

"But surely your parents spoke Chinese to you," I persisted. However, especially when he was small, Liu's parents had been busy setting up the new business and his Japanese Amah looked after Liu. His first words were in Japanese. Liu was left most of the time with their Japanese household staff.

During this very early part of the 1930s even Lu Xun, a senior Marxist figure and leader in the League, praised me. I was riding on top of the world. In 1927 Lu had returned from Japan where his indoctrination in left-wing ideology had been thorough. Lu Xun interpreted other people's work along doctrinaire lines. For me, that was the problem. These idiots wanted their politics to dictate literature.

However, Lu Xun was above all an ardent supporter of Chinese nationalism and never did actually join the Communist Party. By the end of his life, despite the sojourn in Japan and despite having settled in the Japanese sector of Shanghai, Lu Xun was regarded as a nationalist first and foremost, against Japanese domination in China and against the corrupt régime of Chiang Kai-shek.

Living in this Japanese, Hongkew area of Shanghai, Lu Xun developed the same passion for that city as I did. (The Lus even gave their son, born in 1929, the name Haiying, Shanghai infant, after the city.) However, Lu Xun's passion was different from mine. He wanted this burgeoning metropolis to be the centre of a nationalist movement that would unite China and convert the whole of China to Communism. I wanted Shanghai, the literary hub of China, to be the centre of freedom to do as you pleased, for writers to soar, and write whatever they wanted in their own way. I wasn't interested in political infighting.

During these magical months one experience struck a sour note. I received an invitation to meet Lu Xun. I thought the method of delivering this message strange. He didn't ask me himself but employed a go-between, my old friend Rou Shi who I knew from the student political discussions and our subsequent talks walking round Yu Yuan garden. He was as ascetic as ever, peering gently at me through those round glasses he always wore, and as devoted to the Communist cause. We hadn't seen each other for a while and on my part there was a reunion that was joyous, but not so friendly on Rou Shi's side. There was nothing in his manner that I could put my finger on, and say that Rou's attitude towards me had changed, but he seemed to be more reserved than before. I wondered why that was. I also wondered: *What kind of an invitation is this? Is this man Lu Xun, supposedly so concerned about equality for all, too stuck up to invite me himself?*

Nevertheless, mindful of the honour, I washed and dressed myself carefully in my best clothes and polished my shoes until, as usual, they shone. Another League member took me to the Uchiyama Bookstore where I expected to meet Lu Xun. But here again I was surprised. The proprietor Uchiyama Kanzo led me out by the back door and we went to Lu Xun's place nearby. I asked myself, *Does this man regard himself as too august to be seen with such a young writer as myself? What on earth is going on?* (My older friends such as Shi and Liu didn't mind openly associating with me—and they were better writers, at the leading edge, not old-fashioned like Lu Xun.) As we climbed up the stairs I asked myself, *What is Lu Xun's problem?*

I soon found out. In the bare living room, very upright on a carved wooden chair with arms, as though it were a throne, sat the austere Lu Xun. He was dressed in Chinese peasant garb with black trousers and a faded blue top. Lu barely acknowledged my presence before he began laying into me: "You are a hypocrite, writing in the proletarian style when you have a *bourgeois* background," he thundered (could I help it if my father was a banker?) going on to criticize my dandyish clothes and racy image. He said, "You spend far too much time taking part in the decadent foreign pastimes of dancing and attending the latest movies from America, hanging around with dance hall girls and smoking an expensive brand of cigarettes."

Lu indicated with some force that he despaired of the younger generation in general and, needless to say, of me in particular. *So that was his problem: the younger generation. This happened to almost everyone in growing older. I'd heard about it already: we were too uncontrolled in our behaviour, too noisy in the music we played, which was not like their music, with too much oil on our hair, drinking, smoking, dancing and gambling too much, too flashy in the way we threw money around, and dressed in modern clothing that was not like theirs in style . . . on and on, blah blah blah, etcetera . . . etcetera.*

I took quite a dislike to this supercilious, angry, depressed and depressing, and also—let's face it—ill-mannered, man in his bare surroundings and truly *dismal* clothes, and lashed back: "In twenty years I have obviously enjoyed myself more than you have in almost three times that length of time. Are you envious of me and of all young people?" I asked, "You should be. One should run to meet life, try out new experiences and be glad, joyful in the younger (and even older) years. Just because you've obviously wasted your youth doesn't mean you can order me to waste mine."

Before I could say any more Lu Xun, with a sour look on his dour face, waved to dismiss me from his presence. I had thought of kowtowing, but decided that such was his conceit he might actually have missed the irony intended. Anyway, kneeling down in my fine suit could have damaged or dirtied it. Therefore, turning my back, I left that place, to continue with my wonderful life

However one day in February 1931, in the middle of all this joy, freedom and self-expression, there came a chilling reminder of the political reality. I was walking along the Bund when I saw a movement of people towards the Huxi western section immediately outside the Settlement. A passerby told me that the KMT were marching five young left-wing writers, all still in their twenties, through the streets of Shanghai to the Lunghua killing grounds. I followed the crowds. And then I saw him, Rou Shi, hands tied behind his back, off balance. Soldiers were pushing Rou along, using their rifle butts.

It was then that I really understood, deep inside myself, that if I landed on the wrong side of some dominant political ideology, this could happen to me. Suddenly, I found tears pouring down my face. "Do you know that one?" asked a man beside me. But I denied any acquaintance with Rou Shi, my dear, gentle friend. For the first time, I was truly afraid.

With eighteen other dissidents, the KMT executed what came to be known as The Five Martyrs. *I've seen him, not long ago, how can he be about to die, actually be dead?* Lu Xun commemorated Rou with a short biography and thundered that not content with their repressive publishing laws, the KMT had resorted to "the lowest tactic of all, arresting . . . left-wing writers and putting them to death in secret—to this day they have not made these 'executions' public."

As mentioned, I had written stories in the Marxist manner to such effect, that at first the Shanghai left wing writers thought I really was from the working underclass. For instance, in *Black Whirlwind*, one of the first proletarian stories I actually had published, I described a rich man's car shooting past and, on purpose, splattering a poor man's clothes with dirty water.

These Shanghai left wing writers lauded my work as a proletarian writer until they found out my actual background, and saw I was developing myself by trying other approaches as well. Then, by the time of The Five Martyrs, they were turning against me. I'd received a salutary shock, but I personally wasn't in trouble with the KMT, *I* wasn't one of those unfortunates. At that moment, I was enjoying my success, felt free to do as I pleased—and that was the main thing. What a nuisance was this politics and its attempted interference with my writing! The best thing was to ignore it. But, again, I am jumping ahead of my story.

Night in the City. At night I walked and walked, watching the action and taking notes of revelers going in and coming out of nightclubs (their muddled conversations and often staggering gait): "We're close to hitting our sales target." "People who have been in the business for Ohh twenty years . . ."

My first impressions were the most striking. The sounds of hysterical laughter haha Ha Ha, wooo wooo jazz and honky-tonky ragtime music, drunken shouting and violent brawls, bang bang gunshots, the eerie silence of an opium den, all combined to form the night sound of this city. Then I breathed in the smells: of alcohol and vomit, scent and sex, the reeking fumes of gasoline, tobacco, marijuana, and opium.

"Wasn't it hilarious? Wong was so drunk he spilled the champagne all over the waiter. Hee, hee, hee," "I think I'm going to be sick," and the age-old, "Do you love me . . . love me . . . love me?"

Flashing neon lights playing on passing faces, cars, clothes and blank lit houses formed the city's night scenery. The whole experience provided me with fodder for my writing, as you can see from *Shanghai Foxtrot* published later, in 1932, where I compare the trees and telephone poles lining roads to the legs of girls dancing in a nightclub.

This new environment had me in a whirl, and that was the main thing. Sometimes it seemed to me that even the buildings of these concessions had something to say. I said it best in *Shanghai Foxtrot* when I wrote about the Shanghai Racing Club's golden horse weathervane kicking out its legs at the moon, and the racing track surrounded by light, full of evil deeds. The Moore Memorial Church seemed to be bowing down and asking forgiveness for people's sins, but the arrogant Great World tower did not accept such forgiveness.

These were heady days for all of us. We continued to have the impression that we were free to write whatever we liked and to bring out translations of the foreign modernists, both Japanese and European. In contradiction to his preoccupation with "decadent" modernism, in 1930 Liu brought out a translation of *The Sociology of Art* by the Soviet literary theorist Vladimir M. Frische. On this translation, the League drastically criticized him for his un-Chinese turn of phrase (he still had the Japanese language churning around in his brain). They accused Liu of being decadent, ideologically different from them in his modernist writing that was different in that it was not written in their own style, nor was it addressing subjects on which they themselves thought everyone should be focusing.

Couldn't these left-wingers *see* themselves for what they were? Didn't they realize that *their* writing was different, very different, from *ours*?

My exploration of Shanghai continued. I knew I'd never really know it through and through. During these wanderings I met the famous Russian writer, actor and singer, Alexander Vertinsky. He always kept his fine hair smoothed down close to his head, and this gave full force to the man's brilliant, dark eyes and actor's presence. Handsome and intelligent, he was a real charmer. The doorman at the Renaissance confided: "Vertinsky is known to be Stalin's favourite singer, and people say he possesses all of the records Vertinsky made before leaving Russia."

"When did he leave?"

"I think it was in 1920 that Vertinsky left with others, including his main clients. Since then, he's wandered about across Europe and even South America before settling in with us."

We respectfully called him Mr V shortening the Russian name that, for those of us who spoke Far Eastern languages, was difficult to pronounce. In him I soon found a kind friend and truly great conversationalist. We talked for hours. Our favourite café was the Renaissance. We talked about writing. Mr V had written many plays and poems and lyrics for songs. I had the impression he wrote in a more traditional way than I did, but I respected Mr V's views, in particular about aiming for high standards. He seemed sad, and spoke with longing of his "Mother Russia."

One evening I asked, "As you love it so much, why did you leave? Why don't you go back?"

"I left because I didn't like the violent turn of events in the Revolution. I can't go back without permission. The violence could turn against me. I would be killed, perhaps imprisoned for life, sent to a work camp in Siberia and worked to death. I would never practice my art again. I know what goes on there, and yet I cannot overcome my love of country: it is my native land. But I have hope," he said with his brilliant smile, "I write constantly to Stalin asking for forgiveness, and to return to the beloved country to entertain the Russian people again. One day, one day soon . . ."

I very much admired Alexander's beautiful singing voice. One evening, Mr V appeared in a Pierrot costume. "That's the way he always appeared as a young man," said an older Russian sitting at a table beside mine. By now Mr V seemed in his early forties.

As the Pierrot began singing, there was a nostalgia, a sadness about his performance that started me thinking seriously about the image of the Pierrot: that of a person hiding his sadness under the bright black and white costume, and makeup.

In between Mr V's performances, we talked about the Pierrot in literary allusions: "I can see a certain amount of him in the slapstick, comical but sad figure of Charlie Chaplin's tramp in the American movies," said Mr V, and I agreed, being assiduous in attending such films.

"Here seems to be someone whom life had treated badly," I said, "A powerless, lower class sort of person who rolls with the punches and keeps his outer calm." I didn't regard myself as lower class and powerless, far from it. At this time I myself was developing the image in Shanghai of a rich, fast-living sophisticate, a smoker of the high-end Craven A cigarettes.

With Mr V and my writer friends I began to explore the concept of the Pierrot and its application to the writer, and in particular to the writer in Shanghai. Later, feeling he hid his concern over the current political situation behind a smiling appearance, I was to refer to the poet Dai Wangshu as the smiling Pierrot. I dedicated my story of that name to him. Indeed I dedicated to Dai the whole of a collection of stories, *Public Cemetery*, containing the one about Pierrot.

This figure of the Pierrot became quite fascinating, and I wondered how to transpose him to the streets of Shanghai and even to myself, while still preserving the other, dandyish, image I had developed. Even in my story, "Pierrot" I was still consumed by the idea of a modern Shanghai, especially among the literary crowd. I described my Pierrot figure Pan Heling as a solitary writer, attending a party in a room filled with symbols of modernity such as a statue of Tolstoy, a small transistor radio, cigarettes and cigarette smoke, laughter, (American materialism and culture), and a photo of Greta Garbo.

Over a number of discussions, and aided by Mr V's perceptive prodding (but not dictating, I wouldn't have allowed that) of my thoughts in different directions, my own view of the Pierrot took shape. In wandering about the city I increasingly abandoned the previous view of myself as flâneur, albeit one honed to a tight wariness by the fast pace and dangers of everything around me, especially at night. Now, in my mind's eye, I became Pierrot, perceptive of people and their foibles, hiding my sorrow and cynicism behind a playful, often self-deprecating, disguise.

11 (1932)

The year 1932 was a momentous one for the world. From the point of view of building tensions between the European powers and also with Japan, this year marked the first time during that period that a major power unleashed its war machines specifically against civilian populations. After the invasion of Manchuria, Japan now dropped bombs and diseases from the air on our defenceless people, leading to international sanctions.

At the same time, the Japanese set up in Manchuria the notorious Epidemic Prevention & Water Supply Unit (Unit 731) to be kept a secret. They could designate such a killing place as top secret, but we knew about it. Before the Japanese strengthened the fortifications round the Unit, some people had escaped and informed those outside about what was really going on.

Here, Japanese surgeons conducted the vivisection of our civilians of all ages that they had infected or otherwise processed (e.g. by freezing a leg). The doctors administered no anaesthetic. Word leaked out that surgeons joked about being in a logging operation, asking each other over the evening meal how many logs they had cut (i.e. sentient human beings they had vivisected, slowly murdered) that day. Later, the Japanese located subsections of this nightmarish place, as required, in major cities such as Nanking. They named the Nanking section, Tama Unit Ei 1644. We knew what they were doing all right.

The January 1932 bombings laid waste to the Chinese sections of Shanghai. They also all but destroyed the publishing industry concentrated in Chapei. Many publishing houses there were left in ruins. Closer to our group, Liu's bookstore was severely damaged.

He asked me to have lunch with him, and during the meal said, "I have met with such heavy financial losses, both from publishing ventures and especially in the bombings, that I have decided I can no longer continue in Shanghai and so am returning to Japan."

I took the news rather badly but said: "I quite understand that you have to do this, and I hope we'll keep in touch . . . I'm so sorry to lose you." At the time, I wondered how I could survive as a writer without Liu's example and encouragement. However, as they say, life goes on and from Japan I received an enthusiastic letter from Liu saying: "I have decided to change my focus to films. I'm fielding offers to write reviews, scripts and to take part in making them. From now on, this will be my life."

After the destruction, Dai Wangshu returned to his hometown in Chekiang province. There he made arrangements for travel starting later in 1932, to study and write poetry in France. Dai said he would be returning in 1935. Shi returned to his own hometown of Songjiang to teach middle school, virtually giving up all writing for the time being. Du also retreated, but within Shanghai, concentrating on the work of translating foreign texts.

There was a lull of a few months for rebuilding, not only of the physical infrastructure but also of the literary publishing industry. In some ways the physical destruction of older, dominant publishing houses, notably the Commercial Press and its valuable library of Chinese and Western books, opened up the way for new endeavours. As Dai (writing from France) said in his poetic way: "From the ashes of the old publishing houses, new shoots are growing, like a forest renewing itself after a fire." This lull gave me a breathing space to continue with my writing, experimenting in the new style of more visual techniques, describing scenes, rather than producing stories written in the older way.

After only about three months, the small Xiandai (Contemporary) Bookstore decided to start a new literary magazine and persuaded our distinguished writer and editor, Shi

Zhecun, to leave Songjiang and return to Shanghai as its editor. In him they made a good choice. Shi had the *gravitas*, the total reliability in what he said and did, that I certainly lacked (not that I was in the running for that job). He was exactly what the publishers wanted in their chief editor.

In a back room of the bookstore, the Xiandai managers held a meeting of our coterie, now reduced to Shi, Du Heng and as a very junior presence, myself. Their president said, "We have some ideas of our own, but first we would like to hear from you how we can create a new magazine to compete with the Commercial Press *Short Story Monthly*." The ideas came quickly: "It has to be non-partisan . . . with an international focus" "And with an excellent content" "And set up in informal, non-glitzy premises." "Yes, where as long time friends, we can relax and do our best."

The new magazine was called *Les Contemporains* and was carefully explained to the reading public. Shi printed a manifesto on the inside front cover to the effect that the publication was to be non-partisan, and would accept only articles written to a high literary standard. In this way, the publisher hoped the new magazine would stand out from the scores of other literary journals of that time. These other journals all aimed at a high standard, but tended to be run by cliques with particular views

At the editorial office in an alley off the International Settlement's Gordon Road, Shi brought out thoughtfully balanced issues of the magazine. If there was one on the European or Japanese modernists, he followed it with another on the Soviet writers. Shi held brainstorming editorial meetings with Du Heng and (sometimes) me to consider, in a measured way, what possible problems or censure could arise from our magazine's content in the upcoming issue, and how to avoid trouble.

From France, where he had arranged to go in October of 1932, Dai contributed his work and also acted as liaison between the magazine and the French writers he knew. There was a column from him consisting of news about authors internationally, bolstering the magazine's leading edge, cosmopolitan image. Shi aimed at having literary news from different countries worldwide. From Japan, Liu contributed some translations.

So the previous group was again united. Under Shi Zhecun's responsible leadership we were unbeatable. Starting with a first issue in May, *Les Contemporains* soon had almost as many sales as Shanghai's leading newspaper *Shen bao*. In readership, *Les Contemporains* stood head and shoulders above the scores of competing literary magazines and hundreds of popular magazines and newspapers that were available in the city. This fact propelled Shi Zhecun into even greater fame in literary Shanghai. My own work was now regarded as being not only very like that of Liu, but also (dare I say? Yes I do dare) *superior* to it, so that in effect I took his place in our latest joint effort.

The League of Left Wing Writers' ideology was becoming increasingly inflexible, forcing out of their membership more (politically) middle-of-the-road writers and editors such as Du Heng. With the support of Shi Zhecun, Du reacted by conducting a debate, in the pages of *Les Contemporains*, about the Third Category writers posited in our previous magazine *Trackless Train*. In this discussion, the idea of a Third Category person who developed himself as a writer only, to meet the demands of his writing and without regard to ideology, won hands down. "Hurray! A win for the good guys," I exulted.

We went ahead accordingly. Shi continued carefully balancing the magazine's content and making it quite clear that his coterie was no in-group, excluding other talented writers coming from all fronts of opinion. For the next two years we had conversations with major modernists from North America, Japan and Europe as well as China. They visited our city and we published translations of their works. This continued to be an expansive period for Shanghai's literati.

My first collection of stories, *Poles Apart*, came out to great acclaim. It contained five stories in the working class style, stories such as "Black Whirlwind" that portrayed macho male men from the country fighting the corrupting influence of an effete urban capitalism. This story portrayed capitalism as exploiting the poor who came to work in factories. They congregated in teahouses, smoking and waiting for the day when men of integrity would rise up and drive out the corrupt Chinese and also the "foreign devils".

Undeterred, the League of Left Wing Writers produced a positive avalanche of criticism of me in my new persona as a modernist writer. They accused me of turning away from revolutionary concerns and betraying the Nationalist and Communist causes with my adoption of Western pleasures and portrayal of them in new stories. According to the League my writing, in particular about the modern woman with the increasing focus on details about her body, was degenerating into a purveying of trash and pornography. They said I was polluting the Chinese language by using some words from other languages. I was a fencesitter, the trash of society, and (my favourite) a red turnip with the skin peeled: weird! Even the right wing had their say, characterizing my writing as a bastardized version of Western literature, as essentially fake . . . on and on . . . blah blah blah . . . etcetera . . . etcetera . . .

In a short essay for *Modern Publishing*'s August issue, I defended myself along Third Category lines, saying that I was young, finding my way in trying out all sorts of different ideas, and that writing should take on whatever form best served the subject (not some political ideology).

That said, I went on my merry way.

12 (1932 continued-January1934)

Through the many published stories, which appealed to all sections of the reading public, I had become well known as a writer, and was even hailed as the Chinese Yokomitsu Riichi, after the leading Japanese modernist. However, after *Les Contemporains* printed my photograph, I came to know the heady status of being a celebrity.

Wow! That was quite something. Wherever I went, women mobbed me. They flocked to the offices of *Les Contemporains*, hanging around outside the door. The female fans also discovered the places I was known to frequent such as the Renaissance café and Moon Palace nightclub. There they watched my famous foxtrot dancing, asked for my autograph, took snapshots and even tried to tear buttons off my clothes. The destruction of clothing did *not* please me. The rrrip of tearing cloth became my least preferred sound. A beautiful lining material showing through a hole in fine cloth became my least preferred spectacle. Outside the Renaissance café, the Cossack doorman regularly had to come to my rescue. I thought these women were a bunch of crazies. What was so wonderful about my appearance? It was the same as it had always been. Why this sudden frenzy?

From the point of view of my writing career, I had my ups and downs. There were several more editions of the *Poles Apart* collection and also another one, with stories written in the modernist style, called *Public Cemetery* (with the Pierrot story). As a preface to some of these I *again* explained my approach (how tedious this was becoming): it was to give my work the form that the *subjects* demanded, and to ignore *all* political ideologies in choosing the subject matter and writing.

1932 was an extremely hard-working and prosperous year for me. In particular, one of the stories in the *Public Cemetery* collection had come out to great acclaim. It was *Shanghai Foxtrot* that I intended to include in a larger book depicting China in 1931. In the estimation of others, and also for me, *Shanghai Foxtrot* was my finest, most mind-blowing work to date and depicted Shanghai in all its glory and squalor. I had it published separately as a booklet, which people bought eagerly. In fact they snapped up anything I wrote. I couldn't lose. Despite the carping complaints of the Leftists, I was enjoying myself, which was the main thing. The money, including cheques from my father, kept rolling in.

I should also point out that I had the perfect infrastructure for developing myself as a writer: I knew all the best literary figures of my time (they brought me along) and above all I had Liu Na'ou's example. All I had to do was follow in his footsteps and try to improve on Liu's style. Also, let's give credit where credit's due, I was in the best city in the world for being a writer. Firecrackers and gongs galore for Shanghai!

1933. On a personal level this was a truly horrible year. Father died in 1933 when I was twenty-one, and Mother's huge grief was beyond all description. When I returned home, I found our mother in bed with her face turned to the wall. "Your mother is refusing all food," said Amah, wringing her hands, "I don't know how to persuade her to eat. Your mother won't even speak to anyone."

"I'll try," I said, entering my mother's bedroom. "Mother, it's Shiying," I said softly. My mother turned and let out her sorrow to me:

"Your father was my first and only love," she cried, the tears welling up. "I am filled with sorrow. How can I live the rest of my life without him? His death came too early. I need my dear husband to come back. I must have more time with him before I can say goodbye." This hopeless pining continued for several months. Amah and Ah Shi-Yuan watched Mother carefully in case she tried to commit suicide.

At the big dining table we held a family conference without our mother, who we felt was in no state to make any decisions. My uncle sat at one end of the table, and as the eldest son I sat at the other. Our Uncle said portentously, "The Ningpo Commercial Bank provided a small pension for your Father, that they will continue to provide to your mother until her death. However, it is not enough to allow you to continue with your current standard of living. There are problems."

"What problems?"

Round about the time I had turned seventeen, disaster fell, and unknown to the family, our magical life began to turn sour. "Wall Street Crash, Read All About It," shouted the newspaper boys on every street corner, but we never connected these cries with our father.

What we didn't know was that the steady banker had started over-reaching himself. My father decided to engage in gold trading, and worse, to gamble his carefully saved money on the stock market. He had mentioned that to me without letting me know about the down side. Father's measured decision-making did not fit the split second reactions needed for the roller-coaster ups and downs of the new ventures. I thought: *I'd have been better at that sort of thing. What great fun it would have been!*

Soon, our father was in serious financial trouble, which was later exacerbated when his stocks lost value in the 1929-1930 market crash. Then came the depression in China which hit even Shanghai with the credit crunch by the early 1930s. Nevertheless Father always gave me more than adequate spending money, keeping the true extent of the financial situation from all of us. *I'm glad he did that. I had a terrific time as a university student.*

"To support you in your usual manner your Father went into considerable debt, which must now be paid off," said Uncle. "I shall be advising your Mother to sell the big house, invest any surplus after debt repayment to provide some further income, and move in to the family compound in central Ningpo where I run my import/export business."

The sale and clearing out of our family home was a sorrowful time. We spent it in a dreary haze of whittling down our possessions to the minimum for settling into much smaller quarters. We had to give up the childhood treasures Mother had been storing, such as my early drawings and writings (I kept some of those) and also much of our furniture that could not fit in the space Mother would now have.

The second day after Father's death, I had gone through his apartments opening the curtains and windows, letting in the air and light. However my mother arrived in tears. "Stop that!" she said in fury, "We are going to leave your dear father's rooms as they were." So the depressing, shadowed environment that prevailed during Father's illness had continued.

Shiyan had no interest in further education and after a discussion about his intentions, went to work as a clerk in our uncle's Ningpo business. Shijie continued in Shanghai with his education. Lijuan, the youngest and only sixteen years old, was to live with Shijie and me and also continue with her schooling. Mother hoped she would make a good marriage. They trusted that, with help from Uncle, and as I was now doing well in Shanghai's publishing community, I could cover expenses for my brother and sister and also provide Lijuan with a dowry. As events turned out, I even provided her with a husband, a friend from the literary community whom she married. But I run ahead of myself.

I accompanied my brother Shiyan, mother, Amah and Ah Shi-Yuan to Ningpo where they were to live with the extended family. When she went to live in Ningpo, the other women in the Mu family immediately rallied round Mother. "Welcome," they said, and took her away with them to the family kitchen where they were preparing the food for our next meal.

Mother took a seat at the table to help. The Mu women immediately involved our mother in the life, and also gossip, of the compound: "Did you know that the Ching's youngest is suddenly getting married next week? People say his wife is already

expecting!" "And their eldest has had her third child, a boy."
"The Wongs are terribly worried about their middle daughter.
She doesn't seem to be in good health, and there are no children.
They say her husband is thinking of taking a concubine." "The
weather has been terrible and our vegetable garden is not doing
well, maybe you will bring us good luck."

By the time I left again for Shanghai, Mother had already
somewhat recovered, but I doubted she would long outlive our
father. Shiyan promised to write regularly, and we on our side
said we would keep in touch.

Shijie, Lijuan and I rented a small apartment in the International
Settlement, and we began to face the challenges of real life and
fending for ourselves. We all sat round our table (What would we
do without tables for having family conferences?) and decided
on the food for the week. "How much rice will we need?" "I've
no idea."

"I'll buy three pounds in Hongkew market and see how long
it lasts," said Lijuan who, as the only female, was going to do the
grocery shopping.

"I think the laundry should go out to a shop," I said, thinking
of piles of sheets and shirts to be washed and ironed every
week.

Shijie's contribution was practical, "We can take down all our
expenses for the next week and then do a weekly budget," he
said.

As you may have gathered by now, I am an outgoing sort of
person. I regularly attended meetings and networked among
other literary people at the Chinese Cultural Association. The
many friends I had made in the publishing community rallied
round and I was soon working harder than ever and making
even more than before. Over the next two years I was prolific,
bringing my publishing total to over fifty stories, and doing other
editorial work and translating.

In three short stories about love of family and the memories we all have, titled "Father", "The Old Home" and "The Hundredth Day", all written in the older, traditional style, I wrote out my sorrow about my father's illness, the sale of our family home and our mother's grief. According to the critics, these stories revealed a deeper side of me, a more solid aspect of my character than had been evident in the light-hearted man-about-town, frequenter of nightclubs, racecourses and gambling houses, and chaser of dance hall girls. Maybe, one reviewer speculated, I would soon mature, give up my raffish, rackety way of life and settle down. *Fat chance!*

In early 1933 I had brought out two stories to great critical acclaim, and they formed part of further editions of the *Public Cemetery* collection. The first was "Five in a Nightclub" about five people in trouble who had gone to a nightclub to drown their sorrows, and about what happened to them the next day. It employed the cinematic technique of panning round a room from one person to another. In the opening scene I had the verbal camera showing exhausted gold traders panicking and rushing around as the price of gold fell rapidly. Then it panned to Hi Junyi, who laughed and called them idiots for worrying, as the price would be back up in a few minutes. (He was wrong.)

The other story was about a sophisticated Shanghai girl called Craven A, also the title of the story. In it I described the body of Craven A in geographical terms, describing her hair as being like black evergreen forests, her eyes like lakes, her mouth like a volcano and her lower body as a fertile plain terminating in a harbour for the docking of long boats.

This caused a storm of protest about my morals from the politicos, with whom I was becoming thoroughly fed up. What was wrong with them? Had they never *seen* a naked woman—on the other hand, probably not. They needed a good shaking, the idiots!

My detractors had another angle. The nationalist writing had compared the Japanese ravaging of Manchuria to the rape of a woman's body. Astonishingly Lu Xun in his nationalist guise, and his cohorts, thought that my writing in "Craven A" was an unpatriotic put down of this image, whereas such a thought had never once occurred to me. They thought everyone was as obsessed with politics as *they* were. Everything anyone wrote had to be about *them* and their obsessions.

I decided to continue explaining my views about the need for artistic freedom of experimentation and expression, unfettered by considerations, or even worse the *dictates*, of politics. In the introduction to the revised edition of *Poles Apart* (1933) I said: "I wrote the stories in this collection with the purpose of experimenting and exercising my techniques . . ."

In other places I explained that I wasn't anti-Marxist, but I believed artistic freedom to be a necessary condition for all writers, and for other workers in the field of culture. In an effort to beat them at their own game, I even used Marxist terms and arguments in defence of myself.

In the January issue of *Modern Publishing*, Du Heng published a justification of me. In it he coined the term split, or dual, personality to describe my approach. He argued that a unified personality was a form of hypocrisy in a writer. Some (perhaps deliberately) misinterpreted his comments to mean that he was making me out to be mentally ill or confused. I followed up with an essay stating that I was living an infinitely layered life as a writer, student and son, frequenter of dance halls and schoolteacher. I added that even I could not understand all of these layers as being one, unified whole.

My continued lack of interest in settling down to one way of writing did not reflect a dual personality at all. In articles, and prefaces to collections of my short stories, I again pointed out that to the contrary, it was the desire of a very young writer to try out various different techniques. I couldn't get enough of this experimentation. It became an obsession with me, in a way my very life's blood.

It was then that I met my perfect *modeng* muse: Qiu Peipei. But how was I going to keep her attention long enough to really study this wonderful young woman?

13 (1934 continued)

I thought back to when I first met Peipei at the Zengs' salon. She had discussed *Shanghai Foxtrot* with such intelligence. Here was no beautiful face and figure with nothing behind it. And then there was that wonderful first dance. I even remembered the tune: "Always". She came only up to my shoulder, but as a partner Peipei fitted me perfectly. Her dancing was as good as mine. Was there anything this wonderful *modeng* girl couldn't do?

I decided to show her the Shanghai sights, take her to different places, give Qiu Peipei a wider life than she'd had up until now as a dance hall hostess, observe her in different settings—for my writing of course.

So the following afternoon, Peipei was again in my arms, dancing in the beautiful ballroom of the Cathay Hotel, where they held their afternoon *thés dansants* during the colder months. This setting was more luxurious than that provided by Moon Palace. I loved to go there and enjoy dancing to another excellent orchestra.

When we sat at our table, Peipei gave a little pleased stretch and said, "I love the service one has from the waiters here, and the beautiful china on which they serve tea, the subdued lighting from those gorgeous Lalique glass light fixtures, and best of all the superb dance floor."

"So you've been here before," I said, surprised and a bit deflated.

"Oh yes, it's one of my favourite places."

We danced and danced, but above all, we talked. Today, the day after our meeting at Moon Palace, we were discussing our early years. I was enchanted by Peipei's: this tiny perfect girl, la-la-la playing the pipa and tip-tap dancing her way through her childhood in her father's house of antiques.

My friend Liu Na'ou came over and I introduced him. "Honoured," he said to Peipei, bowing in the Japanese manner. I invited him to sit with us but he was on his way to join some other friends. "Charmed to meet you," Liu said again, bowing to Peipei as he left.

"He looks Chinese, so why does he speak with a Japanese accent?"

I explained about Liu's background in Japan. "After the 1932 bombing he left for Japan to pursue studies in cinema. However, now he's back in Shanghai and we're planning to put out a film magazine together. Given this city's obsession with movies, it's bound to do well. . . . Let's have another dance."

When we returned to our table, I turned and signalled for the waiter to bring more tea and things to eat. Peipei ate very little, nibbling daintily, but seemed to enjoy the little iced cakes and sandwiches. "Do you mind if I finish everything?" On her nod, I wolfed it all down.

While the waiter was clearing away, Peipei recalled that like her, I was born in a Treaty Port. "Of course mine, Canton, is a long way south of Ningpo, on the Pearl River in from Hong Kong."

"I think I can remember enough school Geography to know where it is," I said, giving a droll smile to show I wasn't being sarcastic.

"Of course, like Ningpo, Shanghai is a Treaty Port, but with a much more varied foreign presence. So did it feel the same after you moved?"

Shanghai. That jazzy, dancing city, that was to become my writing muse. When I was six, Father transferred a few miles north to the Shanghai office of the Ningpo Commercial bank and we all moved to another large house similar to the one in Ningpo, and backing on some undeveloped land. It was in the Hungjao area south of the International Settlement. There life continued very much as before. The house was different, but not the household. We did not have to lose dear Ah Shi-Yuan or our kind Amah.

I remember well the same sort of experience of foreigners in both cities: during trips downtown in Ningpo with Amah or Mother to shop or buy clothes, we Mu children could see that the British were there. You couldn't miss them. Their banks, business offices and houses, so different in building style from our own, dominated the downtown area (like the Bund).

You couldn't miss the foreign wives either. Talking in loud voices, they went about in public more often than my mother and other Chinese women that we knew. They regarded themselves as being quite something, a cut above us.

The British wives dressed in light coloured, frilly clothes that looked like a real pain to keep clean and starched. However, they didn't have to do the work. It was the duty of their Chinese servants whom they often kicked around. Of course both our families, and those like us, also had the work done by Chinese servants, and some families abuse their servants also, but that's different. Here in Shanghai some of the foreign wives behaved in the same fashion as the ones in Ningpo.

"So in a way, Shanghai feels the same," I said, then becoming lyrical, which is all right for a writer, "But oh, I miss the gulls' cries high in the summer skies by Ningpo, the autumn breezes fanning off the river, muffling the city streets in their early morning shawl of mist. I still miss the soft, blurred outlines of our old house drowsing in its comfortable cradle of twilight. Somehow, the old house we had in Shanghai wasn't the same."

There were other aspects I missed, the varied, hilly terrain was one: "On the windswept Yong Hill by Ningpo, the air is so pure it's like wine . . . one feels intoxicated by it. On Yong Hill, the air is to the birds, for their soaring and singing. The Hill's sides are for the streams, murmuring against stones as they rush to join the Yong River on its stately sweep to the sea."

To be more practical, I pointed out that in central Shanghai there is not much of Nature. In Shanghai's level plain, the fetid smoke from factory chimneys hovers above. Songbirds are in cages and man's racing pigeons own the sky. In Ningpo, the land is for the wealth of burrowing creatures and wild bushes, lichens, ferns and flowers that grow beyond the cultivated gardens. "Of course, Shanghai started off as marshy mudflats so that even now, tunnels soon become filled with water, and the land is blanketed with man's buildings and ornamental grounds. Streams are covered over. Shanghai is such a desolate place for wild animals. However, in this city I can observe a much wider variety of the human animal than was possible in Ningpo," I said, brightening up.

Peipei seemed entranced by my descriptions of Nature. I could have gone on and on, but we both had to get back to work. I paid the bill, and arm-in-arm we walked out to the street to hail rickshaws.

Early in 1934, I had joined in producing a magazine *Literature and Art Pictorial* oriented towards cinema. In fact in *Shen bao* I published many film reviews and even articles about the making and theory of movies.

That year the credit crunch, caused through actions by the United States in buying up silver on which our currency was based, didn't affect me. As usual I was lucky. Later, when my good friend for life, Liu Na'ou, who had plenty of cash, returned from Japan, I left *Literature and Art Pictorial* to join him in a new venture directed at films called *Six Skills*. At this juncture the League accused me of joining Liu in advocating "comfort" (i.e. soft porn) movies. They constantly questioned my morals. The League did their best to ruin my personal reputation—the jerks! As proof of my lack of a moral approach, they quoted part of "Five in a Nightclub" where I wrote that on Saturday nights all inhibitions are removed. That even the top legal men are tempted towards crime and even God enters Hell.

In 1934, the Shanghai obsession with movies, and that of our group, continued unabated. A major hit of the Chinese film industry was *Song of the Fishermen*. Released at the height of a severe heat wave, with temperatures reaching 104 degrees, and without any cooling, not even fans, it nevertheless ran to packed houses for eighty-four days.

For our group, these years were ones of change in the political environment in which we worked. The KMT and CCP were becoming more insistent that we writers should write only what was agreeable to *their* views. Now that the Communists had massacred thousands of rich landowners and the richer peasants, and had retreated to the north, the KMT was the more powerful of the two factions. There was change also in our personal lives, including my own. But there I go, jumping ahead as usual.

After one of several visits from a KMT representative (thug?) to inform the senior management of Xiandai bookstore that they should not be publishing left wing material, our chief editor Shi Zhecun called Liu, Du and me to the editorial office. "Chiang Kai-shek is tightening the screws, but then so are the Communists. I'm so worried by the left wing attacks on my experimental writing that I'm stopping my explorations into the areas of Gothic, Freudian and mystic writing. After all, they're more the field of European, rather than Chinese, writers"

"*Why?* That would be terrible. We're part of a *worldwide* modernist movement in writing. You don't have to limit yourself like that!" I protested.

"Oh but I do. Assassinations are increasing, even in the Treaty Port area. My wife is expecting a child and I feel afraid for the future of my family if anything should happen to me." We all shook our heads. Through 1934 we continued as before with *Les Contemporains*. However, several times more, the KMT sent along a "representative". We joked nervously that at least we still had our lives, and our lives did continue.

The discovery of Peipei hadn't stopped me from exploring my co-muse: the streets of Shanghai. Outside the dance halls, nightclubs, cafés and cinemas, there were the street scenes, all business during the day: "Name your price." "Listen, the figures are going through the roof, they're . . ." "In advertising, there are the subliminal, emotional contacts that . . . consumer product adoption . . ." "We'll say it's a done deal."

But at night, when the neon lights went on, everything aimed towards a jazz-rhythmed attempt at enjoyment. The huge Johnny Walker and cigarette, real estate and perfume advertisements dripped their bright colours on the people passing by, flowing down to pave the sidewalks in green, blue and red. I took in all the sights and then used them in my later writing. I painted this scene in "Five in a Nightclub" and showed a newsboy's mouth changing colour as he opened it to cry out the name of his newspaper, looking blue (from a blue neon high-heeled shoe sign) and then appearing to catch on his tongue some red wine from another neon-lit commercial.

But one day I saw another side of Shanghai as it was developing, even in the relatively safe foreign concessions of the Treaty Port area, and realized that what Shi had been saying had sound reason behind it. On my way to the *Les Contemporains* office, I noticed a group of people round an object on the sidewalk.

"Who is it?"

"Don't know—some political person, maybe a writer."

"Must be pretty recent, there's still sweat on his forehead."

"Ugh, they've cut off an ear."

"They send them to people they disagree with."

"Maybe let the police know."

"Better get away . . ." and they all left.

Then I saw it, a severed human head with one ear missing: a gruesome reminder of what was going on behind the glittering façade of the International Settlement. I had a premonition of what the situation was becoming. Agents for the political parties would be stepping up their assassinations, with gangsters from Korea and Taiwan fighting our own for control of the city's rackets, and the Japanese stepping up their incursions into our opium and gambling schemes. There would be killing and counter-killing. The Police Forces would be unable to cope, even within their own jurisdictions, far less in the Huxi western area that was even now becoming a lawless no man's land where rival gangs and police forces tried to assert their authority.

What was happening to my vision of a long, happy and unfettered life in writing? When I told the others about the head, Shi shook his head and smiled sadly. "That's why I've given up the other, more experimental, more European types of writing. It's getting too dangerous. Putting out *Les Contemporains* could also be too dangerous."

I didn't want to think about it. All this was too depressing. I wanted to enjoy my life, believe (pretend?) the wonderful years since my first publication in 1930 would go on forever.

A few days later I decided to take Peipei to yet another setting quite unlike the last one. The pretext was to find a present for her. We penetrated through the filth and stench of Nantao, the Old City's alleys, to the streets of soapstone carvers, dodging drips from washing hanging overhead as we went. It was the really small items that fascinated Peipei. Brandishing a large carving of monkeys and flowers and jungle plants, I asked, "Don't you want something big, like this?"

"No thank you, I adore the small ones. They take greater skill to make," and she chose a tiny carving of a boy playing a flute.

"Can't I find you another one, perhaps suitable for your birth year?"

It turned out that Peipei was born in 1916 (a year of the dragon). I mentioned that I was born in 1912 (a year of the rat).

"In that year (I boasted) Sun Yat-sen overthrew the Manchus and became head of the new Republic of China. To show the end of Confucianism and the Manchus, Yuan Shi-kai, had his queue cut off in public."

"He'd need to have a good hairdresser on hand after the cutting," said Peipei, and we collapsed, laughing.

"So we're a rat and a dragon," and we smiled, both knowing that these signs are very compatible for marriage. Of course there could be no marriage between us. That would spoil things for me using her alongside the City as my personal *modeng* muse.

Both Peipei and I were mad about movies. I informed Peipei that I had written many of the originals and translations of the plots summarized in the programs. Watching the movies, I studied filming techniques such as the panning back and forth across scenes, and close-ups. On a visit to the prominent movie maker Zhang's Xinhua movie company, I saw a cameraman actually using this technique. The immediate result was to inspire me to try reproducing the effect in my writing. In my famous story, "Five in a Nightclub", I used the same approach, panning from one person to another as they talked, and across to the woman they were discussing (Daisy Huang).

A major social event Peipei and I attended with my literary friends, was the wedding of Shi Zhecun's sister, Jiangnian. She had been engaged to the poet Dai Wangshu who had left Shanghai two years earlier to study in France. Jiangnian had created quite a scene at the wharf in October 1932 when he departed by steamer. I told Peipei: "She ran after the boat as it turned away, weeping and trying to catch a written message from Dai that he had thrown to her. Needless to say it landed in the river. What a fool! Now, she's marrying a refrigerator salesman. Some say it's for the regular income and social status, which don't come to a young poet—so much for her true love of Dai."

And so we all put on our best clothes to attend the Western type of wedding. Chiang Kai-shek, and his wife Soong Mei-ling, were encouraging young couples to marry in this way rather than taking the traditional Chinese approach involving a year of (financial) betrothal negotiations between the parents, consultations with astrologers about the suitability of the match, and the days of feasting, gongs, firecrackers and jokes played on the newly married couple.

With a reception in the ballroom of the Cathay Hotel no less, Shi did well by his sister. Everyone, high or low, on the staff of *Les Contemporains* came. Peipei and I had a memorable time, sitting and talking to Liu and Du Heng. We discussed the next issue of their magazine and gossiped about Dai's protégé, Xu

Chi, and his latest girlfriend. (We could see them both at another table.)

"She's a lovely type of person and good looking," said Du, "Xu is a lucky fellow, unlike his mentor Dai who is losing his fiancée."

I shrugged, "What does that matter: if Shi's sister can switch so quickly to someone else, is she worth bothering about?"

Again reminiscent of our first experience in Moon Palace, but with such different surroundings, I took Peipei's hand and led her out to dance in what was widely regarded as the world's most beautiful ballroom. Lit by the Lalique glass fixtures, its rose-coloured curtains and gold-splashed carpet and walls gave off a soft glow, as I whirled round with Peipei in my arms, on the white maple wood dance floor.

14 (1934 continued)

Peipei loved musicals. By this time, she had not only the *modeng* Fred Astaire and Ginger Rogers, but also a new singer/ dancer called Jeanette MacDonald. When Jeanette later teamed with the handsome baritone Nelson Eddy, acting in period costume, Peipei was delighted. To her, the new leading man was the best one so far for Jeanette, and Peipei already had some of his records. This was all grist to my mill in connection with *Six Skills*, the movie magazine Liu and I were putting out.

One time when we were taking a break, Liu said casually: "You're mixing in very expensive company."

"What company?"

"Well Qiu Peipei of course."

"Expensive, she has hardly cost me anything . . . chose an inexpensive present. She's my new muse alongside Shanghai."

"It's a bit more than that. What about her profession?"

"As a dance hostess? What about it? You know I study them."

"Huh, don't you know what she *really* does for a living?"

"Being a dance hostess."

"You'd better get yourself better informed. Do you mean to say she hasn't told you?"

"Told me *what?*"

"Well maybe I shouldn't say anything . . ."

"No, no, *tell* me." I felt worried. *What had I missed? What could be so bad that Liu didn't want to repeat what he knew?*

"All right then, under the name of Lin Daiyu she's a well known courtesan. Some say Qiu Peipei is the best there is. I heard about her from a client of the other one at her house, who has the name, Xue Baochai. I was going to arrange an introduction, but I won't, now that I know you're so interested." So that was it: Lin Daiyu was sometimes a courtesan's chosen name (but she must be really outstanding). Like the name Xue Baochai, it came from *Dream of the Red Chamber.*

I reeled back to digest the information: *So that explains her beautiful clothes, exquisite manners and appearance.* For the sake of not losing face with Liu, I recovered enough to say, "Surely this is the best possible news: at eighteen Peipei is even more the *modeng* girl than I thought." I pointed out to Liu that Peipei was exactly the perfect girl he featured in his stories: seeking pleasure and money, attractive, precocious and above all unfaithful, with the free will to pursue her own desires and path in life.

"There's something more that you have to consider very carefully: Peipei's coming to the end of her time when she can continue as a courtesan. She'll be looking for a good alternative. Why hasn't Peipei told you yet? It's obvious that young woman is deliberately hiding her background from you. I'll bet you anything that she wants more than to be merely a concubine, which is what so many courtesans become. Qiu Peipei *has* to be thinking along the lines of marriage."

I was staggered: me, get married, what with? I had to support my sister and continue to help my brother who had only a starting job, making not much. Again to save face I said the first thing that came into my head: "Oh there's no chance of that. Marriage would spoil her as my muse."

I really needed more time to think about the feelings I had experienced when Liu told me about Peipei. They were really quite surprising. One was that of jealousy. With the other girls I had hung around with and, let's be frank, slept with, I hadn't bothered who else they might be seeing. There were many more beautiful girls where they came from. But by now, so soon, I knew that for me Peipei was different.

At that time, work was very demanding. I dashed about freelancing for newspapers, up the Yangtze to the fire on the ship Weitung. With over two hundred lives lost, this was quite a story. Then there was what was going on in Germany where the

Lebensborn policy had been announced. It was to encourage young women of pure blood to volunteer themselves as mates for SS officers to produce blue-eyed blond children for the pure Nordic race. And there were rumours to follow up about a development in air travel. I had been interested in that subject since my student days. A proposal was afoot to create a network of air routes linking the United States with Pacific Rim countries and of course China. This was wonderful—such an exciting time to be alive!

However, at the back of my mind, thoughts of Peipei went round and round. I could not deny I was becoming fond of her, but there was the social situation: what would people think of a liaison with a courtesan? But then what did they think anyway? My reputation was hardly the best. What it all boiled down to was that I was too young at twenty-two to tie myself down. In fact we were both too young for a permanent arrangement, Peipei being only eighteen. I couldn't afford such a wealthy bride. I needed more time to be free, to look around. I'd tackle Peipei about this as soon as I had some time. . . .

With all the others, Peipei and I quickly stepped off the crowded elevator at the top of the Cathay Hotel. It reminded me of the lines in *Shanghai Foxtrot* about an elevator ride taking fifteen seconds a trip, moving people like goods and throwing them up to the roof garden.

The weather was warming, and the hotel's *thés dansants* were once again being held in the open. We sat at a table, and after ordering, I decided this was the moment to come to the point: "Why on earth didn't you tell me about your real profession?"

"I was going to—but was looking for the best time. I was afraid you'd disapprove."

"Oh nonsense! Of course not, it makes you even more valuable to me as my muse, the perfect *modeng* girl for my research, like Liu's *modeng* girl: independent, something new, different, and above all unfaithful," I said smiling. "Talking of trying something different. We keep on having the usual snacks when we're here, but you can also have a new delicacy: pancakes . . . different from our savoury ones. They're from the United States where they make them huge, taking up the whole frying pan, and have them with sweet maple syrup.

*

Didn't he realize he had just delivered to me a verbal slap in the face? I could hardly breathe Shiying called a waiter and asked whether they had pancakes and the genuine maple syrup available. Yes, they had, so we waited a few minutes before they came, then ate before resuming our conversation. To start, he put some on a fork and fed me my first bite. "Let me be the first to offer you a taste," he said, again with his irresistible smile. Playing along, I told Shiying I'd serve these to my American foreign clients.

And all the time I smiled. And all the time I thought *So that's what Shiying thinks of me: something new, different, another "thing" to study for his writing, to add to his muse, Shanghai—and above all, unfaithful.* I wondered whether Time and Patience were the best weapons not only for obtaining what I wanted, but also for coming to a real understanding of a person, *this particular person.*

Far from taking me to my goal of marriage, were these two weapons giving me a deeper knowledge of Shiying's character and turning me against him? I was beginning to dislike Shiying. He had this clinical approach to the beggars we saw in the street, taking out his notebook and describing them for his future writing, but never giving them a coin. Then there were his remarks about his poor, sick father who had supported him so well during his university years. I thought: *How can I possibly think of marriage to a man so self-centred and lacking in compassion?* This type of thinking was more that of the experienced courtesan, Lin Daiyu, but the *feeling* I had for Shiying involved an overwhelming physical attraction, an adoration of this man, that I had never before experienced. For the first time I, a young girl called Peipei, had fallen head-over-heels in love.

Then I began to discover another side of Shiying: his gambling. "I'll bet you ten dollars on that player winning. What are the odds on player number three?" Shiying and I were at the *hai alai* game in the French Concession, and he was all excited. Above the thock, thock sound of the balls and cheers of the spectators, came my companion's voice again, "Oh no, better luck for me next time!" and so on. As usual, Shiying was losing money on his bets. He would put money on anything: whether a player would drop the ball in a game, how many times, who would start first . . .

Meanwhile the men dashed about with nets attached to their arms to catch the ball and quickly lob it against a wall for the next player. There was not much time for talking about ourselves. However, later Shiying hailed a rickshaw and we went on to DD's Café on Bubbling Well Road. There we took a table for two to begin again. We couldn't find out enough about each other. For a few minutes, Shiying left our table.

At that point I glanced out of the window across the frantic traffic on Bubbling Well Road, a mixture of modern cars and trams with wheelbarrow transport and even pedestrians carrying goods on poles slung over their shoulders. It was the very old style of transport mixed with the new, and it made me think of Auntie Lo and her older views side by side with our (and some of her own) newer ones.

When my companion returned I said, "Looking out at Bubbling Well, I suddenly thought about Auntie Lo . . . how someone so traditional in outlook has survived up to now without changing." From school, I knew that in the past, China was a world leader in hydraulic technology, road building and the invention of printing, gunpowder, the magnet, the kite and weaving looms. Yet now we were behind the rest of the world.

"Oh, that'll pass. Your Aunt is like my mother, and doesn't go out much in public. That generation will go . . . probably a leftover from before the opposition overthrew the Manchus and Confucianism—which to them is not that long ago. As a nation, we have some distance to travel. Don't blame your Auntie Lo.

She can't adjust now. We're the generation that has to achieve the next step forward."

We discussed the modern background of Shanghai. Most modern manufacturing development was in the hands of foreigners, especially the Japanese factories now surviving after the Japanese bombings of the early 1930s. The current credit squeeze had made it difficult for anyone else to build more. As he ordered another round of coffee and yet more little Western-style iced cakes, (Shiying had an enormous appetite—but for snacks, always on the run) he said: "We're now part of a world-wide culture and economy, but we need to get rid of the unequal trade treaties, be masters in our own country."

I watched Shiying. He was so utterly beautiful, yet also seemed unaware of those exceptional looks. Mu Shiying took in his stride the adoration of the women who hung around his known haunts hoping for a sight of him. Shiying seemed rather puzzled by the fuss.

And then there was his other obsession: writing. Shiying had made it plain that he was only spending time with me to further his writing. Shiying loved to frequent places mentioned in his colleagues' stories, that he knew by heart, to feel part of the Shanghai portrayed in their literature. One afternoon we were having tea and snacks in the garden at Rio Rita's, the café made famous by leftist writer Mao Dun through his description of it in his book *Midnight, A Romance of China in 1930*. Shiying quoted from memory the comments about the excellent music and wine, also the White Russian princesses, fine gardens and the small lake for rowing to be found at Rio Rita's. Mao Dun had felt this background reminded him of blissful times beside the Seine.

"I love the cosmopolitan atmosphere of this café. The first paragraph of Mao Dun's famous novel goes like this—and from his briefcase he took a copy of *Midnight* and showed me the opening passage about the sun setting over the Garden Bridge in a mist, and across the Whangpoo, the monstrous forms of foreign godowns squatting in the industrial area, Pootung, their lights shining like eyes. "What a description!"

Shiying also loved the ultra modern artifacts featured in Mao Dun's writing, such as radios, cars, guns, perfume, high-heeled shoes, and dances such as the tango and foxtrot, as well as roulette, greyhound racing and film stars. All these trappings of modernity were to him so attractive, so exciting.

"But I can't stand, I *hate*, the way that given the current atmosphere of Shanghai, literary discussions all tend to provide political labels for writers, as in 'the leftist writer' for Mao Dun," As we sat sipping iced tea and looking across the velvety lawn to the pleasure lake for boating, he said, "We need to be free to write as we wish, and experiment in our stories, try different approaches. I *won't* be put into a political box."

But on a later expedition we had an encounter, which led me to to understand there was another problem with my association with Shiying: the danger. When we arrived early at the Heart-of-Lake Pavilion, I giving change to the beggars in the zigzag bridge to the teahouse on the way, it was almost empty. Shi Zhecun, editor in chief of *Les Contemporains,* was already there, and we sat down beside him to talk, when in rushed the young poet friend and protégé of Dai Wangshu, Xu Chi. We smiled because we thought we were in for another of his enthusiastic accounts of exploring Shanghai to which he was a relative newcomer. Like Shiying, Xu adored the city with its exciting variety of attractions, and high-rise buildings. However, this time he didn't talk at all. Xu sat down at a table next to us and put his head in his hands.

"What's the matter?" said Shi going and bending over him.

"I've just seen a murder . . . in Yu Yuan garden," he gasped, and again put his head down. Then he continued, "The assassin was all in black. He took out a gun and shot a man. Someone said it was the Green Gang, but who did it? How do you find them to punish them?"

"The Green Gang, they're the thugs who do the dirty work for Chiang and his KMT," said Shi turning to Xu and frowning.

"I've heard about their leader Du Yuesheng sending a coffin to someone he didn't like, and thought it was pretty amusing . . . black humour like Pockmarked Huang's idea of leaving a gap at the top of the Great World for people to jump through after they've spent all their money on amusements at the lower floors. But this is different . . . horrible. Du actually has them killed." Xu shook his head. Plainly this was another side to the wonderful city of Shanghai, a side he did not like one bit.

Shi turned to us and said quietly, "I'll handle this. You two go on with your afternoon. I think he's missing Dai since he left for France." Shi decided to distract Xu by taking him out to Kelly & Walsh on a book-buying expedition, a favourite pastime for all of us who were writers.

I was shaken by Xu Chi's experience, and looked at Shiying, aghast. "Lately, there's been too much of this type of thing. It's another step to a political takeover by the KMT," he said, "Soon we'll all have to write as *they* want. When it's not the League of Left Wing Writers, it's the KMT." There Shiying went again, seeing everything only in terms of the pursuit of his writing. Shiying showed no concern for either the murdered man or for Xu Chi. Again, how could I think of permanence with someone so lacking in concern for the wellbeing of others, and so self-indulgent, (pursuing his gambling and writing), as not to worry about his own financial health and personal safety?

"Well, it's all part of life in our City as it is right now," I said, trying to be as unmoved as Shiying, and changing the subject, mentioned how interested I had been to hear about his experiences with being out in the country.

But then I knew that in Shanghai Shiying had seen all that violence and more, I thought of some lines from Shanghai Foxtrot about meeting a woman who offered her daughter-in-law in exchange for food for both of them.

"What a wonderful place Shanghai is. If only we could be free of the political factions. Obviously things are becoming more dangerous again," sighed Shiying, "Let's go and look for somewhere to dance and have dinner."

That night I dreamed again of the Japanese Sandman. That night he seemed nearer; what I had perceived to be his overalls was actually a more formal, Western-style suit, or perhaps a uniform of some sort.

15 (1934 continued-May 1934)

In a taxi, Peipei and I were bowling along Gordon Road, running north off Bubbling Well Road in the International Settlement. I was on my way to deliver a story to *Les Contemporains*, whose offices were in an alleyway off Gordon. "Why are we going in a taxi? What's wrong with a rickshaw?"

"It's to make a fast getaway," I said with a mischievous smile, "You'll see," and after we stopped, I asked the driver to keep the engine running and dashed into the alleyway closely pursued by a crowd of young women who had been loitering around the alleyway entrance. They tried to surround me and tear buttons off my clothes, but two printers from *Les Contemporains* had been alerted in advance. They took the envelope and quickly escorted me back to the car, which accelerated off to our next destination. For a change, we were going to the Palace Hotel. As it featured a banjo section, the Palace's orchestra was different from that in the Cathay.

"That was exactly like a spy thriller."

"We'll take in one of those at the Odeon after tea," and I started to laugh.

I couldn't see enough of Qiu Peipe—to study her of course—but she was so pleasant, so amusing to be with—quite unlike what I had imagined in a hard-nosed, *modeng* girl. This time we were back at Rio Rita's. Walking in the door, we could see that it was packed, and a lively argument was going on about the current situation in our country. In April the Japanese had declared China to be under their protection (i.e. domination) and that no other nation was to interfere.

"Why doesn't Chiang pull himself together and throw out the Japanese . . . use his troops?" was the first remark we heard, from the young poet, Xu Chi.

"Don't be simple-minded. He can't. The Japanese have broken his army, they've overrun Manchuria and there's nothing Chiang or anyone else in China can do. Besides, Chiang feels he has to defeat the Communists as well. They are getting a hold over the rural people . . . we *are* still mainly agrarian." "It's hopeless, the idea of a united front with the CCP is simply not going to happen now." "Why not? Chiang should join the CCP and with their combined resources they could make a good fight and throw out the Japanese." Many nodded and said they agreed with this comment.

"The Japanese atrocities become worse and worse. They're even saying that with the Germans, they'll soon leave the League of Nations. Then they won't have any other authority to answer to," said Xu.

I joined in: "Right now, all I care about is my own freedom to write *what* I want *as* I want. Right now, we're supposed to please two opposing political ideologies: Chiang's KMT and Mao's CCP. It's not possible, or desirable. And then the Japanese are flexing their muscles. Soon it'll be *three* opposing ideologies we have to think about. If I had my way, I'd throw out the whole lot." Then turning to Peipei, "Come on, this discussion could go round in circles forever. The situation is a total mess. There's no effective leadership. Let's order some snacks and talk about past, better times." And I waved to a waiter, ordering some *petit fours* and lemonade.

I ate each cake at a bite. "In case you need it for next time at the Zengs' that means small oven in French," I said with a grin.

"I know that you idiot!" Peipei said, swatting me with her menu, or trying, because I was too quick for her, dodging out of the way.

We got along so well together. It reminded me of the way my parents were with each other. I wondered whether this was what real love was all about. But then there was Peipei's occupation, quite unlike my mother's. Could I really love someone like that—marry a courtesan? In even thinking about it, I wondered whether I was falling in love, whether I really was moving towards marriage with Peipei.

As a courtesan, she must have great wealth, although she never mentioned it. Such a woman would only agree to be the concubine of a very wealthy man. The only thing I could offer was the better social status of marriage. After all, the comments of the gossips if I did, couldn't be any worse than those of the League. I had developed a pretty thick skin.

*

We were such friends, but that was all. I wondered when—if—Shiying would ever fall in love with me, or with anyone else for that matter. It was always *him* and his writing, getting money for his gambling. I had decided never to mention the times when I made love with a client—and then wait. (Time and Patience) *But did I really want a man like Shiying?*

In our talks, we discussed all Shiying's interests, many of which were the same as mine. The others *became* mine. In one of our conversations about his writing Shiying looked longingly at the ceiling and said: "Sometimes I think my writing would benefit from me living for a while in a remote place, like Tibet." My heart sank. "But no, that would never do for me because the City is my writing muse. How could I ever write without it—or now without *you* for that matter?"

We were walking together near where I lived when Shiying said impatiently, "How can I have Shanghai as my muse when I don't know about the alleyway life where *you* live. I've never lived in one myself."

And there was something Shiying did not yet know: in the City's alleyways was a sweet anomaly, respected and protected as bringing good luck. There, the little golden ferrets went about their lives.

"You could always rent an alleyway room for a month and find out."

Maybe living nearby he would realize an understanding of ordinary people, and a love for me. But also there was the question: would he expect me to be only his concubine? Would I really be happy with, even married to, a man like Shiying who was so focused on his writing above all else? Could I be content playing second fiddle to that?

And then it began to happen. There was an increasing sexual tension between us that we didn't consummate. Every time I thought Shiying was going to kiss me, he developed a cold, calculating look in his eyes, and withdrew. I wondered whether I should take the lead. There was also the unspoken problem of my profession. I hadn't chosen it for myself, but had fallen into it by an unfortunate accident of fate. Given my profession, did Shiying think he should offer to pay me? Would he rather not, with someone who occasionally slept with other men? But then I suspected that, if anything, he was more experienced than I was.

My thoughts and feelings went round and round, up and down. Of course it was better to wait, to really get to know the person you wanted for a husband. This must be what truly falling in love was like. *Did Shiying love me?* That's what I wanted to know. I knew that despite the drawbacks I had noticed, I had fallen in love with him. This was quite a different feeling from that I'd had for anyone else, even dear Cheng Ziyao who had bought me from my family for my first sexual experience.

One afternoon when we arrived at Moon Palace, the orchestra had started to play, and we took a break on the dance floor.

Shiying asked the leader to play his favourite, a foxtrot. Soon we were whirling around, losing ourselves in each other and in the rhythm of the music, then returning to our table out of breath. For several days I hadn't seen Shiying, so we had some catching up to do on our current lives.

"Last week my first ever client, Cheng Ziyao, was in Shanghai from Canton. We discussed my financial situation, which seems to be going well. Cheng Ziyao thinks I should transfer some more of my American dollars into gold bars."

Shiying went white with rage: "I can't bear the thought of you with that old man."

"But I didn't actually sleep with him this time," I fibbed, "I only saw him for the afternoon and then he had other business meetings. What I do sexually with clients isn't frequent and is not at all important to my feelings." Then Shiying said the words I had been waiting for all along, and that I'd been dying to ask of *him*,

"Peipei, I've fallen in love with you. Do you really love me as I love you?'

I put aside my concerns about his character. My overwhelming attraction to Shiying rushed to the fore.

"How could you doubt it?"

"I want you to tell me everything about how you became a courtesan (I assume it had something to do with your father's illness) and how you came to Shanghai, what your first impressions were, everything," said Shiying, "And I want you to give up the courtesan's life. At that, the whole world seemed to dissolve into one, overwhelming sensation of having found my place in life, of coming home to Shiying.

Then he said: "I've given it some thought, and have decided to overlook your past: sleeping with strange men, which will be known in Shanghai. After all, I must consider my social position. But in spite of everything I am not asking you to become a concubine, as someone in your position would normally become, I am asking you to marry me. I want something more permanent. It'll be wonderful to have you on-the-spot, save time in my research."

Anger welled up in me and came bursting out: "Who do you think you are, to insult me like this—and you said you loved me, but you despise me, regard me only as an object for study. What do you want? Is it a subject for study at your elbow, or perhaps a subservient woman who never reads or takes an interest in anything? Is that what you *really* want? Well look elsewhere."

I told Shiying that my family background was every bit as good as his. And if *I* had to think about things before marrying him, it would be about Shiying's current gambling, putting his writing before all else, the increasing danger to intellectuals, and possibly their families, in Shanghai, and Shiying's rakish reputation.

"Why, I believe that *you* have slept, and very casually, with many more women than I have men!" And I swept out of Moon Palace.

16 (June 1934-September 1934)

When I proposed and Peipei said she loved me, and kissed me, the whole world seemed to dissolve in that moment. I felt an overwhelming sensation of calmness and belonging.

And then Peipei actually refused my honourable proposal of marriage, a proposal from me, the most sought after bachelor in Shanghai. I couldn't believe it!

I went along to see Liu Na'ou and told him about the whole affair. He seemed faintly amused: "So I was wrong about her. Now that her courtesan days are numbered, I thought she'd be delighted to marry. You're probably not rich enough for her. Has she had much in the way of American dollars or jewels from you?"

"No, Peipei refuses anything expensive. She knows I don't have the funds. When we went to buy a soapstone carving for her, Peipei chose an inexpensive one."

"Aha! So she's not been gold-digging. However there's the social status, and she's even refused that. What are you going to do now?"

"I don't *knoowww* . . ."

"If I were you, I'd try to get her back. You have a good one there. She has character."

Liu smiled broadly now, and suggested we get down to work on our magazine.

Beside myself with regret, I felt I must make amends, and decided to woo Peipei in the conventional way: with flowers and poetry. I even brushed up my art skills, practised day and night to get my hand in, and sent her a drawing of a bulbul bird that I knew was one of her favourites. How could I have treated this exquisite young woman in such a shabby way: regarding her merely as a part of my research, even condescending about Peipei's profession as if I didn't know she must have been forced into it?

Later I decided to follow Peipei's earlier suggestion, taking a room in an alleyway near, but not too near, to hers. I couldn't believe the almost twenty-four hour action outside. There was this constant stream of peddlers, each with their own pretty song about their wares, selling food, haircuts and household services such as knife sharpening and in the evening a soothing snack of porridge made from rice with lotus seeds. I thought: *It's like having a gang of servants catering to your every need, day and night.*

Instead of going to the back door at night, I followed the custom of the other tenants and let down a basket on a string, with money and an empty bowl in it. The porridge seller took the money and put the snack in the bowl.

The cheerful din did not subside until after midnight. Now, I truly understood why Shanghai is regarded as never sleeping. In the afternoon, I could wave to the local barber, and go outside to sit surrounded by a pristine white cloth and have my hair trimmed, all in a few minutes.

One day, I decided to visit old haunts and stood outside the alleyway entrance looking for transportation. Finally a rickshaw came and I went for a tour of the area around Soochow Creek south from the alleyway. As I bowled along I saw people, who also lived in the alleyway, and who waved or bowed politely. There's a lot to be said for alleyway living: it's so friendly.

We were going east to the North Nanking-Shanghai Railway Station. That was where I'd observed the material for the famous images in *Shanghai Foxtrot*, of the Shanghai Express like a dragon, the whistle shrieking, clattering across the railway ties in the rhythm of a foxtrot.

Now the rickshaw reached the stench, diseases and squalor of the shanty area round the station itself. Here, by the station, lived the poorest of the poor. . . . I looked at people existing in *gundilong* (rolling earth dragons). These small huts made of reed mats, had no sanitation and in many cases their occupants had no hope except that of escape from being either starved by famine or killed by wars that raged in the rural areas outside the City.

I felt sorry for these people, who used the creek water for washing, drinking and throwing away their garbage and sewage. Many who came there earlier had been killed in the 1932 Japanese bombing. I reached in my pocket for coins to give.

Looking over the side of the rickshaw, I could see sickly looking children, chickens and dogs wandering around. I had seen sights like these before in my wanderings about Shanghai, but had not really *seen*, or rather *felt*, them. Now, I looked in my pocket for more money.

I re-examined the bitter laughter, the pain and shallowness of the urbanites I wrote about. In their own way, didn't they suffer too? I was reminded of some lines from Liu Na'ou's *Scène*. They describe someone laughing at a friend who asked why he was laughing. The reply was that the friend's eyes looked so comical when he was crying.

Wasn't *I* suffering now? Ohh . . . but I well deserved my suffering.

I continued with my penance, leaving flowers and drawings for Peipei with Madam Wong.

At first, Liu Na'ou continued to take a humorous approach saying, "How is our sad lover today?" and clapping me on the shoulder. However, one day when I was mooning about, thinking of Peipei, he said: "Oh for goodness sake, stop that and concentrate. You're like a lovesick teenager. Have you sincerely apologised for insulting her as you did? Have you said how much you love and in particular respect her?"

"No, I've written to say I'm sorry in a general way. But I think about her all the time. All the time, her face floats before me."

"Well write the letter—and draw a portrait of Peipei. Have it beautifully framed and sent to her. Anything . . . anything to stop this! Your career will be in ruins!"

It was the portrait that did it. Soon after I had it delivered, I heard from Peipei that maybe we could meet again. I invited her to the Cathay Hotel for the *thé dansant*. I told her of my adventures since moving in to the alleyway, and the trips I'd taken round about, my reaction to the poor people I saw.

This time, I was careful to listen to what Peipei said, and not constantly interrupt with my own views. This time I told her of my love and respect. This time, I had asked the orchestra leader to switch to playing "Always" when we walked onto the dance floor.

And so again that perfect girl took my hand and walked out with me, as the band in their immaculate dinner suits started playing, and held me, in public, on the dance floor of the Cathay Hotel. We circled the space to the slow tune, and the singer crooned: "I'll be loving you, always . . ."

This time, she accepted my proposal.

*

I could see that Shiying certainly was taking time to think about me as a person. His apology was sincere. Shiying did understand the insult to me in the way he had worded the proposal. And Shiying's drawing and painting were divine: a new side to his talents. I loved the portrait. However, what really convinced me was one day seeing Shiying give coins to a beggar. He had never done that before, thinking of beggars as merely objects for study (like me). I had missed him so, and decided to try again.

In June we married. When we were discussing our marriage I said, "I'm not thinking along the lines of a big, traditional marriage like my sister's, for one thing both our fathers are deceased and none of my relatives will be attending, and really, I don't want the fuss. Besides, we're part of the new China where weddings are done differently from before"

I mentioned that at Ailing's wedding, however, as a concession to the newlyweds themselves, Bobby's family and ours arranged for a modern dance band to play the latest Western hit tunes for a dance after the banquet, and to my delight "The Japanese Sandman", that had recently been brought out again on a record sung by Rudy Vallée, was one of them.

I had complained to my father about the whispered comments of the old women on how beautiful I was becoming, and what a good match I would make. Father had smiled his golden smile and said, "You have a fine mind. You are meant for a deeper life than Ailing. The right man will come to you and you will know him when you meet him. He will be someone very unusual, very special. You'll see!"

"And you are, aren't you?" I said, flinging myself into Shiying's welcoming arms.

Although our wedding was simple, Peipei and I did have a wedding photo professionally taken, and because of my high profile in Shanghai the press photographers were there. "Just one more for my newspaper," called one news photographer, and wouldn't you know it, that beautiful last wedding photo was in the newspapers and even in literary magazines such as *The Story*. We had a brief, wonderful honeymoon in Hangchow, that glorious place of lakes, pagodas and flowers, and then Peipei came to live with me and Shijie and Lijuan in our apartment.

Two women with equal status cooking in the same kitchen (for Peipei never came the heavy hand with Lijuan because she was my wife) is supposed to be a recipe for disaster. However, this was not so in their case.

"What groceries do you think we should buy for the coming week?" asked Peipei almost as soon as she entered the house. And the two girls went into a huddle about menus. Early that Saturday morning they went shopping together at Hongkew market.

Peipei and Lijuan spent ages sitting at the mirror of Lijuan's room, trying out different hairstyles and also makeup. One morning I was passing my sister's room and I heard Peipei's voice, "Let's try your hair down, now maybe we could sweep it to one side. That would be a nice style for going out in the evening, don't you think?" I have to say Lijuan's appearance became more polished, without having her look too old and worldly wise. With Peipei's guidance, Lijuan soon developed the soignée look people expected of the women of Shanghai. We all also led a more calm, well-run domestic life.

To the extent that she no longer gave sexual favours, Peipei gave up her occupation as a courtesan, but Madam Wong asked if she would continue to be a hostess at the dinners she gave. Peipei was much sought after for enlivening dinners with her bright conversation and music. That entertaining brought in a good continuing income. I insisted that it should be saved in her name and bank account. It was at this point that Peipei settled a sum on her Auntie Lo, large enough to support her and the aging household for the rest of their lives.

*

The early days of our marriage were such fun. On the pond at Rio Rita's Shiying tried his hand at rowing. Our splashy progress had me soaking wet and in fits of laughter.

We decided to take Xu Chi under our wing until his mentor Dai Wangshu should return from France, so invited him and his girlfriend on outings to places such as a favourite one, the French Concession's Canidrome: Bells rang and the dogs were off, racing round the grass oval, which was `shining bright green under spotlights. In the indigo blackness of the night sky, neon advertisements blinked on and off. They had inspired the image in *Shanghai Foxtrot* about large advertisements written on the sky in the ink of neon signs.

Shiying counted up his losses, ("better luck next time"), and that was the problem: the losses. He never did know when to stop. This was no amusing pastime. This was an obsession, an addiction, very dangerous to financial security. But in the back of his mind he felt, and said, that he could make up the losses and *then* stop gambling.

We danced a while among the multinational crowd in European dinner clothes, saris, and silk Chinese dresses. They rivaled the colourful display of the dogs and handlers in their racing colours, parading round in front of bettors before the race.

Then we decided on a meal in the dining room. Shiying led the way, with his dancer's walk. And during the meal the four of us talked through the buzz of conversation in different languages, under a pall of smoke from cigars, and cigarettes in long black lacquered holders.

17 (October 1934-October 1935)

After that commitment to each other, Peipei and I began planning our lives together. We discussed my rising fame as a writer. At the end of a long and productive writing life, it is usual for such people to write an autobiography. Peipei, who is so much better organized than I am, suggested making notes of our talks about our early lives while the memories were fresh, and then adding to them as we went along. In this book, I decided I must, of course, include the love of my life, Peipei, and *her* life. In many ways I'm too busy *living* my life to have the time to *write* about it as well. I'll do a quick job of writing and revise later, at my leisure, when I'm old. I have no doubt that the entries by Peipei will be polished from the start. That's what she is like: meticulous in everything she does.

I could see that my marriage, to a dance hostess of all people (for that is what they called her among other things, such as whore) created a sensation in Shanghai literary circles. The main question was: how could someone so well educated in literature at a Shanghai university, such a connoisseur of women, marry a person like *that?* What would we have to talk about? What interests could we pursue together? I imagined the louche smiles.

Then they met Qiu Peipei, and heard her discuss literature, films, opera, plays, and speak in French and English with the best of them. Then they looked at her: the perfect face, figure, grooming and clothes of this rather reserved eighteen year old, the superior manners and conversational skills. And *then* they understood.

But I alone knew about her love for the poetry of Yu Hsuan-chi. I alone heard it recited from the lips of Qiu Peipei. Now, I alone held her in my arms.

Need I say that the attacks from the League of Left Wing Writers continued? They were again attacking my sexual behaviour just at the point when I had married my one true love and had given up any excursions into other women. I thought this was ironic, and also disrespectful to my marriage. I could hardly stand these slurs on what I regarded as the sanctity of the union of Peipei and me. They drove me wild, and I didn't hesitate to fight back in the press. But what use was it? They had their views. I also realized that now these criticisms actually concentrated more on the subjects I chose for my writing, rather than on my personal behaviour, which had toned down. I no longer racketed about town chasing pleasure and women.

Peipei and I still enjoyed the cultural amenities of the city. In November we attended the Shanghai Art Club's Exhibition, and an International Photographic Art Exhibition held at 80 Nanking Road. In the cinemas *The Goddess* starring our own celebrity actress, Ruan Lingyu, was playing.

In October, *Les Contemporains* had brought out a huge, seminal issue entirely on American literature. In it, we had emphasized that literature's creativity, modernity and liberalism, and advocated a new Chinese literature with an international reach. Editors at the magazine continued to joke that, although other writers, and especially journalists, were losing their lives, we still had ours.

But in November there came a development that turned this into a very black joke when on the thirteenth, during a car journey from Hankow to Shanghai, the editor of *Shen bao*, the premier Shanghai newspaper, that had annoyed the KMT, was assassinated. His young son had escaped by hiding in bushes by the roadside.

Our civil war continued. Instead of cooperating to drive out the Japanese, we were fighting each other. The KMT were wasting their energies winning against the CCP who, having first attacked the KMT troops, since October, were now making a strategic withdrawal, taking a circuitous route around north China. To Shi it seemed best to knuckle down to Chiang Kai-shek's KMT.

By the November 1934 issue of *Les Contemporains*, such was the pressure from the KMT on our publisher to distribute only works that preached to the Nationalist ideology, that Shi and Du Heng brought it out as their swan song with the magazine, still with a balanced content. Then they both resigned.

This last issue edited by Shi Zhecun and Du Heng, included an article titled "Social Realism and Revolutionary Romanticism". Prophetically, this issue also contained an article by the French writer Vaillant Couturier addressed "To the Chinese Intelligentsia," in which he warned about the rise of Fascism in Europe. We were all part of a worldwide brotherhood, turning aside from our usual job of writing to express concern about the rising tide of oppressive politics and possibly war.

The KMT-approved editors who now took over *Les Contemporains* were able to keep it going for only two issues. So perished the premier literary magazine of the modernist period in China. What a farce: the whole business of censorship, especially by politicians. What would they know about literature? They'd probably never read a short story, far less a book!

By 1935 I had brought out two new short story collections. The first was *Platinum Statue of a Female Nude*, in the preface of which I expressed my view of the fast pace of contemporary life, comparing it to a fast moving train that men were compelled to run after until they died.

In the title story of this collection, a male doctor examines a newlywed woman's naked body in a voyeuristic fashion, imagining her as being like a robot, at his command.

The second collection was titled *The Emotions of the Holy Virgins*. You can imagine not only the content, but also the vicious criticism from the League. Thanks to the good offices of an important KMT figure in the cultural and educational fields, Pan Gongzhan, I began to write a supplement, *Twilight*, and also a regular column, *Cultural Front*, for the KMT newspaper. Liu Na'ou, back from Japan, was also working for the KMT. As I've mentioned, after the publication of *Poles Apart*, The League of Left Wing Writers initially hailed me as the spokesperson of the proletarian consciousness. But as the scope of my writing expanded, they changed. I was incensed by what I saw as the narrow minded and unjustified attacks of the Leftists. For instance, they said that I was a problem specific to Shanghai's capitalist economy, but was likely to cause moral harm throughout China because I would persuade the Chinese people to seek, above all, mercenary goals in life. How could they say such things? If only they had read my indictment of Shanghai's capitalism in some of my writings, such as the description in *Shanghai Foxtrot* of the death of a construction worker. It depicted a terribly frail man carrying a heavy beam. He slips and the beam breaks his back, causing him to spit out blood and die. However, the construction continues: placing concrete over the blood, for a new dance palace to rise.

I decided to use the publications for which I wrote as platforms to counter attack and publish many articles roundly criticizing the Leftist cultural viewpoint. These comments also happened to suit the KMT who published them.

However after resigning from *Les Contemporains*, Shi Zhecun was so afraid, that he stopped writing in any kind of modernist vein himself and became editor of a journal called *Literary Vignettes*, which featured the works of deceased writers and avoided modernism completely. By this time Shi felt he owed it to his family to be cautious, to keep safe.

One person I found totally fearless, was the new young political cartoonist for *Xinwenbao*, Huang Yao. His character,

Niubizi, was an outspoken gentleman whose pithy anti-war, anti-Japanese comments were spot on. Like me, Huang was only eighteen when he got his big break, being appointed Art editor for *Xinwenbao in 1935*. Like many other readers, before I read the main news, I turned first to the Huang cartoon. In the political climate we all faced, it seemed a matter of time before Huang would be murdered.

This was a time of wonderful happiness with Qiu Peipei and quite frantic scrambling for work. Because of my new responsibilities, and sheer financial need, I gave up being apolitical in the sense that I became editor of the KMT newspaper, *Morning Post*. In it I tried to explain to the general public what the world was like for our contemporary writers: the confusion, and generally paralytic state they were in as a result, explaining that writers had neither the courage to face the nation's tragedy, nor a firm understanding of its many facets. In their innermost selves, our writers knew they were a lost generation.

"Do *you* really feel so confused and helpless?" said Peipei, looking over my shoulder as I wrote.

"Confused, yes, in the sense of the many-faceted political situation: the Nationalist KMT, the Communists who also say they are nationalists, and the Japanese who are our real enemy—as Huang Yao understands in his cartoon strip." I leaned back in my chair and sighed, "But in the sense that I strongly believe we should not have to bother about the views of politicians on what we write, I'm not confused. If they want a particular type of writing, let them employ their own tame scribes to do it. But politicians should leave us serious writers to our development of ourselves and our craft."

I sipped the tea she had put before me and continued, "Helpless? I'm feeling more and more so. At times I think I am the only one speaking out. The others are too afraid. I wonder where all this will lead?" I took Peipei in my arms and held her tightly for comfort. "Come, bring your tea and sit beside me. Let's talk about something else for a while," and as usual, she smoothed my brow and told me about her day and as usual, I felt calmed.

Then in October of 1935 came the triumphal return of the Communists from what soon came to be known as The Long March. In the meantime there were the news stories about the Red Army's heroic May crossing of the Tatu River, swinging by their bare hands on the chains of the long suspension bridge from which the planks had been removed, and the refusal of their hungry troops to steal food from the farmers. In the countryside, opinion was turning away from Chiang Kai-shek's KMT who sided with the landlords against the ideas of land reform proposed by Mao's CCP. Everywhere, especially in the cities, there was revolt against the KMT for their weak response to invasion by Japan.

There was gossip about the expedition: "You know it was a defeat, with only ten percent of the original force still alive at the end." "Some say Mao was carried part of the way. . . . His senior followers are now indulging in high living. . . ." However, with the stirring stories of The Long March and the troops' good treatment of peasants, the Communists won the hearts of ordinary people and the propaganda war over the KMT. Now the political pendulum had swung the other way and it looked as if the left-wingers were the ones to fear and obey.

Then came Mao's chilling pronouncement: "All art is propaganda for some viewpoint or other, whether it sets out to be or not . . . revolutionary writers should consciously propagate the interests of the proletariat." That meant all of us who were writers were to write only according to the Communist doctrine.

18 (November 1935-November 1936)

A delightful relief from the turbulence of the Shanghai scene was the return from France of our foremost poet Dai Wangshu, accompanied by crates containing thousands of books in French and Spanish. In a private room in Del Monte's on Avenue Haig in the French Concession, he held a special reception for members of our group. These were Shi Zhecun, Du Heng, Liu Na'ou, myself, and Dai's young protégé Xu Chi. As we did not want to leave her in the apartment by herself, my sister Lijuan came along with Peipei and me. There were two other exceptions: Zeng Pu and Zeng Xubai. In gratitude for all the salons we had attended on Rue Massenet they were among the dinner guests.

Dai asked me to come in ahead of time and help him. "Let's make this a lot of fun . . . have you any ideas?"

"We could lay the books out in related piles, but with some of them open at tempting passages."

"Good, let's start . . . we have these two long tables to use. I'll go and get some records I've brought from France and set them up with the gramophone."

So as the other guests entered the room, he put on a record of the contemporary French composer Ravel's "Bolero." With this new musical experience, we all had a wonderful book experience: delectable new volumes displayed to their best advantage, informally, in inviting heaps. When he saw the books, Zeng Xubai clapped in appreciation, and we all joined in.

And then there was the gastronomic experience: on another table were many tasty *hors-d'œuvres* with wine glasses and opened bottles of French and Spanish wines. As we enjoyed the wine and each other's company, Dai reminisced about France. To chat with other writers, he had visited Les Deux Magots many times, and told us it was at the junction of two streets at an oblique angle (not a right angle) to each other: perfect.

When Zeng Pu commented on the background music Dai said, "I'm glad you noticed. You know, "Bolero" was almost Ravel's last composition before he became too ill to work. I think over time it'll probably become his best-known."

After the initial party, being book people, we all agreed to wash our hands before handling the volumes. Dai put on a recording of "Spring" from Vivaldi's *Four Seasons*. For complementing our mood, it was perfect. We couldn't make up our minds where to start reading in this surfeit of riches. We rushed about from one delectable heap to another. Typically, each of us approached a pile of books and rifled through each one. There was silence.

Later we replaced the volumes, but each kept one to read the next day. Over a dinner entirely of French food set at the big table, we chatted in French and Chinese, with the Zengs adding much to the conversation. Dai regaled us further with his experiences in Paris and told us about a new popular singer, Edith Gassion, always in a black dress, who had recently started to perform at a café, Le Gerny, in the Pigalle area. He said she was so tiny, about four feet eight inches in height, that the nightclub's manager had given her a nickname: the Little Sparrow, which had caused her to change her stage name.

Dai said that despite the Little Sparrow's small size she had a wonderfully strong voice, and poignant way of singing that would undoubtedly bring her great fame. Already people of all classes across Paris, and also top French entertainers such as Maurice Chevalier, were raving about her. "You should keep an eye out for her records, under her new stage name: Edith Piaf," he advised.

Looking round the table as dinner progressed in a leisurely succession of courses and matching wines, I saw my oldest and best friends. It was wonderful to be with them again, especially all at the same time! Occasionally Dai rose to put on another record of European music, played quietly. We talked with a background of works by Debussy, Vivaldi, and Handel's Water Music. Candles lit the room, some on tables round us and other short ones along the centre of our feast. There were low arrangements of flowers everywhere, enough to pleasantly scent the room without interfering with our view of each other across the table.

At the head of the long table was Dai, still chatting about Paris to the Zengs on his right. Zeng Pu wanted up-to-date information on all the sights he had read about. One evening I had asked Mr Zeng, "Have you ever journeyed to France, been up the Eiffel Tower, or had a meal in the restaurant at its second level?"

Totally unconcerned by the question, Mr Zeng replied, "No, I don't need to do that, or even go there. . . . All around me there is the French atmosphere and influence of the Concession." Just by looking at his street sign, he could think of the music of the French composer Massenet. (We had a record of his *Agnus Dei* sung by the famous American baritone Nelson Eddy.) Strolling along the street where he lived, Mr Zeng could cross Rue de Molière, which brings to mind a wealth of plays. "In many ways best of all," said Mr Zeng, "Wandering north again, l'Avenue Joffre is my Champs Elysées."

In the middle right, Liu Na'ou, Shi and Du Heng were deep in conversation about the latest movies in which Liu was involved. Down the table, Peipei and Xu Chi were discussing Classical Chinese poetry and I was asking Lijuan about her day at university. When I next looked up, Liu and Shi were involved in praising French literature with the Zengs. And where was Dai? He was paying attention to Lijuan, so I joined the French discussion across the table. After I turned to Peipei and Xu to discuss Classical Chinese poetry I turned to my right and there was Dai, talking to Lijuan. We all started discussing the books we'd chosen to borrow. But where was Dai? He was gazing at Lijuan . . .

This dinner was a time of good-natured fellowship and happiness. We had a wonderful reunion. It was well after midnight before Dai gave a last speech:

"My dear friends, I thank you all for a most wonderful homecoming and reunion with my most valued colleagues . . ." Shi followed by thanking him for the dinner, music and books. With much joyful banter and lingering farewells, the dinner party disbanded and we departed for what was left of the night.

Dai had arranged transport for us, and we slowly drifted home in rickshaws with their sleepy pullers. At this darkest hour of the night, Shanghai slipped into its night's nap before waking at dawn when the *jenao* started.

In a literary sense, Dai Wangshu made a striking re-entry to Shanghai, starting a new poetry magazine, *Modern Poetic Trends*. His return was also notable for my family in that Dai took one look at my sister Lijuan, who was by now almost nineteen, and fell deeply and permanently in love with her. They were soon married, (Hu Chi acting as best man), and started a family with a little girl, adored by her father and mother.

Dai played it safe in the politically grim environment, where random arrests and even assassinations of journalists by the KMT and other political persuasions were becoming common. He wrote only a few poems, and concentrated on editing, translating, and teaching at Guanghua University. I thought there were so many of us they couldn't arrest and murder everyone. Anyway I was editing a KMT newspaper, so I decided not to worry.

Du Heng continued with articles decrying the criticism of writers by political groups. This, he wrote, was causing them to abandon the modernist movement, (which, he pointed out, was worldwide). It was even causing many of them to give up writing altogether. They were turning to teaching and translating, really anything to make a living in the literary field without coming into conflict with the views of the politico ignoramuses.

Meanwhile, in the early part of 1936, my novel, *This Generation of Ours,* that I never completed, was serialized in *Times Daily.* In it I described the January 1932 bombing of Shanghai from the perspective of a rich intellectual who fantasizes that he will be a famous war hero, whereas he doesn't have the courage to actually fight in a war. I titled the Preface, Song of Slaves and in it made an impassioned call for the overthrow of imperialists. Just as my father had advised, what seemed now to be so long ago when I was sixteen, I was becoming more serious about what was happening round about me.

As usual, gossip entertained Shanghai's chattering classes. There was one source of amusement for us, but not at first for the foreigners, whose newspapers did not carry this particular news. It was the romance of Britain's King Edward VIII and Mrs Simpson. One choice piece overheard in Hongkew market was from a servant telling his Briitish employer that: "When Mr Simpson go shipside, plenty men go houseside." With this lighter entertainment, was also the terrifying news of a purge in Russia of about ten thousand of those Stalin regarded as his enemies.

At home, during the years just before 1937 the Japanese threat was becoming more obvious and the urban and international approach taken by Shi Zhecun became warped into a narrow concentration on anti-Japanese nationalism. I was an exception in that although my interests had genuinely turned to film, I still stubbornly defended the right of the writer to pursue his art unfettered by political considerations. I wrote blasts against the hypocrites who chose a party alliance for convenience, to keep out of trouble, and without really believing in the political stance they supported.

At this point, Shi called for a meeting with Du Heng and me in a private room at DD's. After they had served tea and left us alone, Shi spoke: "Can't you see how dangerous your articles are to your personal safety?" he said. "Writers are being beaten up and the violence is escalating. What use are your views, and your courage in stating them, if you are assassinated like the others?"

"But it's our *right* . . ." I started to explain.

"*Right, right* . . . There is no right any more, no rule of law feasible, no rational argument possible against the thugs and gangsters who have taken over." Shi continued in pointing out that we were too naïve. What good was our right of self-expression, what good were we to our wives, or even to literature or films with all the potential we had, if we were dead? "Take my advice, follow my example, use the skills you have developed to teach the young, and you will live long and see your children and grandchildren. These are the real centre of life. You may even outlive the present troubles and again be able to take up your craft. For myself, I'm giving up my attacks on Japanese nationalism."

After that reprimand, Du pulled in his horns, but I didn't—and neither did the cartoonist Huang Yao through the fearless comments of his character Niubizi. As writers, and let's face it as intellectuals, how could we stop saying what we truly thought? And how could I personally give up my writing altogether? Knuckle under to the politicos? Never!

19 (December 1936-Late December 1937)

By the end of 1936, the political net had tightened and, as Shi Zhecun, our friend and former chief editor of *Les Contemporains,* had feared, violence against journalists in particular was becoming more pronounced even to the point of further assassinations. A common approach was to behead the journalist and leave his head outside the offices of the newspaper where he worked. The Green Gang, affiliated to the KMT, was active in this regard. The assassins were commonly believed to dress in black to commit the murders. I have to say, I was afraid.

Peipei was also frightened. We intellectuals were criticising Chiang Kai-shek for wasting resources on the civil war with the Communists and for not doing more to stop the Japanese attacks on our country. However, as he feared it might be turned against him, Chiang was paranoid about allowing people to organize a resistance. After the massive anti-Japanese demonstration at the October funeral of Lu Xun, Chiang had the seven organizers executed.

"I'm positive that Chiang will move against neutral writers like you," said Peipei one day. "You want to live in an ideal world where you can be apolitical and write as you please. We all crave freedom, but right now that simply isn't realistic."

The Japanese were now plotting in the city against the KMT and CCP. Japanese officials handed out drugs in lieu of payment for work, making the local population less able to fight back, and their own murderers, who were also given drugs, just that amount more ruthless. Shanghai with its foreign concessions, neutral like a few other international cities such as Lisbon and Casablanca, was a hotbed of spying, and undercover *agents provocateurs.* Now, more than ever, everyone was carefully watching everyone else.

There was soon no real freedom possible, in particular the lack of restrictions on literary works that I persisted in advocating.

Battle of Shanghai (August to November, 1937): Events came to a head in 1937 when the well trained and armed Japanese soldiers invaded the Chinese section of Shanghai. The highly trained but fewer and less well armed KMT forces put up a strong, desperate resistance, killing far more Japanese than the deaths sustained by their own side. There was the heroic, four-day stand of the (Gujun) Lone Battalion, during which half the 800 soldiers died before Chiang ordered them to withdraw to safety in the Settlement.

In the International Settlement, many foreigners, (to quote an early story of mine, "Black Whirlwind": "those f—ing foreign devils strutting and swaggering in China who must be got rid of before any Chinese can hold his head high."), *those* foreigners, although they did provide safety for many of us in their concessions, treated this war as a spectator event, watching the fighting after dinner from the rooftops of hotels such as the Cathay. However, one midday in August, the inexperienced Chinese airforce, intending to drop bombs on Japanese warships moored in the Whangpoo, miscalculated and dropped them instead on the busy Nanking Road intersection with the Bund and further down near the French Concession. In the carnage that followed, these "expats", with their convenient "extrality", got their comeuppance, but then, so did many of our own people.

When this happened, Peipei was in Sincere's. That morning she was watching a radio anchorman's newscast through a glass partition. With other spectators Peipei sat comfortably listening to it via microphones.

"Oh, he is so good looking," said one woman next to my wife.

"And such a lovely voice, so authoritative," came the reply, when the bomb hit the Sincere's third floor balcony. At first Peipei was knocked unconscious, but when she revived, it was to see a scene of complete carnage. The bomb had shattered

the glass of the broadcasting booth and blown some of the
spectators through it to where they lay dead beside the man they
had been watching.

Standing up with some difficulty, Peipei made for the
stairs, but they had almost completely disappeared. However,
the banisters were still standing, and so hitching up her skirt,
Peipei slid carefully down to the ground floor. When my wife
(I often thought of Peipei as "my wife", the phrase had such a
comforting ring to it) managed to find her way down to ground
level, she saw that the road outside was littered with pieces of
neon lighting, parts of walls and windows and, above all, many
bodies and body parts.

At first Peipei stood outside the store in a daze. Then, working
parties from the Shanghai Municipal Council arrived and started
removing bodies and debris. Medical personnel from the local
hospitals, who could hardly make their way through the midday
crush of traffic and people, wiped blood from Peipei's face and
arms and asked if she felt able to go home by herself. They did
their best to push a way through with help for the injured, but
everything had come to a standstill, causing a massive jam of
traffic.

Peipei had been very fortunate not to be killed like the other
broadcast spectators. A rickshaw puller helped her onto the seat
of his vehicle and took Peipei home to our flat in the Settlement.
But she was very shaken and when I arrived back Peipei said,
"Please, please let's leave Shanghai. For us, the situation can only
become even more dangerous. Can't you see that? Can't you see
how they despise us, regard us as an inferior race, with no human
feelings?" she said, referring to the Japanese.

"No, I've discussed this view of the Japanese with Liu, and
he says they want us to be their equals in the world, and he should
know, having lived there most of his life. He says what is going
on now is what happens in all wars." (Although I tried, I couldn't
really believe in Liu's viewpoint, but wished to stay in Shanghai,
and wanted Peipei to stay with me.)

Such was the atmosphere of mutual distrust that some observers even said Chiang had ordered the bombing to bring America into the war of resistance against the Japanese.

The strong defence and casualties inflicted by the KMT forces infuriated the Japanese, and when defeated, the KMT withdrew to their capital of Nanking. The Japanese troops vented their fury on every building and living thing across the Soochow Creek from the foreign concessions. Incendiary bombs, dropped along the creeks and rivers, had incinerated the poorest of the poor in their shelters made of mats. But now the Japanese soldiers plundered, raped, and laid waste to what was left in the whole area.

Of course, Peipei was particularly terrified of what happened to women in a war. There was the constant reminder in the "street dramas" enacted by our actors to inform ordinary people, who could not read, about the need to mobilise. And then there were the peaceful demonstrations that sprang up. Peipei said she could hardly go out any more without meeting a drama or a demonstration.

As an accredited journalist, I obtained access from the Settlement to Chinese Shanghai. I talked with people. Several men were in tears. One, carrying a small boy, said, "They have raped and murdered my wife, sister and daughters, all I have left is a nephew. My home is in ruins. Look," and he pointed to a pile of smouldering wood.

"But you still have your job. You can rebuild," I said to another man.

"I worked in a factory weaving silk. It is destroyed. I have no way of earning a living." In his arms he held a young child. "My wife and other children died in the bombing. What am I to do?" he asked, "All the Chinese-owned factories have been bombed. There are only a few foreign ones left, and they are mainly Japanese."

I decided to take these people to the safety zone in Nantao, organized by the French Jesuit Father Robert Jacquinot de Bésange. A tall, gaunt and shabby figure with one arm, (his right forearm was a wooden one lost in a laboratory accident), Father Jacquinot was using his famous genial smile and forceful personality to arrange for provision of over 200,000 refugees with clean water, food and safety. Within two years they began to disperse, to jobs and to homes with family members. Our strong family system was a blessing at this time. However, in 1937 Father Jacquinot had a huge task ahead. Despite the dignity of his office, and decoration with the Croix de Guerre for similar service during the 1932 hostilities, Father Jacquinot was not above supplementing his abundant skills in diplomacy with a few hearty clouts from his wooden forearm for recalcitrant Japanese soldiers.

An unusual case I reported was that of Earl Whaley and his jazz band. Japanese soldiers caught and imprisoned the black Americans. Whaley himself was tortured and had his hands broken. Thank goodness that the famous and fearless political cartoonist, Huang Yao, such a thorn in the side of the Japanese, had gone to Chungking and set up his own publishing house.

For those who had not escaped to the neutral foreign sectors, there was nowhere to hide. Hardly anything stood above ground level. The major part of the battle had taken place during the height of the very hot and humid summer period in Shanghai and the stench of dead humans and animals wafted across to the other side of the Soochow Creek. The odour seeped in everywhere, especially when there had been a thunderstorm with rain.

The Shanghai Municipal Council held an emergency meeting, and in the interests of hygiene, the Settlement authorities obtained permission to clear the area. I wandered around, horrified at what I saw: crews of workers had laid out dead people in rows of ten and then on top of these had placed ten more at right angles to the first row, until there were rows of cubes of corpses. The workers piled up animals: dogs, cats, chickens, donkeys . . . then they doused everything with gasoline and set fire to it.

In total contrast to its former bustling busyness, the area across Soochow Creek from the Settlement took on an air of suspended animation. For days, plumes of black smoke, smelling of burning flesh, coiled over the ruins of Chinese Shanghai, and invaded the foreign concessions where the pervasive foul odour in streets and dwellings alike, harassed people for weeks. Only with the onset of colder weather at the end of December and the following January, did the constant feeling in the air of something indefinable, disgusting and evil, gradually withdraw.

After the Japanese secured the Chinese section of Shanghai for themselves, they pursued the KMT army across country looting, raping, murdering and burning as they went. During these days we sat in DD's discussing the news. Information came in fast and furious: "Did you know that one of the Japanese generals involved in the push towards Nanking, General Nakajima, is described as a beast, and very violent? I heard what he packed to take with him: barrels of a special oil, for burning humans," "Yes, they deliberately brutalize and underfeed the troops to make them more cruel" "Our beautiful Soochow has been razed to the ground, priceless treasures destroyed." "Taking the airforce, Chiang Kai-shek has fled Nanking by air, leaving the ground troops without air support or intelligence."

There was a further turn of public opinion against Chiang Kai-shek.

Then reports and smuggled out pictures came back to us, and Peipei was even more frightened, sickened by the continuing stench in Shanghai, terrified by the continuous Japanese atrocities, and desperate to leave.

"We are safe enough in the Settlement for the time being. Let's see what happens next," I said.

"No . . . no . . . the situation with the Japanese can only become worse. I am going to Hong Kong and you must come with me," and Peipei clung to me, beseeching me to leave. I could not abandon my muse, my special city, but my wife was too afraid to stay. However, wasn't Peipei part of my writing muse?

So the Hongkong and Shanghai Bank transferred Peipei's wealth to their branch in Hong Kong and by early December,

Peipei had returned to Cheng Ziyao and the elegant Madam Shen, her antiques and "daughters", "sisters" to Peipei.

The leave-taking was wrenching for both of us.

"Shanghai, Shanghai," said Peipei to me as we clung together in parting, "Always it's your muse that comes before me, always," she repeated bitterly.

"But you are my wife, you are supposed to stay with me and you are also my muse," I said, "Do you think I would ask that of you if I didn't believe you would be safe?"

"Also your muse! No, no . . . not enough of one. Your main inspiration is still Shanghai, even when your very life is at stake."

"If I left Shanghai, my writing life, my life's blood, would die." I went the whole dreary way to the wharf with Peipei and helped her board.

"At least cut your stay in Hong Kong as short as possible," I pled.

"I can't, it's not safe here. Please, please come with me, or follow soon." . . . And so our argument continued as before.

On the same boat were my sister Lijuan and her husband Dai Wangshu, with their little daughter. Before the boat went, Peipei and I had a farewell party in their cabin.

"I'm lucky as I have a job to go to as a newspaper editor in Hong Kong," said Dai, "Don't worry about Peipei on the journey, we'll take good care of her and see her safely to her house."

Why was I so stubborn? *Why* couldn't I leave the city? Was it because Shanghai was the life's blood of my writing? Did I really put it before my wife? But Peipei was my very heart. As the boat turned down the Whangpoo I felt that heart was being torn out. As I went home, I looked at all the other people around me, buying lunch at a local stand, walking to work, talking to each other, and thought: *How can all the ordinary things be continuing in the world, when I am in such despair?*

Now, Shi Zhecun and Du Heng from our group decided to go into the hinterlands of China. They wanted to be as far away as possible from territories occupied by Japanese troops. They believed they could make their living somehow by teaching, or doing anything else at all to support themselves and families—if necessary buying land and becoming farmers. Anything was better than facing the terror of being tortured and murdered, having one's women raped by the Japanese soldiers. In many ways Liu was culturally Japanese, spoke their language like one of them. He stayed, but he had the option of again returning to his family in Japan.

After Peipei left, my other friends rallied round and I had plenty of company, but nevertheless I spent my life in a haze of bitter longing for her. Stubborn to the end, I continued to write, concentrating on books. *The Fate of a Nobody* ran in *Six Skills* as an instalment for each issue. By early in 1938 I had completed three sections. During this time I was also writing my novel depicting China of our era, to be my *chef d'œuvre*, provisionally titled *China 1931*. It was highly experimental in style of writing and also presentation, involving different type faces and even sizes of type, as well as different languages where appropriate (an approach much scorned by the League who believed that in introducing languages other than Chinese in my work I was acting against the cause of nationalism).

After their massacres in Nanking, the Japanese censors demanded that all Chinese newspapers published in the foreign concessions be submitted to them. This led to the closing of the papers and new ones opening under nominal American ownership. There was much work, even in *Century Wind*, the literary section of *Wenhui bao*.

Throughout this whole weary time without Peipei I wrote her daily letters, many with thoughts from her favourite poet Yu Hsuan-chi: letters that told of my love of Peipei and despair in living alone, without her, the love of my life. Using the words of the poet, I described myself, without Peipei, as being like a boat with no mooring, drifting along.

The only colleague from our coterie that I now had left in Shanghai was Liu Na'ou. He was very optimistic about the prospects for an early peace with Japan and reiterated his view that war was war. "The atrocities we're hearing about are no different from the usual ones in any armed conflict. Reports of Japanese cruelty and mass murders are grossly exaggerated," he told me. "I have it on the best authority." And another time: "These photos from the Japanese newspapers, are the correct ones," Liu said, handing me some clippings he'd made. "See? There's nothing fake about them. They show little Chinese children in Nanking being given candies and other treats and kindly patted on the head by visiting dignitaries from Japan. These photos are what accurately represents the situation there."

However, I found it difficult to agree with Liu, given the almost daily incidents in the later months of 1937 and early 1938, within and near the International Settlement. These involved the following news flashes in Chinese papers: "Two Chinese men were stabbed to death in the Huxi western area, that foreigners called the Badlands, after they had come to the rescue of a Chinese woman being raped by Japanese soldiers." and, "A group of armed Japanese arrested four Chinese in Great Eastern Hotel (attached to Wing On's department store). The soldiers transported their prisoners across Soochow Creek for questioning in Bridge House, from which they were later released."

Reports were commonplace of looting of what little the Chinese had left, including clothes, bedding, cooking utensils, even paper depictions of the Kitchen God. Needless to say, there were many citings of the rape of Chinese women.

Across the road from their torture centre at Bridge House, the Japanese set up the headquarters of a terrorist organisation, called The Yellow Way Association, consisting of about one thousand Chinese thugs. They were ready to promote the Japanese cause in the foreign areas through terrorism.

Almost all of us writers were receiving in the mail decaying hands and ears, or even bullets, with a warning letter. I myself received one such revolting parcel. For me the last straw was a newsflash in February: "In the French Concession, six severed heads of Chinese men have been found and handed to the police. They have identified one of the heads as that of a journalist, Mr Tsai Tiao Tu, publisher of the *Social Evening News*." His head had been hung from a lamppost opposite the police station in the French Concession, with a placard announcing that this was the penalty for those who were anti-Japanese.

I was on the point of leaving for Hong Kong when news came from Ningpo that our mother had died suddenly (the Mus were surprised as she had appeared to be recovering well from Father's death over four years previously). I packed up my belongings and prepared to join Peipei. However, first my brother Shijie and I took a train to Ningpo to attend our mother's funeral.

Although it was my responsibility as the eldest son to plan it, my uncle and brother Shiyan had completed the preparations for Mother's interment, saying that they quite understood this was for the best, especially as I was continuing on to join Peipei in Hong Kong. I officiated at the funeral, which was held at the family burial site on a hill overlooking the city.

Travel was still possible outside the occupied areas. Lijuan had managed to attend, and when it was over, she joined me in boarding a ship going south. Shijie returned to his job in Shanghai. It was a heavy time of mourning: for the beautiful mother we had lost, and for the separation from my muse, Shanghai. But at last I would see Peipei again, and as I realised now, that meant more to me than anything.

*

HONG KONG, NANKING AND JAPAN
(January 1938-November 1939)

East
China

Peking

Yellow
Sea

Yangtze River

Nanking

Soochow

Shanghai

Hangchow

Ningpo

Canton

Tung Shan
Park

Pearl River

Shameen

China
Sea

Formosa
(Taiwan)

Canton

Hong Kong

20 (January 1938-November 1939)

U sually, I obeyed Shiying's wishes, but was so terrified by
what was happening in Shanghai that, for once in my life
with him, I struck out on my own, rejoining Madam Shen's
household as she said I had worn well, and looked younger than
my age of twenty-one. Living as I did in the secure house run
by Madam Shen, with my courtesan sisters all around and kindly
taking care of me as before, I should have felt safer in Hong
Kong: farther from war, nearer to my birthplace and family in
Canton. But that year's unusually chill winds slicing in from the
north failed to scour Shanghai's charnel house stench from my
nostrils, and in their wild wailing down the tree-lined streets, they
brought rumours of what the Japanese were doing in Nanking,
dark whispers that echoed in my dreams . . .

Trying to keep up with her parents and little brother, the tiny girl,
Ga Bo, struggled along the uneven path up Purple Mountain.
They had long ago passed the shining white Sun Yat Sen
mausoleum at the foot and were now well up toward the summit.
The family went past the burning machine gun emplacements
and munitions depots, past the piles of dead soldiers. Her father
said: "Don't look, turn your head away, Ga Bo," but the corpses
were everywhere. So she looked down at her stumbling feet
instead.

The night before, the whole mountain appeared to be in
flames. Ga Bo's mother had looked out of the window and said,
"Aie, the ancient saying is coming true."

"What saying?" asked Ga Bo.

"The one that says the Yangtze to the west and the Purple
Mountain to the east shield our city, like a coiling dragon

and a crouching tiger, and that: 'When the Purple Mountain burns . . . then the city is lost.' That night Ga Bo's parents dressed her in her warmest clothes, for a journey, they said. But first, they hid their money in the thatched roof of their house, tucking it under so that no one could find it. Then, Ga Bo's mother strapped a large bag of rice on the child's back.

"Here, take the new chair your grandmother gave you. You can manage to carry that as well."

Now Ga Bo climbed up the crouching tiger dragging along her little painted chair by the top rung of its back. They were all exhausted and soon would have to find a place to sleep. At last Ga Bo's father said, "We must stop and eat and rest." Ga Bo and her mother looked for wood to make a fire for cooking. "We must make a small fire, so as not to draw attention to ourselves," said the mother, and made a fire and cooked some rice with vegetables.

After eating, Ga Bo's father said, "We must find brushwood to put underneath us for protection against the cold ground, and also put it over ourselves to shield us from the wind . . . and prying eyes." The family lay down behind a large rock. Round her, Ga Bo rolled a blanket Mother had brought. The little chair placed on its side formed an angle in which she curled up and soon fell asleep. That night, from the Purple Mountain, her parents watched the city behind them burning.

Below, to the west, heavy wooden gates slammed shut in the high walls. Japanese soldiers thrust home the bolts, and drove long nails through the wood with a staccato finality. No one could leave. The city held its breath. Then the soldiers' work and the civilians' experiences of war began: chasing, fleeing, hiding, finding; shooting, screaming, rape, burning, terrorising, murdering . . . sobbing . . . silence. Narrow streets choked with bodies, faces down, hands clawing forward, feet stretched out ready to run even in death. *Horror: Nanking.*

Why, in Hong Kong, were my dreams beset by images from another city? Even my other dream, of the Japanese Sandman, was frightening: it had taken on a rather sinister, claustrophobic atmosphere. He seemed to be coming closer, more in focus, and was different somehow, but I still couldn't see the Japanese Sandman well enough to make out clearly what it was about his attire that had changed.

I also wondered why, in my waking hours, Shiying seemed to be with me all the time in this place where he had never been. I knew the answer to this question from Shiying's letters, many carrying a love thought from my poetess heroine. One was that after spending many loving nights together, he had never suspected that his true love would leave (from "Farewell").

To Shiying I sent my own poetry from Yu Hsuan-chi: that all my attractions could not interrupt his quest for fame (from "Thoughts at Heart Sent to Him").

I wanted to live. I wanted Shiying to live also. He was constantly in my thoughts. Yet, paralysed with fear, I could not return to the terror of Shanghai, with its odour of death, to try once again to bring him away. Instead of going myself, I sent letters daily.

A welcome visitor who soon came from Canton was Cheng Ziyao. I was so relieved to have his calm presence and good judgement to rely on. Over tea in Madam Shen's beautiful reception room, the news my mentor brought was not altogether reassuring: "Peipei, I have to tell you that the safe refuge in Hong Kong is only temporary. I have inside information that the British believe it cannot be defended against a Japanese attack, and that after securing Nanking, the Japanese will turn their attention to Hong Kong and Singapore." Biting delicately into a cake, Cheng Ziyao then wiped his mouth on a napkin before informing me that as a concrete indication of their concern, in 1935 when they went off the silver standard to gold, the newly built Hongkong and Shanghai Bank shipped their own reserves of silver bars to Britain for sale.

Rinsing his hands in rosewater in a silver bowl, Cheng Ziyao continued, "Right now, the British are taking precautions worldwide to protect their country's wealth, and I am sure the gold bullion cannot be far behind in being shipped away from Japanese looting." This would represent millions of pounds of profit from trade in the Far East where, partly because of the influx of both rich and poor refugees fleeing Japanese violence, business was booming. The British must not risk such wealth potentially falling into Japanese hands.

This raised the question of how to protect my own store of gold bars and American currency. My mentor presented me with a plan that reminded me of my father's approach to the depredations of the KMT (it seemed like so many years ago): "I suggest a two-step plan to protect your wealth, as well as you if you do not get away in time. As a first step, I suggest that you convert some of the gold to American currency, leaving a healthy balance in your account firstly to use for an escape or, failing that, for the Japanese to loot. Once you've done that, you should ask the Hongkong and Shanghai bank to transfer all the balance of your wealth to a bank in Vancouver, Canada."

"I have friends in the Chinatown of Vancouver," continued Cheng Ziyao. "Also, I have business interests in Vancouver and am allowed to send my family there. We have visas, and you and Mu Shiying are welcome to go with us. You could probably get a visitors' visa and hope to upgrade . . . or else we could simply hide you until the war's end." The Canadian government were tightening controls and it was possible we would not be able legally to extend our stay. However, we would be hidden among our own people there.

I asked Shiying by letter to consider Cheng Ziyao's proposal for us, but his reply by return post was unequivocal: "You go if you wish with my blessing. It will relieve my mind to think of you safe with good people that you know. However, China is coming into a period of terrible misfortune and I cannot abandon my country and run away to be safe under foreign skies."

Within a few weeks my dilemma with respect to Shanghai resolved itself, when Shiying wrote me a brief letter:

My dearest Peipei, I have some sad news: my mother has died suddenly and I am going to Ningpo for her funeral rites. After that I am coming to join you. You were right about the situation in Shanghai. It becomes increasingly dangerous and in particular for writers. But not to worry, as usual, I am well. However, I still can't stand the idea of you as a courtesan. Even though you may not sleep with a client, nevertheless, in people's minds there is that possibility. Once we are together again, I'd like you to leave Madam Shen's establishment and come to live with me.

Of course I could understand his feelings. This time there was no financial rescue in the form of my being asked to continue with Madam Shen as a hostess for events. Madam Shen's establishment was much larger than the one in which I had lived with Madam Wong. We were going to have to make our living somehow without that support.

Many people had come to Hong Kong for safety. Especially in Victoria, accommodation was scarce and rents high. Dai Wangshu and Shiying's sister Lijuan had bought a bungalow on Pokfulam Road, overlooking the sea and in the countryside on the other side of the island from Kowloon. Lijuan and I had fun thinking up a name for the house such as Seaview Bungalow, or Our Home, (both too obvious). "It's near a wood and there's a stream running through the garden," said Lijuan, "Why not name our house Woodbrook Villa?" That's what the Dais did, and there they lived in idyllic happiness.

Given Shiying's stubborn pride and refusal to use what he referred to as my pension, the same kind of course was not open to us. Before Shiying's arrival, I found a room with shared cooking facilities in a house at the foot of the Peak, and furnished it simply with a bed and other necessities.

Our reunion was ecstatic. On our first night we lay for hours fulfilled, wholly each other's, limbs entwined, in a dreamlike state of total relaxation. From the cool darkness outside came the deep tones of a temple gong and the monks' intoned prayers. The spring rain falling from clouds on The Peak filled the air with a light thrumming sound.

I decided to use my sewing skills, and looked for dressmaking work from households on the Peak. Every morning I walked up the winding road and knocked at the servants' door to ask to see the "Missee". There was a tramway up the mountain, but they wouldn't allow me to buy a ticket. We Chinese had to walk.

Decorated as it was by ferns and other plants, the pathway up was not at all like a public road and I found the journey a pleasant one. I could imagine how pretty it would be when the masses of jasmine and wild indigo and rhododendron flowered. There would be butterflies and kites and long-tailed magpies—and cicadas with their singing in the hot air and mists. I looked down across the stunning vistas of Hong Kong's many islands, with the hills of Canton looming blue-violet in the distance.

The servants I talked with did not want to help me. However, there was one woman who seemed rather sympathetic. "Why, when I go to the service entrance are people always turning me away?" I asked.

It's because you are so beautiful. You may take our jobs, and besides, *we* can sew."

"But I don't want your job, only the chance to do some occasional dress-making."

"I'll see what I can do, but at another house you should try at the front door. The Missee will know you are there, and the maid will not dare turn you away without her permission." She went to ask her mistress if she needed dress-making, but the answer was no.

There was one compound of three houses where I had my first commission. The maid ushered me in and I was astonished to see a *Chinese* "Missee". "You seem surprised," she said, appearing to be amused.

"No, certainly, I am pleased to come in," I stammered, "Thank you for agreeing to see me."

She put me out of my misery by saying, "We are Chinese here. This is the Ho-tung compound. And where are you from?" So I had happened upon the house of Sir Robert Ho-tung, a multi-millionaire, who with his wife Clara gave large donations to good causes. He was famous also for being the only one of us allowed to live on the Peak.

"I am from Canton originally, and have come back from Shanghai."

"Ah, it's very dangerous right now. We have property there as well."

Then we discussed clothes, and from that house I obtained my first commission: to help in making clothes for the servants.

Much encouraged by my work for the Ho-tungs, I persevered, going to the front doors. Eventually my good appearance and beautiful clothes impressed the foreign ladies and I had several more commissions. However, this work did not pay well. People expected me to work long hours for practically nothing. The relatively easy money of the courtesan's life had spoiled me. Now I learned what others had to do to make a living: working hard, fast and for long hours.

Shiying soon joined up with the literary group from Shanghai, notably his brother-in-law Dai, who had quickly made a solid mark in Hong Kong. Recently, given the influx of literary refugees from other parts of China, Hong Kong had developed as a cultural centre. Shiying told me that the film industry in Hong Kong was booming, and that he would try and break into it with some scripts for films. In the meantime, he searched for work in journalism where he had more experience, and soon had a job as editor of a news magazine *World Forecast*.

When Shiying came in from accepting his new job he was in high spirits. That evening we were going to see Lijuan and Wangshu. "Let's celebrate," said Shiying, "And take along a bottle of French wine." Another few weeks saw Shiying with more work writing literary supplements for other newspapers such as *China Evening Post*. I thought we could move to a bigger place, but my husband soon turned to his other love and started to gamble again.

He was good-natured, staying out late, utterly charming as usual, polishing his shoes to perfection as usual. Then one day I came home from a fitting for a coat, and noticed a chest of drawers was missing. My heart sank: I knew he was in debt again and had sold the furniture. Other items: china, a chair, tablecloths and further household necessities, started to disappear. In China there's always a place where you can gamble, a fan tan game where you can lose all your money.

The October 1938 Japanese invasion of my home city of Canton led to an even greater flight of refugees to Hong Kong, driving up food prices and also our rent. The authorities estimated that half a million people were now sleeping in the streets. After the Japanese invasion of Nanking, Chiang Kai-shek had already withdrawn his entourage and troops to the mountains in Chungking, making it the new capital. But first, in June of 1938, to try and stop the enemy advance he had shocked our nation by ordering the blowing up of some Yangtze dikes, creating floods that killed millions of peasants. It seemed that now, the only people fighting the Japanese were the Communists. There were rumours of a Canadian doctor named Bethune, who was attached to the Communists, but who also gave medical help to wounded Japanese and Chinese equally.

Now, something else happened: I had to visit a doctor, and asked Lijuan for the name of theirs. As I waited, I fidgeted in my chair, I suspected what the verdict would be and soon that fear was confirmed. When the doctor came into the consulting room after washing his hands, he was smiling. "Congratulations Mrs Mu, you are expecting a baby," he said, "It should be due in about seven months. You must eat well and rest." *Eat well and rest, how can I do that?*

I left the medical building and walked blindly along. The winter air seemed colder and meaner than usual. It blew through the light raincoat I wore and numbed my hands in their dark cotton gloves. Pulling the collar of the coat up around my face, and bending into the wind, I decided I had to come to grips with this information right away, and turned into a shop serving tea. On the one hand I was delighted, overjoyed to be expecting Shiying's child, but this did not seem to be the best time for a new little person to come into our lives. I decided that of course it was only fair, to him and to our marriage, to discuss this with Shiying.

When I told him the news, Shiying took me in his arms and asked me what I wanted. He agreed with my view of the situation: "This is an important decision that affects you more than it affects me, and we'll think about it for a few days. I'm delighted at the idea of a baby . . . that permanently joins us together. . . . But I think one course we'd better consider is for you to have an abortion. It's up to you. . . . You're only twenty-two and there'll be plenty of time for children when we're more settled, after the war . . . which looks like it's coming. . . ." I could see that Shiying still hoped for some kind of peace between Japan and the European powers, but from what Cheng Ziyao had told me, that seemed unlikely.

So we scraped together the money, mainly from a bank loan, for an abortion performed by a doctor recommended by the one I had seen. It was expensive, but we knew there would be no more children possible if I had a less skilled abortionist and something went wrong.

On our return from the procedure, (such a sterile word), Shiying and I clung together. We tried to comfort each other: "It won't be long before it'll be safe for us to start another child," said Shiying, as he brought me a cup of tea he had made.

"I feel miserable, I didn't know the awful effect an abortion would have. I thought I'd be relieved, and in a way I am. I'm all mixed up."

"So am I. So am I," sighed Shiying, shaking his head.

From this experience we both knew that we most desperately wanted a child some day. That feeling was confirmed on the following week when we were having dinner with the Dais. We were sitting in their living room overlooking the Lamma Channel, watching the ships go through, when I turned and saw them both looking at their little daughter. How devoted they were to her, what joy she brought them. My eyes filled with tears and I pretended to have an ash from the fire in my eye. *How could we confide in them?*

We struggled on through the next year (1939). In August I received a letter from Cheng Ziyao with the news that: "I have learned that when the squadron of British cruisers left Hong Kong, the cruiser Birmingham was carrying all of the island's British gold reserves." The squadron had steamed out through the broad West Lamma Channel, for large ships, which we could not see from the Dais' villa that overlooked the narrower East Channel. To allow the banks to continue with trade, more bullion came from India, but my mentor said that most of that shipment continued on to Canada for safekeeping.

Now, Shiying stayed at home in the evenings. He was morose, fidgety and bad-tempered, quite unlike his usual self. I suspected Shiying was giving up gambling to cover the loan he had taken out to meet our medical bill for the abortion. But then he was again staying out more "to work" and returned to his cheerful self. I was sure he was also again gambling.

When I returned one day to find even our bed gone, with us left to sleep on a mattress on the floor, I felt we had come to an ultimate low point. Shiying looked so sad that I could not bear to say anything about our furniture and other household belongings disappearing. All I had left were my clothes and sewing machine. All he had left were his beautifully kept clothes and shoes, and his light, graceful walk. *Shiying still dances as he walks,* I thought, *His whole way of moving is a dance.* As he watched me looking at the devastation, Shiying said, "I'm going to make up my gambling losses, return to Shanghai and get a job that pays more than I can make in Hong Kong. We can then start a family," he promised, optimistic as usual,

I froze in fear. *Did Shiying really think he could recoup his gambling losses? Did he not know what happened to those who didn't pay their gambling debts: the way gangsters followed a debtor from city to city? Did he not remember why we had left Shanghai: the danger there?*

21 (January 1938-November 1939)

I was overjoyed to be with Peipei again but couldn't stand Hong Kong: that sleepy colonial town where nothing much took place, fit only for shoppers. It was not a great and vibrant city like Shanghai. Certainly, there were some of the Shanghai crowd, but their less sophisticated Cantonese counterparts outnumbered them. There was no life, nothing like the bustling streets and high buildings of Shanghai. Why, the highest was the Hongkong and Shanghai Bank at twelve storeys. What good was that? And there was no Art Deco architecture, only the dull, two-storey old style shops and genteel slow pace of the tree-lined streets.

I couldn't even expand my interest in films. The two scripts I wrote, *Long Live China* and *Fifteen Patriots* didn't get anywhere. No one wanted either them or my ideas for presenting films in new and exciting ways. These people were stuck in a rut and, so far as being in Hong Kong was concerned, so was I.

I had written an early novel *The Fate of a Nobody* that wasn't worth much, my juvenilia, and after running a few installments in *Six Skills*, had abandoned it partway to go to Hong Kong. I *did* work extensively on that third novel which was to be my *chef d'œuvre*, and so far as I was aware, the *only* novel of the modernist writers, who tended to write shorter pieces. It was a panoramic depiction of China in recent times and included *Shanghai Foxtrot*. I now changed the title from *China 31* to *China March*. The book was so experimental in its writing style, and also presentation, that I couldn't take the time to make a copy, as one should do with a work of some length, which would be difficult to write over again if something happened to it such as being misplaced, stolen or lost in a fire.

The nearest I could get to the dash and danger of Shanghai was in the bazaars near the waterfront where only single men lived and where I went to gamble. Given the heavy losses, I had to stop until I had paid off the abortion loan, at which point, to make back the money I'd lost, I started to gamble again. When I had gone to the point of selling our bed and reducing us to sleeping on a mattress on the floor, I knew I *had* to do something about our financial situation.

In October I was sitting in a café feeling sorry for myself, and mulling over an offer I'd had of a political job, when who should come along but my old friend Ji.

"Hello, Ji," I said, delighted.

"I knew I'd come across you sometime. I was going to start looking."

"So what are you doing here in Hong Kong?"

"Just taking a break from Shanghai."

"Well let's have dinner this evening."

Thinking about Ji, I remembered he seemed a quiet person, with no particularly outstanding characteristics either in his appearance or behaviour, the kind of man who, in a group, fades into the background. Like most writers he was very observant and I respected his opinions and advice. Maybe I could ask him, in confidence, what to do.

Over dinner, Ji told me he was still writing under the pen name of Kang Yi. "Do you remember taking me to the Zengs'?" I asked.

"'I certainly do, but you were more of the man-about-town than I ever was."

"There's not much of that now I'm married. In fact I first met my wife at the Zengs', so I have you to thank for that as well."

"But those were good days when we were students—not like the situation in Shanghai now."

"I have something I'd like to ask you about."

"Go ahead."

"Very confidentially, I've had an offer from Lin Bosheng. Lin is in Shanghai again. He is joining Wang Jingwei's government in Nanking and has asked me to work with their propaganda bureau. It's a good job, paying well, but I'm concerned about disloyalty to my country, joining a collaborationist régime like that. Also, I know I'll be worried sick about my safety and that of Peipei." Ji looked grave. He felt I certainly had much to be concerned about. Perhaps I didn't know much about the activities of the KMT Green Gang. Then there were also the Communists to take into account. Since I had come to Hong Kong, between them they had carried out hundreds of assassinations of Japanese or their sympathisers. "The Japanese military retaliate by selecting at random into the teens of our people and executing them."

"I've told Lin about my worries, especially about Peipei, and he has assured me they will protect us and provide me with a bullet-proof car for travelling the streets. You remember my good friend Liu Na'ou, don't you?"

Ji laughed, "You two were inseparable. I'm amazed he didn't come with you to Hong Kong."

"Well no, Liu is very well in with the Japanese, having spent most of his life there and speaking the language so well. Anyway, I couldn't bear to be separated from Peipei, which is why I came to Hong Kong. Of course there's the increasing danger in Shanghai . . . but we're literally almost starving here. If it weren't for the Dais (you know he's married to my sister) we probably *would* starve. Our rent keeps going up. We can't both keep a roof over our heads and also eat."

"Mmm, things are very difficult. I can see you have to do something," Ji murmured, "But what were you going to say about Liu?"

"He's taking over as editor-in-chief of the newspaper the collaborationists have bought, *Wenhui bao*. He says he's dying for me to come back and be his senior editor. It would be wonderful to see him and work together again."

Ji continued to look serious. "I'm afraid Lin's protection won't keep you safe. They may not go after Peipei, but you won't stand a chance. These assassins are very powerful, very fast. They do their work in a minute and disappear right away. They never get caught."

"How would Peipei survive without me? We love each other."

"Love," spat out Ji, with a cynical smile, "It certainly doesn't go very far toward keeping food on the table, or you in safety." Then he continued: "Well I'm keeping to myself your concerns about collaborating, and I want you to keep to *yourself* what I'm going to tell you. It's why I came here to see you," and he leaned forward, speaking closer to my ear. "I'm going to be working undercover for the KMT, collecting information from several agents and sending it on. Why don't I arrange for you to be one of my agents, as well as doing your propaganda jobs? That way, you'll be protected by both sides and have an even better income. I could pick up your information and pass it on with the rest. You won't have to run the risk of being in direct contact with KMT people. As old friends we'll be seeing each other anyway, and no one will suspect a thing."

Ji paused again, "I tell you what, in a week or two I'm going to Shanghai. Why don't you come with me? We'll work out the details on the boat . . . and then you can go on to Nanking to see Wang Jingwei."

I brightened up immediately. "That would be wonderful. It makes me feel better to be also helping my own country. Maybe, by liaising with both sides, I could help bring about understanding and peace," I said, "I think it's the role of writers to do that here."

Ji again looked cynical. "There you go as usual, the wide-eyed idealist. The Japanese desire for empire has gone too far and I doubt that anything we can do will make any difference. Since you left they've even set up a centre for torturing people at 76

Jessfield Road in the Huxi. It has quickly become known simply as No. 76. Look, too many journalists have already been murdered. We'll have our work cut out to save our own skins. But have it your own way," he said, giving his usual quiet smile.

When I told Peipei she was relieved about the safety issue but said, "I've been thinking that we could go to Canada, where my money is, and live there for a while until we see how things go at home."

I reacted strongly, "We'd be fish out of water. I wouldn't be able to write. We'd be dependent on your money and I cannot have that. I must make a living for myself and support my wife. I can never leave my homeland."

"But there's a large Chinese community in Vancouver. In effect we would be at home, among our own people. We'd know the Chengs. That's where they are going. Cheng Ziyao told me he's transferring his family there."

"I'm not interested in keeping contact with that man. The less we have to do with him the better."

Peipei came and stroked my face, kissed me, "I understand you want to stay in our own country and so do I. I want to stay with you. We can face whatever happens together. But what about having a baby?"

"It's not the most urgent priority right now. First we should enjoy life together. Then when we have saved some money from our incomes, not your retirement money from being a courtesan, and then when we're a bit older and have had some fun together, we can settle down and start a family." We agreed that in Shanghai we would live modestly on our incomes and save to have the baby we, and especially Peipei, so much wanted.

That settled, in early November of 1939, Ji and I journeyed to Shanghai on the American President liner Cleveland.

In Shanghai I stayed overnight with Liu and the next morning went to Nanking. On the train, I shifted in my seat, remembering the stories of massacres and rapes, indignities to the dead, bloated bodies of Chinese soldiers with their hands tied drifting down the Yangtze, and worse, the photographs. These were from film handed in by Japanese soldiers at Shanghai, to be made into snaps for relatives. The photofinishers had kept copies. I wondered, *Was I doing the right thing?* As we pulled in to the city I looked out of the compartment window. The place was devastated. *Where are the people, and where do they live?* For a few minutes I stood on the deserted platform and then went outside to the street.

Nanking. After *two years,* there was still an indefinable stench of death about the place. It had followed the Japanese from Shanghai. It followed them everywhere. Smashed into the muddy, bloody underpinnings of the new streets they were laying, mixed with the bricks and mortar of the new buildings, seeping into the air. Some said you got used to it, but *I* never would. Some said you didn't smell it after a while, but *I* did.

Fear. You could hear it in the silence, see it in the way the people crept about, and sense its acrid stench in their breaths, blowing whitely in the frosty air like the ghosts of their dead. Their dead: piled up high in the streets, rolled over . . . and over . . . by the tanks, and then shoveled at last into mass graves. I almost vomited. I almost turned back. But the black car came for me, honk honking its horn. The uniformed men ushered me into it. And I went to my meeting with Wang Jingwei

Wang Jingwei. I had heard he was very handsome, impeccably dressed, but when I was shown in to see Wang I was quite unprepared for his look of boyish innocence. I was expecting a devious plotter, not this charming, open and apparently honest man. Generals in full regalia with medals surrounded him; like jailers they seemed. It had the appearance of a military meeting, rather than one about propaganda. *But then,* I thought, *Both aspects needed campaigns.*

However, after being introduced to the generals, I did meet the publicity officials led by Lin Bosheng, who discussed the propaganda approach we would be taking: "To sum up, we should promote the angle of friendship between all Asian people and the idea of a co-operative Co-prosperity Sphere," said Lin, "We want prosperity, not war. Look at the European powers, squabbling and fighting. That isn't the way *we* should be. Hammer it home!" he repeated at the end of the meeting. I found myself becoming enthusiastic about this whole idea of peace and co-prosperity.

Wang asked the others to leave us alone for a while. The generals clinked their medals as they turned smartly and marched out. The publicity men snapped shut their briefcases, filing out in order. Wang took me over to the window of the large room we were in.

Looking out over the still devastated city, Wang said quietly, "I have a feeling you're concerned about collaborating with this longtime enemy of China. Aren't we all concerned about that in some way? But I'll be frank with you. Our beloved country is divided. In the countryside, despite the efforts of the Communists, warlords are still fighting each other. The Communists themselves are at loggerheads with the Nationalists as they so wrongly call themselves. All the KMT are doing is to back the rural landlords and plunder the nation's coffers. And then there's their Green Gang."

I turned to him in amazement. "But aren't the Japanese plundering and murdering us as well?"

"Yes, and I can see you're puzzled. You must be wondering where *I* come in." He took a short walk around the room before continuing: "Here, I have the beginnings of a centralized government, a structure that will be in place by this coming March, and can be used to bring the whole country under one rule—I trust, over time, one *Chinese* rule. Ultimately, I aim to throw out not only the Western imperialists, but the Japanese as well, Yes, I have to do as I'm told. However I am getting my own way about some things, and hope to continue with that. Having set me up as their puppet, the Japanese have to support me, at least in public, or they would lose face."

He rubbed his brow in a worried gesture. "Please, think about what I've said, and keep it to yourself. Please help me!" said Wang. *I, help Wang?* "I am going to need all the help I can get." With that, he led the way out to his aides. I had a feeling Wang was afraid to spend too much time talking to me alone, that he felt spied upon and controlled. I now became more convinced of the rightness of supporting Wang. He *was* right. This was the only way to have a central Chinese effort for freedom, peace and prosperity. I never saw this remarkable man again.

Japan. No sooner had I arrived back in Shanghai than I was on a ship (literally the next day) to Japan as the journalist representative for a Chinese delegation representing the "Temporary New Government". I must say I did not like the designation of Wang Jingwei's government as temporary, but decided to do my best to promote peace between China and Japan.

We were in Japan for a week. Our schedule was a rigid one and we were not allowed to wander around by ourselves seeing the sights. During this visit we toured several places. One of these was a small town called Odawara. Here I found myself sitting up on the back of the seats of an open car, and waving a Japanese flag at some school children lining the route. "Banzai! Banzai!" yelled the children. (They were waving the flag at us.) "Banzai! Banzai!" I shouted back. I had a twinge of misgiving at this waving of the Japanese flag and shouting of their war cry, but decided it was necessary for future peace and China's hope of independence.

I myself was honoured at an entertainment for the leading literary figures of Japan. We had an absolutely marvelous time together. "I have to welcome with some trepidation my Chinese opposite number," said Yokomitsu, reminding me that I was called the Chinese Yokomitsu Riichi. Kataoka, Hayashi, the Kon brothers, Hidemi and Toko, Kikuchi Kan and many other famous Japanese writers were at the dinner.

The meal had many courses. There was a different type of drink with each new course, and service was leisurely. Different Japanese literary figures made a point of leaving their places to come and talk to me, so I got to know them all. Drinks and conversation seemed to go on forever, well past midnight.

In so many ways, this dinner reminded me of the one we had in Shanghai on the return of Dai Wangshu. There was the same feeling of friendship and enjoyment in each other's company.

We talked about all aspects of literature past and present, but in particular the modernist movement. Whereas I saw it as a worldwide wave, the Japanese envisioned it more as one where the Eastern modernist movement in writing was different, more oriented to cementing friendship and co-operation between the Far Eastern countries. This gave me food for further thought. To writer and critic Kon Hedemi I said, "I can't remember having a more pleasant evening than this one." I liked these people so much, and I strongly felt that it was mutual.

From this experience, I was sure that through cultural cooperation we could deepen understanding, friendship and peace between our countries. I vowed that every time I started to have doubts, these doubts would be overcome. I even began to think that perhaps, if the European countries had focused on cultural exchanges and unity, they would have avoided the war they were presently fighting with each other. The pen *was* mightier than the sword and we writers must use our talents to bring about understanding and peace.

In several letters I later sent to Kon, I said I thought it was positively the responsibility of the cultural industries to deepen understanding, and above all peace, between our two countries. From then on the best policy for promoting peace seemed to be to act as if it really was the case. Perhaps in this way we could achieve Wang's dream of independence and freedom for China.

SHANGHAI
(December 1939-End 1941)

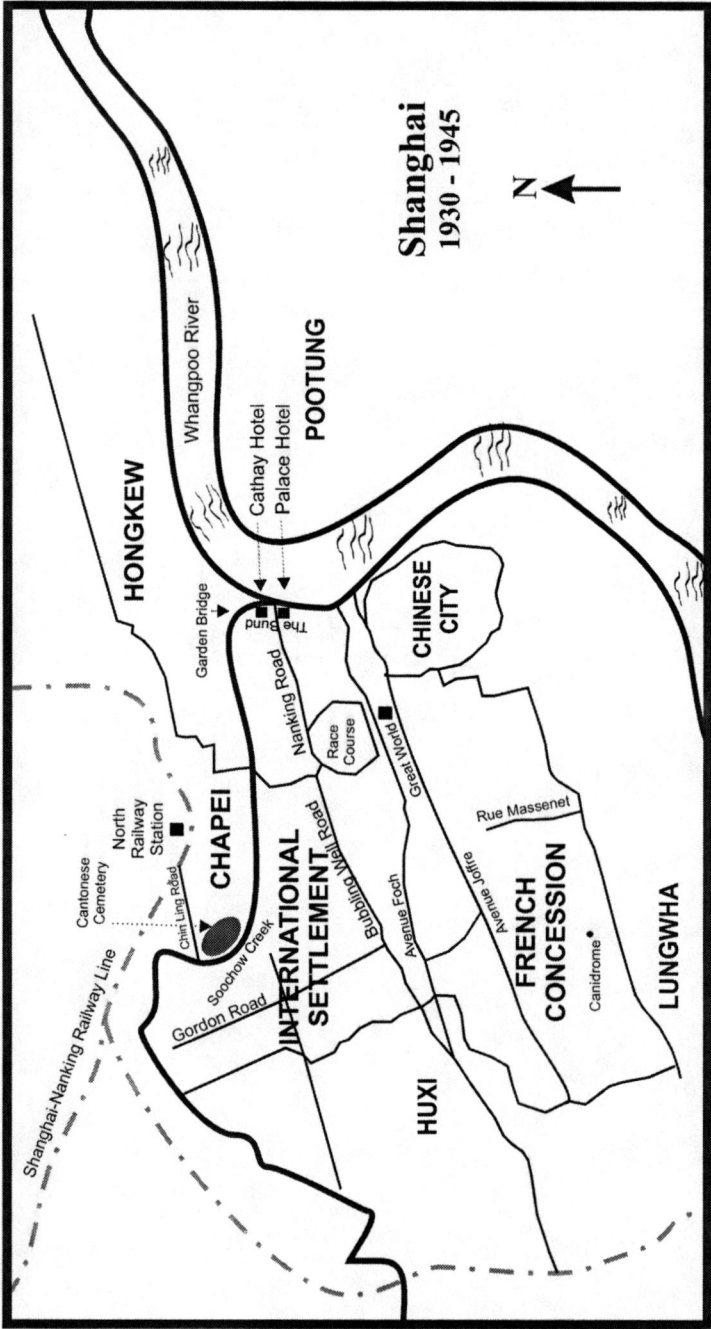

Shanghai
1930 - 1945

N

Whangpoo River

HONGKEW

POOTUNG

Cathay Hotel
Palace Hotel

Garden Bridge

The Bund

Nanking Road

CHINESE
CITY

Race
Course

Great World

North
Railway
Station

CHAPEI

Rue Massenet

Cantonese
Cemetery

Chin Ling Road

INTERNATIONAL
SETTLEMENT

Bubbling Well Road

Avenue Foch

Avenue Joffre

FRENCH
CONCESSION

Soochow Creek

Gordon Road

HUXI

Canidrome

LUNGWHA

Shanghai-Nanking Railway Line

22 (December 1939-May 1940)

Our new home. When I returned from Japan, I received a handsome cheque in advance of my services to the Wang régime, with which I paid my debts. Then I looked around for a place for Peipei and myself. I believed the International Settlement was not only the safest part of the city, but also of course, central. However, space was scarce and at a premium. Accommodation was not only hard to find, but the landlords were very choosy about who they would have as tenants. Eventually I found a roomy pavilion room for us in one of the large old alleyway houses.

I encountered the typical enquiries about not only my job, but also family background: occupations, relatives and where we came from . . . on and on. It turned out that the owner of the house, Mr Ho, had known my father. The Ho family were business people and Mr Ho's father had come from Ningpo and bought the alleyway house as a home and investment. They banked at the Ningpo Commercial Bank.

When we had established all this, Mrs Ho, who ran the renting out of parts of the house, showed me again to our new abode, situated above the large kitchen and accessed by some stairs leading up from the kitchen. It was larger than most and very private, being across a small backyard from the main house and its central courtyard. Mrs Ho took me over to the courtyard. It had pretty carved and painted woodwork, and chairs and tables to sit at. I had a few questions of my own: "Forgive me for asking, Mrs Ho, but are your neighbours likely to be people we would like? Are they and your other tenants quiet people? I need a peaceful atmosphere for my writing."

Mrs Ho touched my shoulder in a comforting and friendly gesture, "You have no need to worry. I would never rent to you if I thought you would not like the other tenants or neighbours. I like to have long-term renters. And besides, we know your family. You are one of us. The only other tenant rents the floor above where we live ourselves. He is a quiet Russian gentleman who has his own nightclub and sleeps most of the day." I thought the Russian gentleman sounded vaguely familiar, but I couldn't put my finger on what it was. "You and your wife will be welcome to come to our courtyard to sit and talk to the other people in this house. We are like a family," said Mrs Ho, again using the word.

Continuing to talk about our relatives and mutual friends, Mrs Ho led me to the alleyway, which gave out onto Ningpo Road. This was a predominantly Chinese street parallel to the major foreign one called Nanking Road. Within a few days, Peipei would be with me again, and I was sure she would be happy here.

As I was leaving, after six, I realised what sounded so familiar about the other tenant when I saw my old friend Mr V. "My dear Shiying," he said, putting his arm around my shoulders, "What a pleasant surprise to see you. I heard you'd left Shanghai. I hope this means you are coming to live with the Hos." I nodded. "Wonderful, wonderful. We must get together, but I'm afraid my schedule is different from yours. I expect you're writing and editing again."

"Well, yes," I said, getting a word in at last, "But we'll manage to see each other, and you must meet my wife when she comes. At the moment she's in Hong Kong."

"I look forward to more marvellous times together," he said, "But you know, times are changing here. It reminds me of the way they became in my beloved Russia before I left: distrust, violence, . . ." and he shook his head sadly.

My new jobs: The next day I visited Liu Na'ou. Over lunch we reminisced about our past times together: "Do you remember unpacking the books from Japan? What a job that was," I said.

"Those idiots who had us under surveillance! Their disguises were a joke."

"How frustrated I was over not being published yet."

"The Third Category writer was a good idea, but its time hasn't come."

"*Les Contemperains,* that was the best."

"Dai's wonderful homecoming dinner . . . Ahh those were the days . . . What happened to you in Hong Kong? You didn't keep very closely in touch."

"I had an editor's job, and worked as a journalist, but couldn't break into the story writing scene whether in print or movies . . . I fell into my old bad habit of gambling."

"Not good when you have a family to support," said Liu shaking his head. "The political situation is becoming even more tense and dangerous than it was before you left. To win over the local population . . . to the side of peace and co-operation under the Japanese . . . we urgently need a really good senior editor for *Wenhui bao.* Have you considered whether you want to take it on? (Of course, you remember that it used to be the KMT paper. We thought it a good idea to buy it and its name.) If you take it on, you will be well protected. As editor-in-chief I'll have my own bulletproof car. You can have one too, and bodyguards for you and Peipei." (a repeat of the protection offer from the Nanking people). "Think about it, but not for too long. It's so urgent I may have to take on someone else—or even do it myself with the editor-in-chief's work. I'll hope to hear from you tomorrow." And so Liu and I renewed our friendship. He paid the bill (plenty of money as usual) and shook my hand in parting.

I had already done my thinking, but to double check about security, again got in touch with Ji. "Yes, it's all arranged. The KMT central intelligence people know about you. I informed them while you were away in Japan. You can go ahead with *Wenhui bao,* secure in the knowledge that both sides are looking out for your safety." I couldn't thank him enough, but Ji shrugged off my appreciation: "That's what old friends are for. Maybe you can do me a good turn some day, and I know if you can, you will."

The next afternoon, I contacted Liu, and what with one thing and another, I was soon very busy and prosperous as well. In the morning of my first day at the newspaper, a large bulletproof car, provided by the Japanese authorities, drew up at Ningpo Road across from our alleyway. The driver knocked on our pavilion room door. I was amazed that they knew where to come. I wondered whether I was under Japanese surveillance, but no, that was a paranoid reaction: of course they knew our address from my paperwork with them over the editor's position. They were only making sure I was comfortable and safe. "Many, many thanks for coming to take me to work," I said to the driver, "But I shall be going to work by rickshaw every day." I gave a correct Japanese bow. To be friends, you had to understand and practice the particular forms of the other culture.

Being protected by both sides (not that the Japanese side knew it) I felt perfectly safe. By behaving as if there was no danger, I believed I could better serve the cause of mutual trust. This attitude provoked an avalanche of letters from Japan, written by people like Kon and Kikuchi Kan, warning me that my approach was foolhardy. I wondered how they knew the every day details of what I was doing. Peipei, who had returned immediately I had a job, joined the chorus of concern. She had just witnessed Japanese soldiers rounding up fourteen of our men at random from Ningpo Road. They were to be executed in reprisal for the assassination of a Japanese journalist. Following one of the men were his wife and children in tears, pleading for his release. Beating them with bayonets, the soldiers added the woman and little ones to the group for execution.

On my side, I felt I *must* have the courage of my convictions by showing trust in both the Chinese factions and Japanese. How else could we have mutual co-operation? How else could Peipei and I taste the joys of Shanghai? That would not work if we were always worrying about safety.

Cultural co-operation for peace. As far as I could, given my many work commitments, and also the desire to spend as much time as possible with Peipei, I tried to use my influence and good reputation to persuade the Shanghai cultural community to think well of the Japanese, to join me in bringing about peace through cultural understanding. I hung around the various café meeting places as well as the Chinese Cultural Association and explained my ideas: "We need to be friends with the Japanese, use our writing to join our two nations together. Look at what has happened in Europe with all this squabbling and fighting!"

"Are you crazy?" asked my old friend Feng, he who had invented the concept of the Third Category writer. "The Communists are the only people who can unite our country." *Oh no, he had become a committed Communist!* Feng pointed out that the Japanese were our old, sworn enemies. They had been persecuting us for centuries, and that had not changed lately. "Think of the news from Soochow and all the other places they have laid waste, Manchuria and Nanking! They want to rape, murder and loot, not help us to greater prosperity!"

The other writers were the same as Feng. They showed no hesitation in telling me I was out of my mind to believe mutual understanding could be possible between us, and a country that was murdering our countrymen in such numbers and with such barbarity as we spoke. "Things have gone too far," said one, "The Japanese have shown their true aim, which is total domination, a Japanese empire (not co-operation) throughout the East."

My magnum opus. I had trouble finding a printer and publisher for *China March*. They all said that given the different typefaces and sizes of print, it was too experimental and too difficult to typeset. However, from the way they looked at me, I suspected the real reason was that they thought of me as *persona non grata*: the editor of *Wenhui bao*, a collaborator and traitor to China.

Finally, I did find someone. In his small shop in a back alley, the printer bowed and said, "Sir, I would be honoured to print the book of so distinguished a writer as yourself. I'll produce the book, but with your experience in the industry you must realize how difficult it will be to set the type. It'll take a very long time.

I'll have to charge you a little extra," and he bowed again, "But it will be a labour of love."

"From the trouble I've had in physically writing it down, I understand that," I said, "In fact, for that reason I haven't made a copy. Are you sure this one will be safe with you?"

"Oh yes! Sir, we have a night watchman, it'll be perfectly safe."

This was a wonderful time for Peipei and me. Gone was the unhappiness from my gambling. I didn't have much time for that! I had the gambling passion under control and tried only an occasional flutter. Luck was against me as usual, but I knew it would change over time. Some people gambled as a profession. What a great life that must be: listening to the click of the Mah Jong tiles, the clatter of the roulette balls as they found their slots. As for the lack of money and sleeping on a mattress on the floor, that was a thing of the past. With the salaries I made, Peipei was able to buy anything she liked for our pavilion room.

My wife had a marvellous home-making talent. Her taste was towards simple rather than ornate furniture. Peipei bought an old clock with pendulums, to hang on the wall. One evening she said, "Shiying, I've found the most beautiful, carved and comfortable antique desk for your writing. It was expensive, but worth it." Peipei arranged everything so that while we were at ease together, we had space enough in the large room. Nevertheless, I had my desk and private corner for writing. (I did give a glancing thought to how on earth I'd ever have peace to think with a crying baby around, even in larger quarters.) My adorable wife even made a pretty miniature garden in a bowl, in the Japanese way.

One late night, the man who always came round selling snacks called softly at our window. Peipei let down our basket with money and pulled up the food. As we talked and ate before bed, I thought I had never been so happy, and so thoroughly contented with my life, so at peace. "The newspaper is increasing its circulation, especially in the Settlement where the intelligentsia live. Maybe they'll see that we must join together in peace."

"I so enjoy the dancing at Moon Palace. I'm being paid the same as before. Of course the best times are when you are there." . . . "Xuan and I were looking at baby clothes. Maybe I could start buying some."

"Sometime . . . why don't you buy a little chest to put them in?"

We were saving to have a baby, but we didn't have to think of that right now. This was the pleasant life: lots of fun, no worries. Why jump just yet into parenthood with its responsibilities and sleepless nights? Why not enjoy ourselves while we were young? Early in 1940, like everyone else in Shanghai, we went to see *Gone with the Wind* over and over—so romantic!

In May, Liu had the wonderful idea of having a belated celebration of our appointment to *Wenhui bao*. "Let's book a table for all of us at Sun Ya's. The times are so tense just now. We need to relax . . . enjoy ourselves." So the editors and staff of our newspaper dressed up and went to the renowned Cantonese restaurant on Nanking Road. Peipei was especially looking forward to the cuisine from her own town.

We were no sooner seated, with some security people standing behind Liu and me, when there was a dull plop sound from the restaurant stairs. Liu fell forward onto the table, blood gushing from his forehead. The security men chased someone who had fired a gun with a silencer, but he had disappeared into the crowd outside. Liu was dead, my dear, dear friend. The guards hustled us into the bulletproof car and took us home.

Peipei was in hysterics. I tred to calm her, holding her close in my arms, pressing her head against my shoulder, rocking her gently. "I am safe," I said, "I am perfectly safe and so are you. He could have shot me as well but he didn't."

"Safe. Who is safe . . . and where?" sobbed Peipei, "There is no safe place."

Confusion. By the time of my second visit to Japan in May, again representing my newspaper, (now as editor-in-chief), on a Chinese delegation, I was becoming discouraged. My idealism was being challenged by the facts emerging from the Japanese actions in the war, to the point that I wondered about the validity of my own actions.

Also, I was confused about exactly who *was* the enemy. Was it the CCP who were also claiming to be (and were) fighting for the Chinese national cause, or was the enemy the KMT—with the CCP being the real nationalists? Peipei had told me of the so-called voluntary contributions required by the KMT in Canton, and well-founded rumours were coming of the corruption at the top of the KMT administration. I asked myself how on earth such a political party could be good for the Chinese people. However, they had the support of America, a very powerful ally indeed against the Japanese. Of course the Japanese would qualify as an enemy. That is if we could not all get along well together and there *was* an enemy. My thoughts went round and round.

However, after my return, I continued my policy of showing trust. I did not take precautions for my own safety. Was I being brave, or merely foolhardy? I had my principles to protect, and that was the main thing to do. I needed freedom to write *what* I wished, *as* I wished, and so did all the other writers in China. But was overt collaboration the right way (even though, through my trusted position, I was able to obtain and feed useful information to the KMT Nationalists?). I simply was not sure any more. I think my state of mind was clear to the Japanese on my second visit in May.

"You're having doubts about us aren't you, my friend?" said Kon Hademi over lunch together (I am not good at hiding my feelings). "Are you really in favour of the two nations being as one?" Now I had another worry: I wondered if the Japanese would continue to trust me. I wondered again whether I could trust them.

Peipei continued to be concerned. "I think we should go ahead and have the baby," she said repeatedly, "And not worry about saving so much for it. What if something happens to you and I have nothing, nothing of you to keep with me to remember you by?"

"We have time. We are young. We should enjoy our time together and have a last fling before taking on the responsibility of a child. I want to be the provider and pay at least my share of clothes and food and accommodation for you and the child." I said, over and over. It was the same circular discussion.

"But *why*. I have so much put away in the Hongkong and Shanghai Bank for us all. We don't really need to save. You must learn to *take* from me as well as giving."

*

23 (December 1939-May 1940)

When I returned to Shanghai early in December of 1939, it was to settle down with Shiying in the alleyway accommodation he had found for us. The first thing I did was to go and see Madam Wong, who hugged me. "I am so glad to see you again," she said, looking me up and down, "And you're the picture of health! The stay in Hong Kong has been good for you." Madam Wong ushered me into her living room, "Come, have some tea and snacks." Sitting there, I felt so secure. *How could Shanghai be dangerous, with people like Madam Wong around?*

When we had had our tea I said, "First and foremost I am here to see you, but I have another purpose. Do you have any hostess work for me as before?"

"Ah, I wondered about that," said Madam Wong with a sigh, "But times are hard. I was able to replace you and have a full house to meet all my needs." Again she sighed regretfully, "But I would love to see you to chat whenever you have the time."

"I would love that too," and I meant it. We parted affectionately.

I thought Moon Palace could always take me on, especially given my husband's celebrity status and well-known dancing skills. So I went to see the manager Mr Chong. As I sat down opposite his desk he gave me an assessing look. "Your looks have not suffered from you being married," he said, spending some time arranging items on his desk. "Let me think, times are hard (shades of Madam Wong without the regret) but you may add to business. Will your husband be coming to dance?" I nodded. "Well then, you're hired on the same pay as before, no more mind, as times are hard," and he turned back to his desk. Mr Chong had dismissed me.

I worried about Shiying's undercover work for the KMT. "How are you going to transfer information to Ji? If you meet too regularly, the spies are bound to notice." (All the signs, of casually dressed men hanging around our home and his office, indicated that we were under surveillance.)

"Don't worry, it'll be all right. Ji and I won't meet regularly . . . only from time to time. Sometimes Shijie will act as a go-between, memorizing information from me and relaying it to Ji. At other times Ji and I will simply meet in a restaurant as friends and quietly converse. Shijie, Ji and I see each other often anyway, so nobody should be any the wiser."

For the first meeting Ji chose the Heart-of-Lake Pavilion next to Yu Yuan garden. As he was leaving, Shiying admitted to me that he was rather nervous, but Ji chose a table near a group of older men. Each one had brought a singing bird in a cage. The noise of their song and of the men's chatter, each claiming that *his* bird was the better singer, completely masked the conversation between Ji and Shiying. The two sat chatting as usual, perfectly relaxed, except that Shiying was telling Ji a few facts he had gleaned, but not published, about the plans of Wang Jingwei. As the facts would probably soon be made public knowledge, Shiying believed there was no particular harm done to Wang: he was only giving Ji a scoop.

Shiying repeated his conversation with Ji: "And so you two are thinking of starting a family. Do you think it's wise in the present situation?"

"No . . . But we have it in mind for later when things settle down—as I'm sure they will soon."

"Always the optimist," said Ji with his rather cynical smile.

One morning about four months after my return, I stood in my dressing gown at the door of the alleyway house seeing Shiying off to work. He was dressed in a light grey European suit with a freshly laundered, white shirt and blue tie. Despite a late night waiting up for me, he looked his freshest (and handsomest) self, the black hair shining with a light application of oil, and bright dark eyes looking down at me. On his way to work Shiying would be buying the pink rosebud he always wore in the lapel of his suit jacket.

We were in the pleasant Summer Monsoon season for Shanghai, and now, in the latter part of April, entered *Ku-yu*, the Corn Rain period. The night soil cart had come hours ago, at about four that morning, and our bucket with the brush for scrubbing it stood out drying beside the door. After the previous evening's long stint in the smoky atmosphere of Moon Palace, the fresh warm feel of April sun on my face was heavenly.

The air was still acrid with smoke from the charcoal fires in small metal containers that many of us had used to cook our breakfast of rice and pickled vegetables. Across the narrow cobbled alleyway, the bubbling cry of a little bulbul bird, perched in a tree behind the wall separating our lane from the main street outside, distracted me. Shiying laughed, "That bird's Japanese. He's saying "*shokuji*" (a meal). "Shokuji, shokuji, shokuji's ready," cried the bird. His black crown and the white nape of his neck reminded me of a photograph Shiying once showed me of the North American black-capped chickadee.

I looked at the sun shining on pink blossoms bursting out all over the tree, with at the end of each branch a small light-green puff of new leaves, "The tree's looking beautiful today."

"Yes, but it won't last out the year. That tree has a disease." Shiying reached up, plucked a leaf and pointed out a tiny grey mark on it. "In a few weeks it'll be showing signs." He hugged me and went off in search of a rickshaw. I watched him as he walked his light, dancing walk, turning to wave at the end of the lane. I returned to our room for some added sleep before the afternoon and evening ahead at Moon Palace.

This was the happiest time of our life together. We were financially secure, living below Shiying's income and saving the money I earned and part of his for the baby we had decided to start very soon. There would be no more visits to an abortionist.

I didn't have to tire myself out taking on extra work. When I told him about Mr Chong's comment, Shiying said, "Of course

I'll come and dance in the afternoon or early evening. They're usually the less busy times, aren't they? Maybe it'll bring in more business then. What else could be more fun?" One afternoon at Moon Palace he said, "This reminds me of when we met at the Zengs' and first came here together."

And so we danced to the wonderful American popular tunes of the1920s and 1930s from composers George Gershwin, Jerome Kern, Irving Berlin, Cole Porter and so many others. We clung, dancing to tunes such as "Cheek to Cheek" and "Dancing in the Dark." Then there was that very special tune, the one playing when we first took the floor together at Moon Palace, Irving Berlin's "Always." As we danced, we whispered our undying love for each other, echoing the words of the tune.

We felt that the Rodgers and Hart tune and lyrics "Where or When," which was playing during our first dance together after our return to Shanghai, held a special significance. We both had the sense of déja vu about our relationship that was so well expressed in the words of the song.

Shiying showed off his spectacular foxtrot. It was something that had really impressed me when I first danced with him. Whenever we took the floor for that particular dance, others stood to one side to watch. We often danced the foxtrot to the tune of "The Japanese Sandman," which was very popular for dancing.

Although he appeared regularly in my dreams, at first I had thought of the Japanese Sandman as a rather benign figure. However I had begun to have misgivings. He seemed to be coming ever closer. Now I could see that the Japanese Sandman was definitely clad in a military uniform, a Japanese military uniform: the same one worn by those who were massacring our people. I shrugged off my unease at the dream (nightmare?) and continued to enjoy life with Shiying. I knew he would think my fears superstitious, not fitting for our new China.

Our favourite tune of all "How Deep is the Ocean? (How High is the Sky?)" came from Irving Berlin. The lyrics so clearly mirrored the depth of the love we felt for each other.

These interludes provided a last romantic fling before settling down to daily life (and disturbed nights) with a young child. I longed for life with another little person, who would be a combination of Shiying and myself, a life of contentment, of fulfillment, a deepening of my love for Mu Shiying.

But then came the assassination of Liu Na'ou. Despite my opposition, Shiying took over the position of editor-in-chief of *Wenhui bao*.

24 (Late May 1940-June 1940)

One morning a month later, after Shiying's second visit to Japan, the printer for *China March* came to the door.

"Sir, Oh my very dear Sir," he said, and burst into tears, "My printing shop and its contents have been completely destroyed by fire."

"But I thought you had a night watchman."

"He's dead . . . murdered the police say." Shiying and the printer consoled each other as best they could. Each had lost his life's work: in the case of the printer his livelihood built up in the printing business, and on the part of Shiying, what he felt was his highest achievement as a writer. Shiying explained that he suspected gangs were trying to destroy his work, and even him, for working on the Japanese collaborationist communications. "But we need to eat," and Shiying said he would go to the bank that morning, and withdraw as much as he could to help the printer.

Then the first death threat came, nailed during the night to the door of *Wenhui bao*. "Idiots! Don't these political gangsters understand that I'm a writer through and through, and not involved in politics? I have to live in Shanghai to be at the centre of things, and like everyone else I also have to make enough to be able to eat." Shiying shook his head. "I'll nail up a reply to explain."

At a restaurant serving Western food, Shiying had dinner again with Ji. Shiying insisted on paying the bill remarking, "I'm using the Wang régime's money to feed a member of the Chungking party," and lowering his voice said, "I ask you to make a point of discreetly spreading this comment around to the right (Nationalist) people who oppose the collaborationist Wang

Jingwei and his *Wenhui bao* daily newspaper. These death threats have to be coming from the KMT. Are you sure that there hasn't been some miscommunication? Have you told them I'm working for them as well?"

"Yes! I don't understand what is going on. . . . Maybe it's the CCP. . . . I'll check again with the party headquarters."

As nothing more happened, we believed that Ji had settled Shiying's position with the right KMT people, and lived the next weeks to the full, enjoying our life. One afternoon at Shiying's lunch time we went for a walk in the cool, winding walkways of the Yu Yuan garden. He stopped at the centuries old Exquisite Jade Rock, running his hand over the suitably scraggly, rough and holey surface. "Well, if this can last here in Shanghai for so long, so can we and our family to be." We felt so happy and secure.

Before we set out, there had been a light rain shower. As we walked along with our arms about each other, Shiying's head brushed against a branch of the garden's four—hundred-year-old gingko tree, spraying our faces with water. "That's a promise from the tree that our family will last," he said, and I smiled. Slowed down by the nine zigzags of the bridges across to it, we raced to the nearby Heart-of-Lake Pavilion for some snacks and tea, and collapsed, breathless, into chairs at a table. Shiying was panting and laughing so much that it was several moments before he could give an order to the waiting attendant.

Then came the second death threat, nailed to the door of *Wenhui bao* as before, but on the inside, so that Shiying would realize he was not safe, even on his own premises. When Shiying told me about the threat, he said, "This morning, I stood in the printing shop looking at the motes going down and down in shafts of sunlight, and a bluebottle blundering round and round, with my own mind going round and round with it, wondering again and again, *Who, who, who, could it be: that person leaving the threat inside my office door, because I'm the only one who has a key.* Today, I found myself looking with suspicion at employees I felt before I could have trusted with my life. Even the rather frail old man, who applies glue to postage stamps before sticking them on the envelopes, now looks sinister."

That night after I came home we worried, and took extra precautions to secure our door. We didn't open our window as usual for the late night seller of snacks, not even after he shone up his lamp, casting dark, elongated shadows on the opposite wall where the old clock ticked. I thought the shadows looked like ghosts, or worse, assassins. I was afraid.

By now, the serious effects of political interference on journalists had again been headlined in the newspapers, when the severed head of the Chinese assistant editor of *Shen bao* turned up on the street in front of their offices. I was so very worried.

In the morning, as usual, I went to see Shiying off to work. When I looked at the tree we could see over the wall, my blood froze. The leaves were withered and falling. A shrike perched on the wall. He was looking for his prey to impale upon a nearby thorny bush. The shrike's foreboding presence and strident call created an added presentiment of evil.

"Look at the tree. It's an omen." I clutched Shiying's arm, "Please, please start using the bulletproof Cadillac limousine they have provided."

"It's really not necessary. Ji assures me the KMT know I'm one of their intelligence people. I'm not in any danger on my way to work, and I'll be on my guard once I'm there."

"As for the tree, we've known for two months it was going to die. This is a new China we're building. There's no room for the superstitions of the past." Shiying gathered me up tightly and kissed me. "I'll be all right," and he waved as usual, going round the corner for his rickshaw.

Half an hour later, as the rickshaw puller ran through crowded Foochow Road, an assassin shot Shiying in the back.

When I returned home that night, he told me about the assassination attempt.

"It'll be in all the papers tomorrow. I was lucky to get away with only a flesh wound at the top of my left arm. With First

Aid, I was able to do a full day's work. . . . But someone really is trying to kill me," he murmured sighing, "I'm beginning to think I won't make it out of this alive."

"Oh please do accept the protection the Japanese have offered."

"From now on I'll take the bulletproof Cadillac to work, and use bodyguards for us both." Shiying sent a message to the Japanese headquarters to that effect, to start with taking him to work the following morning. Gone was the belief that writing, cultural understanding and literature could save us, and our world.

The subsequent lovemaking had a special significance. We knew how precious every moment was from now on. There was no more talk of idiots who didn't understand, or of backward superstitions. There were no more precautions against pregnancy either.

"I feel I can't escape either by leaving my job and ceasing to write the way I want (things have probably gone too far for that) or by running away to some remote part of China. . . . As I said in the preface to *Public Cemetery*, Time goes forward, and those of us who choose not to commit suicide must experience the consequences of what has gone before."

"What about another country? The offer of Canada will still be open,"

"The trouble with Canada, or fleeing upcountry within China for that matter, is that I'll be away from my own creative community, Shanghai, my muse. Look what happened in Hong Kong. I wasn't nearly as successful as I am here."

"But we could both work. You've always liked the idea of the independent, *modeng* woman."

"How do I know we won't be in the kind of poverty we experienced in Hong Kong. What kind of a life would that be? What kind of life—without writing and my muse?"

"Better than waiting to be murdered."

"I doubt I'll be safe anywhere. They'll follow me. By expressing my views in writing as I wish, and in collaborating, I've gone too far."

"Darling Shiying, surely we must try to save you."

"How naïve I've been, how gullible to believe that I could win over people by showing trust. . . . Now I don't believe the Japanese really want peace and prosperity with us. . . . They are after complete domination . . . if they could, complete extermination. . . . There are too many of us . . . but the *intent* is there." At that point I heard the cry of the man selling snacks.

"I'll let down the basket and get us some food. How about rice and pumpkin seeds?"

"Sounds tasty," so down went the basket with our order and payment to the alleyway.

Taking a bite from the food on his chopsticks, Shiying lamented that we had planned for him to have a long, fulfilled life as an author at the end of which he would write his autobiography. "I have been writing it every few months, but now I may not have the time to finish by myself. All I have is notes, especially on the past six years, the wonderful years after meeting you. My book that was to be my masterpiece has already been destroyed, and no doubt my other writing will be suppressed. Who will remember me, or know about me in the future? Who will now write the story of my life?"

Shiying's usually optimistic outlook now gave way to exhaustion, a heavy despair. He was like an animal that has long evaded the huntsman and is now too tired to run any more. (Not that Shiying was the kind to run away . . . more the sort to turn and fight.)

"If the worst happens, *I* will write down your story. I could work with one of your writer friends, Shi or perhaps Dai, to write a fuller and completed biography."

"When would you have the time?"

"I'll find it. This is so important. I know much of what has happened in the past six years. I'll use your notes and then find out more from your friends and colleagues." Shiying seemed to be soothed, and said that I must include myself, and my own life.

I tried to comfort Shiying: "We mustn't lose hope yet. Let's make the most of the time we have left, plan special treats that we'll remember, or that I'll remember if you go." Together, we listened to the ticking of our old clock on the wall. It looked so solid, so stable. I wondered: D*oes the old clock know how many seconds of life we each have left to live?* In the time left to us, I vowed we would live in happiness, and if I survived, and did have a baby, I would have these and other memories to comfort me, and to tell to the child.

As it was built above the kitchen that jutted out from the main building, the pavilion room we'd rented shared no wall or ceiling with any other rooms in the house. We entered it by a stairway. In winter we had only the heat rising from cooking in the kitchen, but our room was very private. That night it hit home that our room was also very isolated.

Later, I looked across at Shiying lying beside me asleep, naked. I could see the outlines of his body, so many angles, so very thin, and so young. I could sense the salty tang of his skin. I felt I must store up every detail in case . . . Shiying opened his eyes. He leaned over to the gramophone, winding it up and setting it to play softly, and soon we were listening to the love song from Saint-Saens' opera *Samson et Dalila* sung by the diminutive Ebe Stignani. The rich mezzo soprano voice filled our consciousness. "As flowers open to Dawn's kisses . . . my heart responds to your voice . . . the solemn promises . . . forever . . ."

"*Mon cœur s'ouvre à ta voix.*" I whispered.

"*Je t'aime.*"

"Tomorrow let's stay near each other all the time so that when they . . . if they . . . we'll be together."

"Shhh," his arms came round me.

"Do you think we'll meet again in another dimension?"

"I think we've met before. Here. We were the same way then. We're woven together in time. If I were to die right now, I've never been happier."

"Yes."

And so Shiying and I comforted each other, sheltered each other, closing out the nightmares with our arms about each other. And so we slept again. We would value the precious days to come and after each one, hope for one more. There was still a chance that soon I would conceive a child.

I woke up to the sound of a scuffle by our bed in the pavilion room. Black-clad figures loomed. Something flashed down. The door slammed.

And then, in slow motion and in terrible detail, I found out what had happened. My husband was not beside me. As I slid endlessly across the bed I could feel the warmth where he had been. What was that smell?

In the moonlight I looked down to see the body and severed head of Shiying on the floor. Supported on one elbow I leaned over, and with the sleeve of my nightgown wiped a bead of sweat from his brow.

Then I started to scream.

25 (June1940 continued-July 1940)

Mr Ho was the first to come. I was paralysed. All I could look at was the pool of blood on the floor, and the bizarre spectacle of my husband's body disconnected from his head. Speaking slowly and in a calm voice, Mr Ho said, "Please, Mrs Mu, move across the bed away from that . . ." I slid obediently back across our bed. Taking my hand, Mr Ho led me to his wife and his mother who were close behind.

"Come," said Mrs Ho putting her arm around me. Carefully, she guided me down the stairs and across to their room. Gently she laid me down. I was shaking so much I couldn't feel or hear or see anything. From a chest under their bed Mrs Ho lifted a padded blanket that she wrapped about me.

Her mother-in-law ran out of the room, saying, "I am going to look in my store of herbs and medicines . . . sprinkle dried flowers and splinters of wood from a peach tree . . . to keep away the devils . . ." Afterwards, she came with a tea. Having in effect lost most of my other senses, I found that my sense of taste was heightened and in the liquid I tasted ginseng and rose oil, and something sharper like licorice. My hands were shaking. I could not hold the cup.

"Here," said Mrs Ho lifting my head, and she spooned the tea into my mouth a little at a time. Her mother-in-law wiped my face with a cool towel that smelled lightly of lemon. Old Mrs Ho stroked my hair. After I'd had some tea, I leaned on one elbow and said, "I must get up to take care of Shiying's body," but the Ho women said, "No, no, you must stay in bed," and continued stroking my hair. They calmed me. Soon, I fell asleep. During this period I dreamed the sounds of chanting: comforting prayers for the dead . . .

May the heroic knowledge healers lead us,
May the bands of the Mothers, the *Dakinis*, be our rear guard . . .

But I didn't wake up. Old Mrs Ho must have given me some
potion dissolved in the tea to make me sleep through the rest of
the night.

The first thing I heard on waking was again the sound of the
prayers from my dreams, intoned by Mr Tang, the Vietnamese
Buddhist priest from the nearby temple, who was aided by his
assistant:

May we be saved from the fearful narrow passage of the *Bardo*,
May we be placed in the state of the perfect Buddhahood . . .

The next time I woke up, it was day and the priests had been
saying their prayers and chants all night. Opening my eyes, I
could see Old Mrs Ho going by my door carrying tea for them.
She came to stand beside my bed, "Good, you are awake. Soon
more holy people from the temple, and friends of Shiying, will
come to take over the task of praying."

It seemed well past daybreak, when usually I would waken to
the birds' dawn chorus. Now, I could hear the muffled daytime
sounds from Ningpo Road coming up the alleyway. I must have
been asleep for some hours.

For a Buddhist, the state of a person's mind at the moment
of death is very important because it has a significant influence
on the next life. I believe that Shiying's murder was so quick that
he had no time to fully wake up and change in consciousness
from the state of utter happiness he had declared before he fell
asleep. From then on, we had treated his body with gentleness
and respect so that his soul could continue calmly and be reborn
to a higher, rather than lower, realm of being. I thought of
another passage from the prayers for the dead, my favourite:

May it come that all the Sounds will be known as one's own
sounds;

May it come that all the Radiances will be known as one's own radiances.

I was positive that Shiying's soul was safe.

It also seemed to me that in dying in such a state of mind, Shiying had escaped his captors: the political people who had tried to dictate what he did with his talent. I so wished he had been able to exercise and develop that talent freely in less of a prison, in a different kind of society, open to, and not threatened by, wide ranging literary forms. *Why couldn't Shiying have earned his living by writing stories that he wanted to write, for literary publications that were free to publish what they liked? They may have offended some people's sense of what was proper, but they weren't political stories.* My thoughts went round and round, wanting a different type of society to live in. But if and when that took place, it would be all too late . . . too late . . . *too late* for Shiying and me.

By the time I was awake the Chinese policeman from the Shanghai Municipal Police Force had come and gone. He had understood the Hos' request not to have Shiying's body touched for at least three hours, to allow his spirit to feel secure and calm. The policeman said the cause of death was obvious. There was no need to bring the body to the police mortuary.

"Who is the murdered person?"

"It is Mu Shiying, the editor of *Wenhui bao*"

"Ah," he had said, shaking his head at the Hos, "Increasing numbers of journalists are dying in the same way. . . . Like the others, this seems to be a gang slaying. . . ." Again he shook his head, "As with the others, we will probably not be able to find the murderers."

Privately we, (the Hos and I), thought it was Du Yuesheng's Green Gang and the Nationalists, that by mistake had murdered Mu, their own undercover agent. However, we had to be very careful about what we said, what we revealed.

This view was confirmed when Shiying's friends came to help in saying prayers. Ji came to see me and he was in tears.

He explained that there actually *had* been a miscommunication. The KMT spying operation had two divisions: that of the Central Committee, whose operations among Shanghai's literary community he controlled, and another one controlled by the KMT military, not all of whom had been informed of Mu's work for the Central Committee. Therefore an order had gone out to have him assassinated. I felt too numb to take this in properly, or to feel angry with Ji and his colleagues. It all seemed so inevitable: if not the assassination now, then when? It had been a matter of time.

My visitors told me that in Japan the literary community were already bringing out a series of commemorative articles, by the poet Kusano, and writers Kataoka and Yokomitsu, praising Shiying as a bridge between the two countries and their cultures, and portraying his death as a sacrifice to co-prosperity, saying that the Japanese takeover of China was really the will of the people of China. Again, the numbness prevented an angry retort, but I thought: *They have to make political hay out of Shiying's murder, the very antithesis of what he himself would have wanted. And what co-prosperity are they thinking about? The Japanese take everything from us . . . even our lives, the only possession we have left.*

The next day, a Japanese policeman came to the door.

"May I come in?" he asked Mrs Ho, bowing and entering the kitchen where we were sitting as usual. "May I speak to Mrs Mu?" he said, and Mrs Ho indicated me. "I have come from the Japanese embassy. They ask that, for your own safety, it is best to finish the funeral arrangements as soon as possible."

"I understand. We will do as you say. Please thank your ambassador for me." Bowing again, he clicked his heels and left.

After several days of prayers, and again sprinkling fresh peach flowers and wood, the funeral came. It was a quiet affair with a minimum of professional mourners, all dressed in white. First, Mr Ho visited the Temple of the Daughter of Heaven on North Honan Road, which is where the Beggars' Guild had their headquarters. Here they worshipped their god Chu Yuan Chang, who according to legend, himself started as a beggar before becoming rich. As was the custom, Mr Ho hired some of the local beggars to help as mourners.

During the period of mourning, Mr Hayashi, an official of the Japanese police came to visit me. He bowed respectfully and informed me: "Due to the possible danger or chance of an attack on the funeral procession, the Japanese would like to arrange security." I again gave my thanks and acquiesced. So accompanied by the usual funerary goods (such as clothes, a car, a pen and pads of paper) that he would need in his spirit life, all expertly made in miniature from paper, and looking like the real objects, Mu Shiying's coffin travelled to the Whitehouse Mortuary in the Japanese police zone. There a funeral took place, with a very few friends from the old coterie in attendance, under guard of the Japanese military and city police.

After the funeral, Matsutani Tatsunosuke, an official of the Japanese cultural institution in Shanghai, wrote a commemorative piece lamenting my husband's untimely death, but typically saying it was not in vain as the assassination of such a Chinese writer, who was so in favour of friendship with Japan, could provide an opportunity to promote unity between the two nations.

Despite the known dangers of Shiying's job, despite the warnings and death threats, we had not been able to believe others didn't understand his view that he was a writer first and foremost who also needed to make a living. I had loved him so much, and wanted so much for him to continue living, that I was astonished when he ceased.

For such a vital person the state of being dead seemed so unnatural, but now that he was gone that state seemed so appropriate—for *me*. It would be so much easier to die, than to continue the heroic daily struggle of living without Shiying. I knew that in murdering him, they had in effect murdered me also, only no one else could see: I still showed signs of being alive. On and on, day after day, and night after wakeful night, my body lived . . . and lived . . .

26 (August 1940)

During this period after Shiying's murder (I could never regard or refer to it simply as a death) I had no appetite. The Ho women encouraged me: "Here is a bowl of rice and steamed vegetables to eat," said Old Mrs Ho.

Mrs Ho joined in, "Fried noodles with shrimp, or chicken broth with an egg broken into it. Which would you prefer?" Old Mrs Ho sat beside me at the rectangular wooden kitchen table where they ate, and fed me like a child with chopsticks or a spoon. Her scent of mint and cinnamon from the kitchen that she crushed in her palms and rubbed on her face and hands after preparing food flavoured with garlic, had a comforting effect on me: it reminded me of old Ah Ling, my mother's former amah, who in the kitchen at Tung-shan told me tales of my mother Lingyu.

I was fortunate to be with such kind, generous and also prosperous people. Late every day, the imperturbable Mr Ho came home from his work as the well-paid manager of house staff at a large estate in Hungjao. "His boss is an American, Mr Arnold Kiehn," said Mrs Ho, "I think Mr Kiehn has an import / export business," she said, bustling about her work cleaning the large alleyway house that the family owned, and occupied with their two young children.

One evening as we sat in the kitchen, Mr Ho said to me, "I love to come home. My wife keeps our house so clean and makes money from renting as well. We are lucky people." He smiled at Old Mrs Ho and took a bite from a cake she had handed him, "With Old Mrs Ho helping, our house is so comfortable and calm, so pleasant to return to," and he stretched and went upstairs to change into less formal clothes.

After Shiying's death, I was overwhelmed by a terrible lassitude. At first the Hos encouraged me to sleep, but then they thought of small tasks that I could do about the house and kitchen. It became my place to help in preparing steamed dumplings filled with minced pork, chopped cabbage, baby *bok choi*, scallions, bamboo shoots, whatever vegetables were available, with some ginger and garlic for flavour.

"Now you must learn to cook steamed dumpling," said Mrs Ho, leading me to the large kitchen table on which she had put out the array of vegetables. While we chopped them finely, Old Mrs Ho minced some pork. Then she spread out a small mound of flour on the kitchen table's wooden surface. Old Mrs Ho took a ball of dough from a bowl and smoothed it out with her floured hands and a rolling pin until it was paper-thin.

Mrs Ho and I each had a glass with which we cut a round of the dough and cupping it in one hand, filled it with a spoonful of pork and with a fork added vegetables. We folded the dough and pinched the edges together ready for steaming.

As I worked, the company of the other women comforted me. I said to Mrs Ho, "You are making many more of the dumplings than I am."

"One step at a time," she replied with a smile. Another time, Old Mrs Ho said, "Peipei, you don't have to be so careful about placing the filling exactly in the centre of the dough. It will come to the centre by itself when you fold the dough." I never stopped trying, and there was no feeling of being judged by my output. I was also able to help with the stir-fry, cutting meat and vegetables and assembling other ingredients such as soy sauce, black bean sauce and bowls of bean sprouts. Here again the Hos were ahead of me with their expert use of the sharp kitchen knives.

As the days passed I came to look forward to our culinary community. These small, easy and repetitive tasks helped me to start my life again, to feel consoled and more energetic. A large paper banner of the kitchen god, Tsao Wang, Prince of the Oven, presided over our efforts.

The coffin remained in place at the Whitehouse Mortuary, to await the geomancers' decision on where in his birthplace in the province of Chekiang, Shiying should be laid to rest. Had we been wealthy, the decision would have been prolonged and expensive. But I had kept my savings from my courtesan work a secret, and as we were not regarded as being rich, this decision came soon. I was able to make arrangements to accompany the coffin south to its burial near the Mu family home in Ningpo, the seaport in the province's northeast where Shiying had spent his idyllic early childhood.

Mrs Ho said, "What good fortune that the journey will be in summer. You know, it's bad luck to transport coffins in cold weather." *Good luck, bad luck*, I thought, *Shiying wouldn't have thought highly of this kind of talk*. But now, dreams of a new China were far in the past.

The Hos let me know that given the many waterways between Shanghai and Ningpo, the least expensive way for me to travel was by the boat train. They found out the cost. So in early July, I went to Soochow Creek to join the 3:00 pm Shanghai-Ningpo boat train. Old Mrs Ho came out to the alleyway carrying parcels of food she had made. "You must take this food," I demurred. "No, I insist," said Old Mrs Ho, and so I was carrying her parcels with me.

"Why is it called a boat train?"

"You'll see when we get there. . . ." And as soon as I saw it, I understood. The boat train consisted of a long line of rather rickety boats tethered together for the journey by very short towropes. As people waited to start their journey, on the bank opposite each boat there were relatives saying goodbye, cooks selling food from roadside kitchens and relatives helping by handing over baggage. The scene was like the departure of a train at the station.

The Hos had said, "This will be a major step in your recovery: You will be going somewhere alone, showing some self-reliance." I was also leaving the quiet, sheltered existence of our alleyway and seeing a much more hurly burly daily aspect of our society than I had experienced before.

"Come along," said Mrs Ho, dodging nimbly past all obstacles of baggage and people selling things and saying goodbye. Following in her wake, I fought my way to the boat through the usual crowd of food vendors. Of course I had brought my own but couldn't resist adding two of the delicious savoury pancakes we sometimes had for breakfast with fried bread. As well we saw tea boys and high priced baggage carriers, beggars and pickpockets, who made up a part of most Shanghai crowds.

The journey would take about three days. Shiying's coffin had gone ahead and was waiting in the hold of the coffin junk that would sail with the boat train. A luxury I allowed myself, was to pay for a narrow wooden bunk to sleep on. It was hardly even confortable: the luxury aspect was provided by a partition about six inches high that separated my head from that of the next bunk sleeper, and the fact that those of us with bunks were to sleep in a small, makeshift cabin on the deck.

I couldn't help longing for a *Fy Teng*, quick boat, used only in my home town of Canton. Originally it had oarsmen, now was motorized, and at first had been designed for rushing sick people to hospital. Nowadays on this boat, the coffins were lowered into the hold through removable planks. For the journey, bereaved relatives travelled in a comfortable midship cabin.

At about 4:00 pm the boat train slowly moved off from the moorings, wending its way into the perilous congestion of junks, sampans, launches and rafts that filled Soochow Creek. I knew timing was not going to be a consideration on the journey as we would arrive when we arrived, after debarking passengers and taking on others at small towns all along the way.

Deep inside, I couldn't believe this was actually happening to me . . . was still in a daze. Apart from eating the food I'd brought for the journey, I spent most of the time sleeping. The morning of my departure, we had made dumplings, but without the usual pork. "If we add pork, it could go bad and you will be sick." With me I also had several small loaves of fresh-baked sesame bread to which Old Mrs Ho had added chopped scallions for extra nourishment.

On the first night I tossed and turned. The throbbing of the engines jarred through my very bones. The fitful doze was interrupted by the snores and grunts of my fellow bunk-sleepers, by the frequent noisy stops and the tinkling of bells attached to children to reassure their parents that they were still on the boat.

On the next day there was a general alarm when a little boy did go into the water. However, the buoy attached to his back kept him afloat until the strap to which he was tethered could be used to pull him in. I noticed his smaller sister had no such buoy. *Typical . . . they value their boy child more than the girl. How backward of them . . . how unlike my dear father, who valued Ailing and me so highly.* And I wept anew for him.

"Why are you crying?" asked an old lady sitting sewing next to me on the deck.

"When I see the parents I am thinking of my father who has died."

"Oh, poor thing, I know all about it. Of course my parents both died a long time ago. My husband . . . but then you won't have *that* sadness for a while. You are too young." I didn't enlighten her. She returned to her sewing.

By day, I could see the crew of two deckhands and two ticket collectors keeping a careful eye on the crowd, doing their job of ensuring the safety of passengers on the transport. "Don't let your children fall into the river," they shouted to any parents aboard, and "Don't walk around so much, you'll have us overturned."

I don't know how I could have survived the journey without two important and entertaining others in the crew: the tea boys. They saved me. I handed over the fee, and went to my bunk to sit. The tea boys for this journey proved themselves to be experts at the Phoenix Nodding Three Times manoeuvre, carefully leaning over many other people to reach me, and tilting the brass kettle's long, gracefully curved spout three times over my teapot to provide a refill, never spilling a drop of boiling water.

They then kept watch until I had finished, and accurately threw a steaming hot towel over the heads of other passengers into my hands for me to clean up after tea and a snack. As on the crowded boat there was not much opportunity for washing, I appreciated these hot towels. When I was finished, the tea boys sent a long, retractable bamboo pole over for me to return the towel. In my waking moments I made frequent use of the tea service. It was worth the cost.

At last the boat train reached Ningpo where the Mu family in full force was waiting by the quayside: Shiying's sister Lijuan and her husband Dai Wangshu had come from Hong Kong with their adorable little daughter. I was glad to see them again: they brought back bittersweet memories of good times at their Woodbrook Villa on Pokfulam Road in the countryside overlooking the sea.

The younger brothers, Shiyan and Shijie, with many aunts, uncles and cousins, were at the wharf to meet my boat. Shijie had gone ahead from Shanghai to help arrange the funeral. Shiying's uncle bustled over to some coolies he had standing by, and supervised them in loading the coffin onto a barrow. "Carefully, carefully . . . you know where our family compound is. Take it there." The coffin would remain overnight at the Mus' before burial the next day.

The place where the Mu extended family now lived provided a more modest accommodation than the house in which Shiying was born. Due to the circumstances of our lives, I had never met most of Shiying's family. "This is our dear Peipei," said Old Mrs Mu, taking my hand to introduce me to each family member.

"Welcome," they said, patting me and smiling. "Eat, eat," they said in unison over the splendid welcoming meal. "Have some egg drop soup." "Here are our famous Ningpo buns," (filled with very much the same ingredients as our Shanghai ones) "Watch you don't burn your mouth on the broth inside, you won't be used to that." "Here, try a little lemon and sesame chicken, crispy duck, fried wonton, beef with black mushrooms and . . . Oh I forgot, some bamboo shoots," they said, putting some on my plate with the reverse side of their chopsticks, and so on . . . to the point that we were all very well fed and needed tea to revive us.

While dining, the relatives discussed memories of Shiying: his boyhood pranks.

"Do you remember how he used to capture insects and frogs and draw them on the kitchen wrapping paper, and even on his school books?"

"Ah yes, I taught him how to catch them with a noose made of grass, and flick them into his jar," said Ah Shi-Yuan.

"And taught me also," smiled Shijie and Shiyan in unison.

"And what about the time Shiying drew a cricket with an indelible ink pencil on Guanglin's bald head while the poor man was asleep in a chair. What a morning he had at the bank. Poor Guanglin couldn't very well keep his hat on all the time . . . the comments and the jokes . . . Shiying was the star turn at the office that morning," and they laughed. "Do you mean to say he actually didn't tell you about that?" they laughed again, "He's a charming one our Shiying!"

"Ahh, but he was a naughty boy, hiding from me at dinner time. But then you all did that sometimes," this from Amah, "And Shiying's language as a young boy! I remember when we were in a rickshaw and saw some foreign ladies. Do you know what he said when I told him they were going to take toys and books to orphans who had European fathers? He said, 'What a godawful idea!' I was glad the women could not hear what we were saying, and rapped his head with my knuckles, told him to speak properly. Ahh, but he had the charm of those born in the Year of the Rat. He always got away with things." And she narrowed her eyes, and wiped away a tear, in remembering. They remembered also his constant writing and telling of stories from a very early age.

Later, friends came in and added their reminiscences. One remembered visiting Shiying at their Cixi house. Modern upholstered furniture was in all the rooms. There was one very comfortable chair, upholstered in fine leather, which gave a soft whooshing sound when anyone sat there. "Shiying imagined the chair didn't want anyone to be on top of it, that we were a burden, so it sighed. He used to avoid that chair to give it some peace. He was so kind."

"Shiying said he knew what it felt like: like he himself did . . . having someone on top of you all the time telling you how to speak, how to behave."

"Ah but we taught him, didn't we, our charming Shiying."

That evening I learned more about his younger life than I had ever known before. It was a gift they gave me.

By reminding themselves of the past, Shiying's friends and family held back time. They took us to earlier years, made him come alive again, inhabiting a happier life story with a different sequel, looking forward to a longer life in another time when no one could have predicted what really *did* happen. I could almost imagine Shiying was in the next room and would walk through the door any minute, or that he was away for a short visit soon to return. I went to bed happy and had the first real sleep I'd had for ages.

But the next morning, when horse-drawn carts came for the coffin and also to transport the family, reality . . . surged . . . back. Of course, Shiying could not be buried in the busy and expanding commercial sea-port, or among the fields nearby, as that would go against the rule of burying a person where his body would not likely be disturbed: dug up again to make way for a new road or building or for agriculture. So the horses wended their way up the hill overlooking Ningpo to the burial ground where most members of the Mu family were interred.

We buried Shiying. We *buried* him. There was a heavy finality about that act that had the effect of adding to my leaden lassitude. At the cemetery's altar the others burned joss paper, carefully folded to distinguish it from real money. Of course, by strict Buddhist belief people in the afterlife have no need of money. But we agreed beforehand that like most people we knew we would accept a mixture of Taoist and the various Buddhist customs: whatever made the mourners most comfortable. To the funerary goods I added an item of my own: some pink paper roses just opening from the bud, like the pink rosebuds Shiying always wore with his suits.

In the oppressive heat that prevailed, even at the top of the hill, I felt the sweat trickle down my back. There was no breeze. The horses waiting to transport us home, hung their heads. We were silent. The birds and animals would have been active in the early morning. Now they were silent also, asleep perhaps in the trees and lush green undergrowth. A tuft of grass moved and out hopped a cricket. All I could hear was the sound of bees. But as we turned to leave, high above us, and knifing through the thick humidity, came the desolate shriek of a single white tailed fish eagle: "Eheu, Hélas . . . Alas!" it cried, in a timeless language each mourner understood.

27 (September 1940)

As I made ready to leave, Old Mrs Mu was helping me put my clothes into a bag and said, "You are most welcome to stay longer with us, Peipei. We have all this food, still. Stay to help us eat it." But despite the urgings of Shiying's family to visit with them a while, that afternoon I caught the boat train back to Shanghai. I promised to return each spring, in the "Pure Brightness' (Ching-Ming) of the early April festival, to clean Shiying's grave.

Like the Hos, the Mu family supplied me well with food for the journey. "Here, take these spring rolls and sesame bread and . . ." On the way back, my sleep was uneasy, with incoherent, menacing dreams, some of the Japanese Sandman, in his military persona, punctuated by the remembered scream of the eagle overhead as we left the burial ground. I woke up with a start. *Wasn't a sandman someone who put people to sleep? Couldn't this mean the long sleep of death, as brought so often to us by the Japanese military? And couldn't the song's words, about the Japanese Sandman giving you the next day to start life over again, really mean the new life we enter after first dying?* With a shudder, I wondered whether the dream was a warning about a real Japanese military person who would murder me, as he had no doubt murdered so many of my countrymen. I felt my muscles tighten, my skin grow cold with fear. But Shiying would not have approved of such thinking. As I lay on my bunk, I thought of the prayer for the dead and hoped that indeed my dearest Shiying was seeing all the Realms of the Buddhas.

When the boat train docked at Soochow Creek, I picked up my baggage, ready to go and look for a rickshaw. But there was Mrs Ho, hurrying along, "Here, over here," she said, waving an umbrella under the rain that was falling, "I have a rickshaw booked." And so she took me home, talking all the time about alleyway gossip, "Did you remember Mrs Ching's second son? Well, he got married last week, big wedding, wealthy bride." "And the Chos across the way have new furniture. I saw it going in. A lot has happened in the alleyway while you were away."

But the next morning she was all business saying, "It is time to get rid of Shiying's clothes that you've kept hanging and on shelves in your cupboard." And the two Ho women took everything away. Still suffering from that total lassitude, I complied, but for warmth and for comfort kept aside one of Shiying's padded jackets. I didn't ask the Hos what they'd done with the other garments.

Despite the scrubbing and sanding of the floor where Shiying's body had been, and the moving of the bed to a different part of the room, I could not forget his image from that awful night. While lying in bed I often thought I heard the scratch of Shiying's pen as I had heard it when he was alive, during the nights when he rose to write down part of a story that had just come to mind.

On a small table by my bed, in a black wooden frame, I placed my only good photograph of Shiying. Seen from my pillow, his intelligent eyes in the long, beautiful face seemed to look straight into mine. At this time I bought an electric torch and placed it on the bedside table.

As I lay awake at night, when the loneliness within me boiled up into a silent howl and I could bear it no longer, I pressed the switch of the torch . . . and there he was, the light of my life, the beat of my heart, Mu Shiying.

Everyone had thought the journey to Shiying's birthplace, and his final burial, would improve my state of mind. However, since returning from Ningpo my terrible tiredness had increased. I said to Old Mrs Ho, "The tear in my heart is so big, I don't think it will ever mend."

"It will, it will. I felt the same way when my husband died."
But he died at an older age. . . . He wasn't assassinated.

Occasionally, Mr Ho brought home the *Shen bao* newspaper, and it was from that, in early autumn, that I learned that after four attacks and bombings, the collaborationist newspaper *Ping bao* had fortified its offices with barbed wire and iron plating. All the editorial staff now had to live inside their workplace, further guarded by thirty-six armed No. 76 agents. I wondered whether Shiying could have tolerated such living conditions.

In the free time I had from helping the Hos with small household duties, I tended to sit in a chair and gaze into the distance, thinking of my lost husband. One morning, Mrs Ho said, "You know, you really should be more active, take walks around the compound and on the streets outside," and I tried taking her advice. I stepped out, and there at the end of the lane sat our acquaintance, the dignified elderly scribe, who read letters for people and wrote out their dictated replies. Mr Chu was dressed in the long black robe with frog closings and domed silk hat worn by men of an advanced age. He reminded me of our old tutor, Mr Wei. When he saw me, Mr Chu settled his hat on his head and tidied the pens, inks and papers of his profession lying on his desk. Then Mr Chu stood up and bowed respectfully saying, "So sorry, so very sorry."

All the people I met in our alleyway village obviously knew what had happened. How could they avoid knowing? Among the literate classes in Shanghai there had been an outpouring of grief and fury at the loss of Mu Shiying, their handsome and charming young literary star. Mayor Fu of the City Government of Greater Shanghai berated the Shanghai Municipal Police for not giving him effective protection, as they must have known Mu's life was being threatened. In Shanghai, the Nanking Régime of Wang Jingwei offered a $10,000 reward for apprehension of Mu's assassin.

Every obituary extolled my husband's gentleness, great personal charm, and beauty.

As I passed, the alleyway residents greeted me with sympathy. I saw the cook selling *dim sum* from his travelling kitchen, the barber shaving his client who was covered in a pristine white sheet, the local women washing clothes and chatting at a communal tap, rickshaw coolies cashing their rice coupons given by their mutual aid association to those unable to work due to illness, people standing round a game of chance, indulging in their favourite alleyway pastime of hanging around with the neighbours, a man on a bicycle selling toilet paper by the piece, and even children and their teachers on their way to the alleyway school. When I appeared, they each stopped what they were doing, and bowed or gestured respectfully.

With the help of Mrs Ho, I gradually began to move around and break out of the lethargy that had held me captive since Shiying's burial. I even began work on Shiying's biography. After several more days of helping with household tasks and filling my spare time wandering round the alleyway, I decided to step outside into Ningpo Road.

When I opened one of the two vertical sections of the divided entrance door to our compound, a wave of noise almost overwhelmed me. Ningpo is the quintessential Shanghai thoroughfare where everyone talks, no—*shout*—all the time. It's like a successful party that has long ago passed its initial stage of people arriving and being introduced.

I looked back at the alleyway name above the *shikumen:* Xingren Li (Alleyway of Prosperity and Benevolence) and thought it perfectly described the Hos, and my neighbourhood. I almost went back inside. Then I remembered Old Mrs Ho's admonitions: "You must return to normal life now. I know: I have been widowed myself." So I closed the door and walked forward. In Ningpo Road I felt more at home, more among my own people, than I did in its parallel street Nanking Road, the main, Westernised, thoroughfare of the International Settlement.

Along the side of Ningpo Road I revisited the familiar sights of peddlers of herbs, and of books supported by string across a bamboo frame, and the beggars exposing their open sores and missing limbs. Soon, the din of people shouting, and banging drums or tinkling two pieces of brass together to attract attention to their wares, seemed too much. Then I turned to the wonderful distraction of the sights and colours.

For several weeks, I had not seen the earthenware shop, and yes, it still had its kongs of many sizes and multiple colours, each bowl splashed with bright reds and yellows and greens. I had changed, but Ningpo Road had not. Baskets of firecrackers in the yellow and red of good fortune still sat out in stalls.

They reminded me of the New Year celebrations on our street when I was a young girl. Each house made a lantern. Ailing and I created ours and added it to the tail of the New Year dragon, supporting the part bearing our lantern, until the tail became longer and longer and everyone on the street was in a procession. The evening ended in everyone snaking round after the dragon in Tung-shan Park nearby, and then watching a display of firecrackers. Ailing and I loved the colours filling the sky. Each year Ah Ling said, "The noise of the crackers is driving off evil spirits: good luck for our neighbourhood," and she smiled.

The sounds, sights and vivid colours of our street energized me. I felt more alive and looked around hungrily: green umbrellas lined a shop and spilled out into the sidewalk. At a grocer's, baskets of flaming orange persimmons, and bright yellow and green and purple vegetables called out to be bought. If I looked up, on the edge of the curved roofs, I could see enchanting carvings of squirrels, foxes, dragons, and dolphins standing on their tails. *How had I missed these details before? Why was I noticing them so vividly now?* I decided that at last I was coming to life again, noticing even more of what was around me than I had before.

As I passed, the fortuneteller rattled his jar of numbered strips of bamboo. "Pick a number from my jar, pick a number, and see the fortune that lies behind it." I turned my head away. Right now I didn't want to contemplate the future. One day at a time was all I could bear.

But then I faced a new reality, or rather unreality, of my widowed state. Walking a few yards ahead of me, I was sure I saw Shiying. He was carrying a little two-year-old boy, the same age our child would have been if I'd had him in Hong Kong. I ran to catch up, and as I drew nearer, the child faded into thin air. The man turned his head and I saw he wasn't Shiying at all.

The experience had me running back to the Hos. "Yes, several times the same thing happened to me. I have been a widow myself; I know," said Old Mrs Ho sagely nodding her head. "It will change. . . . It will change. . . . You'll see."

But when will it change? I'm so used to going everywhere with Shiying: every road I walk along I've walked along with him. I'm so used to being his wife, so accustomed to looking forward to having our child. Now I'm only myself. When will it change? For well I knew that in the short time we had together before Shiying's death, I had not conceived a child. I had had almost four bitter months to think about it. These thoughts brought back to me the end of a poem by Yu Hsuan-chi titled "Gazing Out in Grief": the part about the longing for the other person, a longing that never ends, continually flowing along like a river . . . forever and ever.

28 (October 1940-January 1941)

At the end of the first week after Shiying's assassination, Mrs Ho had come to collect the rent as usual. She knocked on my door and moved to sit beside me. Leaning forward to take my hand in both hers she had said. "Now that you are occupying the room by yourself, I am reducing the rent." But still, after all this time of not working my money was running low, and I was living on our savings for the child. Mu Shiying's decision, that I should keep as a retirement fund the money I'd accumulated before, now seemed sound indeed. I would have to return to work. (Why do I refer to this as "all this time"? It was only about four months since the assassination of Shiying in June, and yet it was the longest four months in my whole life.)

The cold weather of October was setting in: Han-lu (Cold Dew) of early in the month soon to be followed by Shuang-chiang (Frost Descent). So one afternoon I put on my winter coat and gloves and went to Moon Palace to ask for my job back. To save money I walked almost two miles south along Tibet Road, passing the main intersection with Bubbling Well Road (a continuation of Nanking Road) and various lesser roads, one of which was named after my birthplace, Canton, until I crossed the next main intersection, Avenue Edward VII, and passed into the French Concession where Moon Palace was.

When I arrived, the manager Mr Chong said he was busy and I should return the next morning. The next morning I walked there again. As I entered his office Mr Chong gave me a hard stare, "Well, you haven't lost your looks over this." The ruthless eyes scanned me over again, "You can come back but you're a bit pale. Put on more make-up. No sad face now. . . . We give the customers a good time here."

I asked if I could have more work than before. "No more work. Everyone's having it hard. There's plenty of competition. The customers like variety. You can start next week Friday 3:00 pm: the *thé dansant* through the whole evening like before—and buy some new dresses. What you have on looks shabby." He turned back to his desk. The interview was over.

I returned to my Alleyway of Prosperity and Benevolence and met Old Mrs Ho who'd been shopping for vegetables on Ningpo Road. "What's wrong?" she said.

"I can get only part-time work at Moon Palace. I saw Shiying carrying the child ahead of me again, but it wasn't him . . . and the child faded away. Mr Chong at Moon Palace says I must buy new dresses. . . ." I burst into tears.

"We'll see what we can do." Old Mrs Ho looked at me in a neutral but assessing sort of way. I could guess she thought it was time I stopped the tears, and also stopped seeing things. After all, four months had passed and I hadn't even had to do much.

"Work will be good for you," she said. "Leave your coat upstairs and we'll talk in the kitchen." In about fifteen minutes, the Ho women and I had drunk some tea and were sitting round the big table chopping vegetables and discussing my problems.

"First you need nice dresses," said Mrs Ho.

"I can make them from some lengths of material I bought when Shiying was alive." The Hos nodded approval: I was making plans by myself.

"Good, we'll help."

"You see Shiying, and the child you didn't have in Hong Kong," said Old Mrs Ho, "You work hard, sleep well, and that will go away."

Mrs Ho said she had a possible way of finding more work. On the second floor they had a tenant. He was away all evening until the early hours and then slept by day. The tenant was Russian and owned the Gardenia nightclub on Great Western Road, one of the Outside Roads in the Huxi area. Then I remembered Shiying mentioning such a person whom he'd known before.

Given his schedule, the other tenant never joined our summer evening gatherings in the courtyard, but I remembered seeing, from time to time, an elegant, aristocratic figure clad in impeccable evening clothes, strolling to the *shikumen* alleyway's gateway to call a rickshaw on Ningpo Road. I found that his friends, and that included the Hos, called him Sasha. But Mrs Ho said I should call him Mr V to start off with, only V, as his Russian name was hard to pronounce.

Two days later Mrs Ho said Mr V would see me at 6:30 pm before going to his club. In the gathering dusk of early evening I was standing at the kitchen door to the alleyway eating a savoury dumpling and waiting for 6:30 pm to come. As I looked out I saw, a little above ground level and reflecting the dim light from one of the few alleyway lamps, two eyes. They belonged to a little yellow ferret trotting about his evening activities. As we believe it brings bad luck to offend them, the alleyway ferrets are quite tame.

I gently placed the rest of my dumpling on the paving stones in the middle of the narrow alley and stood back. The ferret cautiously ate the food, glancing up at me before scurrying off. Did he blink his thanks, or was I imagining it? "Bring me luck, little ferret," I whispered, then crossed the narrow back yard to the main house and climbed a flight of stairs to see our mysterious Russian club owner.

On my knock, Mr V opened the door and with a graceful gesture said, "Come in and welcome. Do sit at this table." On it was a shining silver samovar, heated by a lamp underneath, which provided us with tea. Mr V was older than I was, about fifty to my twenty-four, and was already dressed in his evening white tie and tails. A top hat lay on a chair.

He spoke in Shanghainese dialect, "I've asked my manager, and he says we have some work for you. You'll find the clientele rather different from Moon Palace's: more Russians," he said, "But not too many more," and he smiled kindly. "It would be a useful idea to pick up some Russian phrases, but then there will be no difficulty. I'll show you. You can come to and from the

Club with me. It's rather a long way and will be safer for you at night." I let him know what nights I could work at Gardenia, and it was arranged.

"I know what has happened," Sasha said, gesturing with his beautiful hands. "I knew your husband when he was younger. He was a most personable and intelligent young man, a truly wonderful writer. We used to talk at the Renaissance café. I know what it's like losing someone we love. It'll work out all right, you'll see," and with a charming smile, he ushered me out of his apartment.

The next evening, Mr V called at my door, and ushered me into a rickshaw at the end of our alleyway. On the way to Gardenia we talked non-stop. "This is the Russian for Hello," he said first. Mr V complimented me on my "ear" for the language, my perfect accent for speaking Russian.

For a few months, life settled down to my working hard most of the time, alternating between Moon Palace and Gardenia. Mr V's singing of nostalgic Russian songs enchanted me. He stood up for the audience, and before Mr V even began, everyone clapped. His expressive hands aided the haunting voice. At the beginning of each song Mr V put them up in a praying gesture, and then the magical performance began. The words were partly sung and, in some songs, partly spoken in his crisp, clear diction.

I learned much from comments overheard from the audience: "You know, he was famous in Russia not only for singing but also for his acting." "Yes, and for writing poetry and plays as well." "Many of the songs he sings Mr V wrote himself." "People called them ariettas, or novellas-in-song."

Another voice from the audience informed me: "Stalin possesses all Mr V's recordings, which he listens to often. Those are the ones made before Mr V left Russia in 1920." (I knew that fact from Mrs Ho.) "It was a mass exit of those who disagreed with the Communist Revolution. Ah, there is his mistress. He calls her Boobee. . . . Isn't she beautiful? What lovely blond hair. . . . Do you think it's dyed? But what a figure . . . and she's so adorable. He's a lucky man!" Mr V in his evening clothes and his Boobee made a striking couple.

"Those were the days, my friends/We thought they'd never end/We'd sing and dance forever and a day . . ." sang Sasha, and tears of nostalgia came to the listeners, whether or not they were Russian. The patrons sat enthralled while he sang a song well-known even to English speaking patrons: "Dark Eyes" (Ochi chornya) and "Matrosi" ("Sailors") about a mythical island sailors know, where there are blue tulips and other wonders. Mr V also sang the popular American songs such as the ones Shiying and I had so loved: "Where or When" and "How Deep Is The Ocean? (How High Is The Sky?)."

He occasionally appeared in a Pierrot costume and makeup, and the Russian émigrés clapped loudly. "Ah I remember him when he was young, he always wore the Pierrot disguise." "Yes, it was his trademark then," they said, tears in their voices.

Seeing Mr V dressed like that reminded me of the good times Shiying and I had with his sister and her husband at Woodbrook Villa, discussing literary trends and, in one conversation, the changing meaning of the Pierrot figure. I remembered Shiying's description of it as one in whom the disguise is a mask for sorrow, whose impulse is frustrated, with an attitude of sometimes anguished passivity. What I didn't know then, was that I was to recognize that quality, of anguished passivity, in Mr V as Pierrot, just before my life was coming to an end.

During this time, I fantasized that Shiying really was alive somewhere, that the assassination had been faked so that he could disappear. Shiying had always believed that he would magically live through its political troubles to see a better China, and be free to write and develop fully as a writer. When that happened, Shiying intended to come out of his hiding place. Sometime, somewhere, I would see Shiying walking in front of me in the street. I would catch up to him, and it really would be Shiying. We would wind our arms around each other and never let go. We would go to cafés and talk and talk and laugh again, make love again, have our child together. We would be happy again, and at the end of a long and distinguished literary career, Shiying would write his autobiography.

It was almost a year before I could admit my mistake, and Mr V was the catalyst:

On one of our journeys to Gardenia, I thought I saw again Shiying and the child, who faded away as we came near. Sasha (he had asked me to call him by that name) must have noticed my reaction and been told by the Hos about my mirages. He turned round to face me in the wide rickshaw seat. Regarding me kindly, Sasha said with great firmness, "This must stop. You are young and will have a baby sometime."

What Sasha said was well timed. It had an instant effect, for woven in air the phantom child came, that child with no body and no name, rested his head on my shoulder in farewell, and slipped away forever to his shadowy other world . . .

Although I knew he implied it in what he said, I appreciated that Sasha didn't actually mention a husband. I couldn't bear to think of loving anyone other than Shiying: to me, he was irreplaceable. As well as all thought of a child, past or future, I felt I had to give up all thought of a husband.

I realized I must go on my way by myself: as Yu Hsuan-chi said in her poem *Sorrow and Worry*, I must forsake the idea of finding another soul mate. I must play my pipa alone, and abandon such desires. Both Hsuan-chi and Shiying had been executed in their twenties. Thinking of them, and looking at what had happened to me and also to Shiying, I knew all too well the fleeting nature of life and of worldly goods.

29 (February 1941-April 1941)

I decided to work hard for a few more years. (At twenty four I was now too old to return to life as a courtesan.) I would save all I could, and with my previous wealth intact, retire to live simply back in the countryside near Canton: I thought I would buy land in the middle reaches of the Pearl River and build a small dwelling of bamboo.

As so often before, the words of Yu Hsuan-chi guided me. In a poem, she had said that she was finished with chasing after money and found her satisfaction in swallows and sparrows.

I imagined myself sitting on a sun-warmed rock overlooking the flowing water, and playing "The Love of the River" on my pipa to an accompaniment from flights of seagulls. Time and Patience had achieved my marriage to Shiying, but they would never make me accept his death. Therefore, I fantasized that I would build another house. It would have walls of mist, the inner surfaces coloured from a rainbow with silver from the moon, and large windows of sunlight: an abode of mist and light where my lost husband could enter. *Shiying, my house is empty without you.*

Early the next year, 1941, Sasha asked me to come and meet with him in his apartment. He welcomed me with his usual polite flourish and poured tea from the samovar. Mr V offered small iced cakes as well and we ate and talked generally. When we had finished, he turned to face me. Mr V looked grave:

"I have some bad news. I am having to close down Gardenia."

"But it seems so successful."

"Yes, it is a gold mine, but is not successful enough. Despite living frugally at the Hos', I have not been able to keep paying for my mistress's cocaine habit on Gardenia's income. I am deeply in debt."

With Gardenia, Sasha lost his enchanting blond Russian mistress. What he never did lose was his calm, confident geniality. He quickly found us both jobs at the Russian club Balalaika on Bubbling Well Road, which featured a balalaika band all in full evening dress. It was also nearer to Moon Palace than Gardenia. There, they billed Mr V as being well known to all the music lovers for his originality. Balalaika was open all day with a café, restaurant, *thé dansant* and nightclub, providing much work for both Sasha and me from the afternoon on into the night

Given the more lax regulations about closing times in the French Concession, Moon Palace stayed open longer than the Balalaika. On the nights I was there, my neighbour started coming to Moon Palace to escort me safely home. On those evenings, Sasha also sang, but mostly the modern American popular songs Moon Palace patrons liked to listen and dance to. To encourage him to continue this arrangement, Mr Chong actually paid a stipend for the singing.

Mr V (Despite our friendship I still often thought of him respectfully as Mr V) was now working all day every day, late into the night. He never stopped working. We soon found the reason for this at the New Year show along Ningpo Road that at this time of year became even more noisy and colourful than usual. Now, brightly dressed actors, clowns, singers and ventriloquists, jugglers and acrobats, wrestlers even, all shouting for attention and asking for money, joined the throng. Two men in long red robes with fur collars led along a bear that growled and grumbled at having to go along muzzled, on his hind legs and in such a racket. At a corner of Ningpo Road, a Big Umbrella dentist extracted teeth that he added to the other teeth on a long string round his huge umbrella that, with a seat for the patient, acted as his dental office.

In the middle of this chaos and din appeared a beautiful nineteen-year-old Russian girl. Mr V gallantly shepherded her with her mother through the crowd, introducing them both to the neighbours as he went. Lidia was a shy, very sweet and proper young woman who lived with her mother in a nearby alley. From the way they acted, we all immediately understood Mr V and Lidia were to be married.

Lidia and I became instant friends. On my afternoon off we went out to enjoy ourselves, sometimes subsidized by Mr V, or Alexander, as Lidia always called him: another more formal, respectful name for Sasha. Despite damage from the 1937 bombing, the Cathay Hotel provided a peaceful and understatedly luxurious respite from the stress of Shanghai's daily life. Much of its Lalique lighting had been saved or replaced and we sometimes visited the hotel for tea, my favourite meal there, with thin cucumber or watercress sandwiches and mouthwatering little cakes. The Big Four department stores had also been repaired and provided us with afternoons spent not so much in shopping as in attending exhibitions of painting or calligraphy, and having the occasional dish of pink ice cream.

But not all our outings involved spending money. We often went for a walk to Yu Yuan, the classic Chinese garden first set up in the sixteenth century, with its winding walks, cool grottoes and famous Jade Rock, full of holes and wrinkles, and the aged gingko tree. It evoked memories of Shiying and our happy excursions there. While we walked, I answered Lidia's questions about makeup and clothes and we discussed trying different hairstyles.

One spring day, before the next day's outing, Lidia, without giving a reason, (it was to be a surprise), suggested we go together very early to the public park along the Bund opposite the British Embassy. So, after only a brief sleep on my part, we took a rickshaw east to the Whangpoo River.

When we walked into the park, the singing of birds was almost deafening. Hung on all the branches of the trees were caged birds whose owners (men) had come before work to chat and boast about their charges' fine singing and appearance. It was also an opportunity for the birds to have some (relatively) fresh air coming off the Whangpoo, and the company of others of their kind. The men thought quite rightly that this daily outing to leafy surroundings helped keep up the happiness and singing, also appearance, of the birds. In my years in Shanghai I had seen people taking their birds for an evening outing in the fresher air, and even to restaurants, but until then was not aware of this early morning happening.

The Pure Brightness of April 1941 arrived, and with it came the necessity for cleaning ancestral graves. As Shiying was buried at Ningpo, I felt obliged to go there rather than to Canton where my own family members were buried. (I followed the traditional view that the woman must become part of her husband's family. And besides, weren't my family ashamed of me?) So, seen off for a change by Lidia, I again joined the boat train to Ningpo.

At that time of year, almost all of China seems to be on the move, returning to the family village to see relatives and help clean the graves. This time there was no question of reserving a bunk. I slept head-to-toe with others on the deck. Especially at night, there was the same jarring feel of the engines as during my previous journey, but the view was so much better than before. As I lay with everyone else I could see the brilliant stars in the black sky that seemed to surround us from above and along the sides of the river. As we slowly moved along, I felt as if I were up among the stars. However, there was no feeling that Shiying was there with me.

This time, in the feasting and reminiscing the night before we cleaned the gravesites, I learned about Shiying's broader family and how they had come from generations of prosperous business people: "Wasn't grandfather such a generous one with all the money he made, never sparing expense in entertaining us and helping us to buy a house of our own," said one Auntie, smiling and nodding her head, "Yes, we all have much to thank him for."

"And wasn't your father the life of a party, playing tricks on people and telling jokes, and so free with his money to relatives," said an Uncle, smiling at Shiying's brothers and sister, "Shiying was just like him."

"He treated that drawing on his head as a bit of a joke, and bought Shiying some books to write in, in case, as Guanglin said, Shiying should think next of *writing* on his head." We all laughed.

"Think of all the art supplies and lessons he also bought—but then the boy turned to writing."

I was able to let them know that Shiying had not wasted the art lessons, but had kept up that aspect as well, and that I had his beautiful drawings of birds and a portrait of myself to prove it.

This gave me another perspective on Shiying's father that was different from the one Shiying himself had presented, drawing on the experience during the teenage years before his father's death.

Seen off back to Shanghai by the Mu family, I promised to return at the same time the following year. But that was not to be.

30 (May 1941-End 1941)

When I returned from Ningpo, Lidia came to meet me. On the way home in a rickshaw, she couldn't wait to tell me the news:

"Alexander and I are to be married."

"When? Where?"

"On June 23rd (my own wedding anniversary) at the Russian Orthodox Church in the French Concession. Will you be my bridesmaid?"

"Of course . . . I'm honoured."

Lidia's mother placed the marriage announcement in both of Shanghai's Russian language newspapers, Shanghai Zaria (Dawn) and Slovo (The Word). From these I learned that Mr V's last name was Vertinsky and Lidia's was Vladimirovna, another V. Lidia explained the service: how the priest would conduct it and also the significance of each part.

"First, we are betrothed with the exchanging of rings, which signifies that as a couple we will compensate for each other's strengths and weaknesses. Then we are immediately married. In our left hands we'll now carry a lit candle and join right hands for the rest of the ceremony."

Lidia explained I would have to hold a crown over her head until the climax of the wedding when the priest crowns the couple as sovereigns over their own marital domain. Lidia advised me to hold the crown in one hand only and then keep switching hands as each arm became tired.

"The ceremony ends with a walk, led by the priest, round a table on which are the Gospel and Cross, signifying the sacrifices a couple must make for each other in the marriage. The priest ends by blessing the man and wife."

The first anniversary of Shiying's murder came, but I was helped over it by the marriage preparations. With the wedding party, for the first time I entered the onion-domed Russian Orthodox Church. The symbols of the Christian religion were quite new to me. They were more colourful than I had expected. Around the Church walls were large, colourful figures of the Saints, and from the domes hung huge crystal chandeliers.

I thought the Orthodox mystery of Holy Matrimony was beautiful, and by the time we had practiced with the Russian best man, we were word and action perfect. On the day, my hands holding Lidia's crown shook only a little from the strain. It was a small wedding and Lidia in white and Mr V in evening dress looked perfect, and so happy.

Before returning to live at the Hos', they honeymooned, as had Shiying and I, in the beautiful lake district of Hangchow with its wonderful gardens, pagodas and templesmostly rebuilt after the Japanese bombing. While they were away, I realized how important Sasha and Lidia had become as friends and companions in my life, that I was not alone. I prayed that the coincidence of their wedding day and where they spent their honeymoon being the same as mine, was not a bad omen, but then realized that such superstitious thinking did not fit in with Shiying's ideas about a new China.

After the wedding, life continued as before. While Mr V worked hard and long, Lidia spent much of her time in the nearby alleyway with her mother. By November of 1941, Lidia and Alexander announced they were expecting their first child. Everyone started to make clothes for the baby. I chose to make a long padded silk garment with frog closings in the Chinese manner. Lidia said she didn't mind Chinese-looking clothes, although of course the child was Russian, and would be issued papers to that effect by the authorities, as another stateless person of Russian origin.

During this month there was an escalation of incidents with Japanese soldiers, reminiscent of the many that occurred before and after the 1937 attack on and takeover of Chinese

Shanghai. The soldiers were increasing their looting of what few belongings the Chinese had left. We found out because some who lost their possessions worked for people in the Settlement. Rape of Chinese women became again a commonplace event. These took place in the Chinese areas under Japanese control and the Shanghai Municipal Police could do nothing. The atmosphere in the International Settlement was tense. It seemed the Japanese were flexing their muscles.

Terror reigned in Shanghai. People scuttled around, going out only on necessary business. They were terrifed of being rounded up for reprisal executions, terrified of being beheaded "for fun" by a Japanese soldier practising his sword skills, terrifed (in the case of women) of being raped and then strangled or bayoneted, terrified (especially in the case of writers) of being tortured for "thought reform" at No. 76 or Bridge House by the psychopathic *Kempeitai*, famous for their water torture. . . . Terrified.

Then it happened: on December 8th we woke up to the muffled sound of gunfire from the Whangpoo. We soon found that the Japanese had captured the British and American gunboats, HMS Peterel and USS Wake, and taken over the whole Settlement. Over all the bank buildings, that the Japanese immediately occupied, Japanese red and white flags (red for the sun and white for honesty and purity) were flying, making a snapping noise in the stiff breeze off the Whangpoo.

One of the first actions of the Japanese was to tear down the statue of my father's hero, Sir Robert Hart. I was so glad he hadn't lived to see the city and the man he so admired, demeaned.

The roads were unusually quiet and empty as the clip-clop sound of Japanese mounted soldiers on parade along the streets echoed round the Settlement, the noise of hooves reaching its height in the chasms between the Art Deco high-rises. Looking south from our alleyway on Ningpo Road, by 10:00 am we could see a steady light grey snow falling over the business and diplomatic area round the Bund. At first we thought it was a continuation of the slight snow (Hsiao-hsueh) of late November, and would be moving west across the rest of Shanghai, but then news came that it wasn't actually snow, but the ash from documents being burned by the embassies and large businesses.

Word went round Shanghai, that in the Hongkong and Shanghai bank on the Bund, Japanese soldiers had lined up along the bank's counter the British staff, (including William Rigg, a member of Foreign Staff on his second tour of the Far East), ready for a firing squad. After over an hour, an officer entered and intervened, ordering the foreigners to return to work.

The Japanese quickly established an initial curfew of 9:00 pm, which affected both the Balalaika and Moon Palace. Later, for nightclubs, the curfew was extended. People stayed in as much as possible, even during the day. The rapes continued, largely among our own women. In a few months foreigners would have been finger-printed, issued with identification papers, and be wearing armbands to show which country they came from.

The late night journeys from work with Mr V took on an extra strain. He advised me to muffle my face, and especially if there were any Japanese around, to speak only in Russian. Mr V said that in my voice, given my excellent accent, I could pass for a native Russian woman.

Once a semblance of order was in place, in the period in early December called Great Snow (Ta-hsueh), (only this day there was no snow at all), Lidia and I were walking along Nanking Road when out of the corner of my eye I saw a displacement of people on the sidewalk across the road. It moved forward like a wave. Beggars and hawkers up against the buildings melted away round corners or into doorways. Those on the side nearest the road, abandoning their belongings, slid seamlessly into the traffic. As the wave came nearer, I could see the cause: a handsome, impeccably dressed Japanese officer with an entourage of six bodyguards.

"Who is *that*?" I asked Lidia.

"Don't look at them. Keep your eyes down. Never meet their eyes," she repeated. I did as Lidia asked.

"It's Tanaka, Director of the *Kempeitai*, the Japanese secret police for the whole city. He has said he can do anything at all to the Chinese, now that the war is official. The Japanese think the Chinese are an inferior race to their own," whispered Lidia. She told me that he called us creatures, not people,

Once we were settled in the Cathay Hotel tearoom, Lidia told me more: that Tanaka was one of those who beheaded people at random in the street, "Only, to avoid blood splatters on his clothes, he directs his bodyguards to do it. Tanaka has his uniforms specially tailored." She also added a horrible rumour: "People believe Tanaka takes Chinese women home with him and later murders them. The bodies of these women have been turning up in ditches around the Huxi. Each one has been murdered in a different way. The police can't do a thing." Lidia shuddered, "He sometimes uses the *zhuizi*." (It was a needle with a handle attached that the Japanese used for torture and slow killing.) "If he comes to Balalaika or Moon Palace leave at once."

I gave a shiver of dread that Lidia noticed. I told her about my recurring dream and how it had changed into a nightmare, that I now believed it was a premonition of my being murdered by a Japanese military person—and in my last dream, he had looked exactly like the man Lidia identified as Tanaka!

I thought back to my original exposure to the tune about the Japanese Sandman. At their *thés dansants* my older sister Ailing and her friends enjoyed circling a dance floor to the latest Western romantic tunes such as "Embraceable You", "Smoke Gets in Your Eyes", and "Cheek to Cheek" from the Fred Astaire and Ginger Rogers film *Top Hat*. But I quickly took a liking to an older, livelier song that had originally been released in 1920, four years after I was born, and later on a record played by the Paul Whiteman orchestra. It was called "The Japanese Sandman".

No matter how hard I tried to avoid it, turning my thoughts to other matters before sleeping, the Japanese Sandman returned in my dreams.

I often hummed it as I did other things. At first he was a benign, slight little figure at a distance, standing in a sunlit garden under a blossoming cherry tree. Dressed in a black cotton peasant's top with trousers, he was holding a beige sun umbrella patterned in red peonies. This Japanese Sandman conformed to the cheerful words of the lively American song to which my older sister Ailing and her friends danced. The part about him giving us the next day to start our life over again didn't seem at all sinister.

Of course, to a Buddhist like me, starting life over again can mean first dying: We are in a revolving process of being born and dying, birth and death, until we stop this cycle by practicing the way Buddha showed us to reach Nirvana: the highest of all happiness.

Over time the Japanese Sandman has changed, becoming ever more sinister. He looms from the shadows behind me. The cotton peasant outfit has given way to an impeccably tailored military dress uniform. No matter how hard I try to avoid it, turning my thoughts to other matters before sleeping, the Japanese Sandman returns in my dreams. Now, I can almost see the face of my nocturnal companion, and with dread I *know* the Japanese Sandman is coming closer. Now, he is my worst nightmare.

The next evening Mr V and I were coming home on foot (rickshaws were no longer available at night) when we saw some Japanese soldiers at a distance. We tried to walk faster to avoid them altogether, but the soldiers outflanked us and moved towards me. Mr V and I talked in Russian. They hesitated, there came a command from behind, and the soldiers moved away again. I was almost fainting in fear. I had heard of what they did to Chinese women afterwards: the thrust of rape quickly replaced by the thrust and twist of a bayonet. I peeped out from my scarf. In the background, did I see an impeccably dressed

Japanese officer? Was it Tanaka, the head of *Kempeitai*? I shivered, remembering Lidia's account of the rumours about him.

As we entered our house, Mr V spoke: "May I suggest that you give Mr Chong notice that from the end of this week you will no longer work in the evenings? Ask for more afternoon work. I think it will be safer," and with his usual polite flourish, Mr V bid me goodnight at my stairway.

By then I had completed much of Shiying's biography and was up-to-date in adding my own in between and round his. But I needed to edit it again—some parts had been hastily written. Before sleeping that night I added my account of the effect of seeing, with Lidia, the head of the *Kempeitai*, the history of the Japanese Sandman dream, now nightmare, over my lifetime and also my near encounter with the Japanese troops and possibly Tanaka.

That night, I dreamed again of the Japanese Sandman. That night, he was definitely dressed in an impeccably tailored Japanese military uniform—exactly like the one I had seen on Tanaka. In that night's dream, the Japanese Sandman seemed very near—and I *almost* saw his face.

When the perfectly groomed, coldly expressionless figure of Lieutenant-Colonel Ryukichi Tanaka entered, terror stalked Moon Palace. I looked around for an escape route but the exits were all at the other end of the room from where we dance hostesses were sitting.

Tanaka sat down at a table with a commanding view, motionless, watchful, like a bird of prey. The only sign of movement was in his eyes that looked around as if searching for someone he knew (people looked away). He soon seemed to recognize one of the dance hostesses. Tanaka came over, bowed and bought dances for the next hour.

Across the club, parties of patrons at tables began to stretch, say how late it was, pay their bill and leave. The move was gradual, surreptitious, calculated not to attract attention. Within half an hour the whole place was cleared of patrons. Some of the hostesses also gradually made their way out. The man who replenished the hot water bottles we hostesses carried to keep warm, no longer came round with his kettle. I was able to slide over along the seats where we were placed, and with relief saw I was one seat from being able to slip away myself without being noticed. However just then Tanaka turned, thanked his partner, and came towards me. He bowed his stiff, Japanese bow and asked me to dance.

By now the dance floor had emptied. The small orchestra played on and Sasha continued to sing his sad Russian songs. As usual he had come from the Balalaika to finish off the night at the Moon Palace and escort me safely home to our alleyway apartments. Tonight he had switched from evening dress to the trademark Pierrot costume and makeup he always wore as a younger singer. By 2:00 am it was well past the closing time legislated by the Japanese, and Tanaka and I were still circling the floor, the only couple, the staff too afraid to leave.

There was an eerie familiarity about the atmosphere: I was back in the claustrophobia of my recurring dream, yet I wasn't asleep. I wondered whether this was my Japanese Sandman, and shuddered. "Are you cold?" he asked in heavily (Japanese) accented Shanghainese dialect, and held me even closer.

By the piano, Sasha was still singing, singing for me. Switching from "Dark Eyes" ("Ochi chornya") in Russian, he started to croon in English the American popular song explaining the depth of his devotion: "How Deep is The Ocean? (How High is The Sky?)" Tanaka gave no sign of understanding either the Russian or English words.

On either side of the red Pierrot mouth, down Sasha's face ran a slow sludge of black eye makeup combining with the white of his cheeks. I thought that the smudges were positioned directly above the two fountains of blood that always spouted from the neck of a Chinese person beheaded at random in the street by a Japanese soldier.

Tanaka and I moved round the floor, dancing slowly, close together. Sasha's haunting voice never faltered, singing that should he ever lose me . . . the measureless sorrow . . . and weeping . . . "How Deep is The Ocean? . . . (How High is The Sky?)"

Acknowledgements

As for my previous book *Gudao, Lone Islet, The War Years in Shanghai*, for their excellent editorial guidance, my sincere thanks go to Meg Masters and Meg Taylor (recommended by Jackie Kaiser). In addition, I now thank the wonderful Jennifer Glossop, and Meg Taylor for putting me in touch. I also appreciate the inimitable Betty Jane Wylie who always helps fellow writers.

There are those who were so kind as to take the time to read and comment on the manuscript. Their conversation and advice enhanced the writing of *Shanghai Scarlet*: Poshek Fu, John Meehan, SJ, Meg Taylor, Helen Thompson and Betty Jane Wylie CM.

For their support, I appreciate Margaret Aanders, Marianne Brandis, able leader of the University Women's Club of Toronto's Writing Group (Dorothy Bremner, Lyn Friesen, Sandra Gentles, Myint Gillespie, Nancy McKillop and Christine Moore) Donald Grant, Helen Thompson and John Rigg, whose father was the member of the Hongkong and Shanghai Bank's foreign staff mentioned towards the end of this book. John's mother's letters to his grandmother, (never mailed) and written during the internment camp experience, are available at the Imperial War Museum in London.

Margaret Aanders gave me the idea of a weekly Mah Jong tournament among grocers. I thank Drs. Beth and Jerry Bentley for adding detail to the section on Chinese calligraphy, Myint Gillespie for fine-tuning the content on Buddhism, David Grant for the detailed map of old Shanghai, and Dr. Greg Leck for sending me the information about the six severed heads found in the French Concession. Carol Mark told me the story of how her mother escaped being murdered in Nanking, and Dorothy

Moller's father played the banjo in the orchestra of the Palace Hotel.

Much of the historical framework comes from Shu-mei Shih's *Lure of the Modern*, Pan Ling's *In Search of Old Shanghai*, Leo Ou-fan Lee's *Shanghai Modern*, Poshek Fu's excellent book on very much the same subject area as this one: *Passivity, Resistance and Collaboration. Intellectual Choices in Occupied Shanghai 1937-1945*, John Meehan's article, "The Savior of Shanghai, Robert Jacquinot, SJ and his safety zone in Shanghai, 1937", and Catherine Vance Yeh's *Shanghai Love*. For translations, which enabled me to read the work of Mu and his contemporaries, I am also indebted to Yomi Braester of Yale University, Jianmei Liu of the University of Maryland, Shu-mei Shih, Randolph Trumbull of Stanford University ("Five in a Nightclub"), Siu-kit Wong of the University of Hong Kong ("Black Whirlwind"), Leo Ou-fan Lee of Harvard University and in particular Sean Macdonald of McGill University for *The Shanghai Foxtrot (a Fragment) by Mu Shiying*. I also acknowledge David Hinton for his exquisite translations of the poetry of Yu Hsuan-chi.

For their special support, I thank long-time friend Lesley Duncan and my husband Ronald.

Q and A with the author

Q What first sparked your interest in the book's main subjects?
A While researching my previous book, *Gudao, Lone Islet*, I came across the Chinese modernist writers, and the tragedy of the assassination of their most brilliant member, Mu Shiying. On further reading, I became intrigued by his wife and wondered about the lack of information about her. (See Wikipedia listing of Mu Shiying for their wedding photo.) These were striking and dark times. In my first book, I of necessity did not cover in any detail the Chinese point of view. Before leaving the subject, there was more writing to do. Old Shanghai is an inherently fascinating topic for Westerners. I regard the two books as complementing each other. They provide a broad impression of Shanghai of the 1920s to 1940s from different points of view.

Q What made you persist in this interest?
A On thinking more deeply about the matter, I realized that here was a good story, which would strike a general chord.

Those who are deeply talented feel compelled to exercise that talent for their whole lives. Most continue to do so despite a lack of financial reward. Such individuals are in considerable danger in "interesting times" when powerful politicians require them to turn their abilities to political ends. Set in the turbulent 1920s and 1930s in China, *Shanghai Scarlet* provides a cameo of what has happened, and still happens, to creative people and their families in times of political turmoil.

The Chinese modernist writers were at their height in this period. Because of them, Shanghai developed as the Far Eastern hub of an important cosmopolitan literary group with links to Japan, other Asian cities, North America and Europe. One cannot help being impressed by their brilliance, and overwhelmed by the short lives and violent deaths of some. In this book I have made a serious attempt to respectfully memorialize these writers in a readable way.

Q But why concentrate on Mu Shiying?
A I have two reasons. The first relates to the sheer talent of Mu and his fervent desire to be free to write as he pleased. This is part of a universal longing for freedom and freedom of expression. We see it coming forward in the world today (2012).

In the narrow prison created by the absolutist philosophies of contemporary rival political groups, few writers of China's early modernist movement were able to stretch their wings fully. None who did so escaped that prison alive. Acknowledged as the most brilliant of his contemporaries, Mu Shiying exercised his abilities freely using innovative forms, and writing as he pleased about various subjects, latterly concentrating on modern urban life and, in particular, its sophisticated women. At least in the beginning, he believed, wrongly, that his patent lack of a political interest or agenda would assure his safety.

The second reason for concentrating on Mu is that he was, and possibly even now still is, characterized as a traitor to China. I wanted to delve into that aspect.

Q Is that everything?
A No, there was the general tragedy of other writers who survived by ceasing to write. I have no doubt that this takes place today in totalitarian states—or, as has happened in the past, that creative writing circulates in secret.

And then in particular, there was his wife, about whom so little seems to be known. I became very interested in Qiu Peipei. I have imagined Mu's true love as the ultimate, modern urban woman, a soignée, rich and well-educated courtesan, who like Mu Shiying enjoyed Western culture and dancing. However, Qiu Peipei was in a prison of her own, created by an increasingly frightening nightmare from which there seemed to be no escape.

Q In a book such as, *Shanghai Scarlet,* where historical fact is interwoven with fiction, the reader may like to know which is historical fact, and also what happened to the real people whose names have been given to the fictional characters.

A Part 1: (Historical Fact)
In addition to the facts mentioned in the Author's Note, the main events of Mu Shiying's life, such as his Ningpo birth, move to Shanghai, marriage to Qiu Peipei and sojourn with her in Hong Kong, also different employments and writings as well as problems he and his group had with political factions are historical fact. Mu's meal with Ji and summons to a meeting with Lu Xun are also historical fact, as are his visits to Japan and funeral at the Japanese headquarters. All these have been brought alive by fiction. Throughout the text there are sprinklings of historical information about events in China and the wider world.

Although the leisurely courtship and entertainment skills of courtesans were going out of fashion in Shanghai, during the frenetic 1920s and 1930s courtesans from Canton, Qiu Peipei's birthplace, lived on the other side of Soochow Creek from the city centre.

In reality, Mu Shiying died when he was shot in the back while on his way to work in a rickshaw, on Foochow Road. This episode is mentioned in the book as a failed assassination attempt.

At the time of publication, Mu's name is not listed on the Chekiang province website among other authors born in the province. Also, although the collected works of Liu Na'ou have been published, those of Mu have not. It seems Mu continues with the stain on his memory (that he was a traitor to China). In the 1970s, however, Mu's friend, Ji Kangyi, revealed his status as a double agent for both the Wang régime and the KMT. As well, Wikipedia cites Professor David Der-Wang of Harvard University as saying that Mu's family came forward with evidence not only for his role as a Nationalist double agent, but also for Mu's underground Marxist work. Perhaps this book will help modify the view of Mu as a traitor.

Golden ferrets are actually found in the Peking (Beijing) hutongs/alleyways, which sadly may not now exist. Most of those remaining were torn down for the 2008 Olympics. At the time of writing, Shanghai's alleyways have been condemned, and are being torn down.

Finally, for another mixing of historical fact and fiction, I cast Ryukichi Tanaka, brutal head of Shanghai's *Kempeitai* (Japanese Secret Police) as the Japanese Sandman.

A Part 2: (What Happened to the Real People)
So far as what happened to Mu's contemporaries is concerned, some such as **Shi Zhecun** survived by withdrawing inland, and forsaking writing, turning to teaching Chinese literature from the remote past. Shi (1905-2003) further survived hard labour during the Cultural Revolution, and lived into his late 90s, a major custodian of this past time.

After 1945, **Dai Wangshu**, who in Hong Kong had been imprisoned then released by the Japanese, moved to Shanghai and then Peking. There he soon died of an accidental overdose of medication for asthma developed during that incarceration at which time **Mu Lijuan** had divorced him, and later married a collaborationist author.

Xu Chi, Dai's protégé and best man at his wedding to Mu Lijuan, converted to Marxism in the late 1930s. He lived to visit the United States in the 1980s, expressing great enthusiasm for Chicago's skyscrapers, which reminded him of the wonderful Shanghai of the past. Xu commited suicide in 1996, by jumping out of a window of his house in Wuhan, reputedly out of *ennui* with old age. He was in his early eighties.

Du Heng went to Taiwan, where he used his influence to prevent the KMT from using the media as a political vehicle and died in 1965 aged 58.

Feng Xuefeng, creator of the Third Category writer, served in the Communist Party for many years but fell foul of their doctrine by advocating greater freedom in writing. The Party sentenced him to forced labour during which he died in 1976.

The outline of **Alexander Vertinsky**'s life during this time is largely historical fact. He never lost that love for Mother Russia and in 1943 the Russian government, via Mr Molotov, finally granted Vertinsky permission to return with his family. Until his death in 1957, Alexander Vertinsky continued as an entertainer much loved throughout Russia. As distinguished actors, his daughters continue their father's tradition.

In early 1944, for treatment of an old wound from a 1939 assassination attempt, **Wang Jingwei** went to Japan. He died there in November of that year. Some were of the opinion that the Japanese doctors had murdered him.

Shortly after the (fictional) party to celebrate Dai Wangshu's return from France, **Zeng Pu** died. His son, **Zeng Xubai**, tied his fortunes to those of the KMT, followed them to Taiwan, and lived to a great age, highly honoured for his literary work.

In 1938 **Father Jacquinot S.J.** was inducted to the Légion d'Honneur. He received the ultimate token of respect when the poor rickshaw puller taking him to this ceremony refused payment, saying that carrying Father Jacquinot was reward in itself. In 1940 Father Jacquinot returned to France to help refugees in the outskirts of Paris and in 1945 headed a Vatican delegation for refugees in Berlin. After his death from exhaustion a few months later, aged 68, the Jacquinot zone was cited in the Commentary to the Geneva Conventions of 1949 as an "encouraging precedent" for a neutral zone in time of war.

The fearless cartoonist **Huang Yao** survived the war and continued with his career as an artist, retiring to Penang and then Kuala Lumpur to be with his son and family, and dying in 1987.

With other Wang régime leaders, **Lin Bosheng**, publicist for the Wang régime, was executed in 1946.

Unlike some members of his band, the jazz musician **Earl Whaley** survived the war and returned to the United States where he lived at least into his sixties.

In 1940, the brilliant entertainment entrepreneur, **Zhang Shankun**, founded the United China Movie Picture Company. He produced the patriotic film *Hua Mulan Joins the Army*. It was a success in Shanghai and in the occupied territories, but at Chinese New Year, in the unoccupied territories, Nationalist sympathizers burned a copy of the film.

Using his business and interpersonal skills, and also his wits, Zhang Shankun kept the Chinese film industry flourishing during the Japanese occupation. With help from the moderate Japanese filmmaker Kawakita Namagasa, Zhang used Japanese funding to entertain the Chinese during this devastating time. (The Chinese people persisted in boycotting all films made entirely by the Japanese.)

After the war, Zhang Shankun relocated to Hong Kong where unlike many other Chinese filmmakers he refused to sell out to the mainland Communists. Instead in 1949 he re-established his company under the original Xinhua (New China Pictures Company) name. Until his death in 1956 aged 51, Zhang concentrated on improving colour photography in films, and also shooting them in foreign locations, namely Japan and Taiwan.

Zhang Ruogu (1905-1960), a prolific literary figure in Shanghai, continually presented Shanghai as part of a European, and indeed world, modern culture. In his "Café Forum" he pointed out that coffee houses provided the stimulus of coffee, long talks among friends (building important social networks among contemporary authors) and the charming presence of coffee house waitresses, similar to those in the Tokyo bars and coffee houses before the 1923 earthquake. (After the earthquake, the Tokyo coffee houses proliferated and became not only the haunts of intellectuals, but also the symbol of modernity for the wider population.)

N.B. For a comprehensive and well-written account of Shanghai's literary scene, read: Poshek Fu, *Passivity, Resistance and Collaboration, Intellectual Choices in Occupied Shanghai, 1937-1945*, Stanford University Press, 1993

You may also like to look at *War and Popular Culture, Resistance in Modern China 1937-1945*, Chang-tai Hung, in the University of California Press E-Books Collection.

For further comprehensive information on writers and other media of the period, consult the writings of Professor Poshek Fu of the University of Illinois.

Suggested Discussion for Book Clubs

- Discuss your overall view of *Shanghai Scarlet*
- What, if anything, do you like about it?
- What, if anything, do you dislike?
- Did the beginning spark your interest?
- What do you think of the book's ending?
- Different Chinese writers reacted to the political situation in which they found themselves in differing ways. Describe the actions you would favour in such a situation.
- In your opinion, was Shiying temperamentally capable of taking an approach that was different from the one he actually followed?
- From the information in this book, do you think he really was a traitor to his country?
- What do you perceive as the <u>main</u> thrust of this novel? Is it a love story, discussion of the political situation in Shanghai (or in China) of that time, simply a good story overall, a tragedy, a story with relevance for today in general . . . a combination of all these . . .

Select Bibliography

Poshek Fu, *Passivity, Resistance and Collaboration, Intellectual Choices in Occupied Shanghai, 1937-1945,* Stanford University Press, 1993

David Hinton, trans., and ed., *Classical Chinese Poetry, An Anthology,* Farrar, Strauss and Giroux, New York

Virgil K.Y. Ho, *Understanding Canton: Rethinking Popular Culture in the Republican Period,* Oxford University Press 2005

Leo Ou-fan Lee, *Shanghai Modern, The Flowering of a New Urban Culture in Shanghai 1930-1945,* Harvard University Press, Cambridge Massachusetts 1999

Hanchao Lu, *Beyond the Neon Lights, Everyday Shanghai in the early Twentieth Century,* University of California Press, 1999

John Meehan, SJ, "The Savior of Shanghai, Robert Jacquinot, SJ and his safety zone in Shanghai, 1937", *Company* magazine, March 2006: 17-21

Anthony Wan-hoi Pak, *The School of New Sensibilities in the 1930s: a study of Liu Na'ou and Mu Shiying's Fiction,* PhD. Dissertation, University of Toronto

Shu-mei Shih, *The Lure of the Modern, writing modernism in semi-colonial China 1917-1937,* University of California Press 2001

Mu Shiying, *Shanghai Foxtrot* translated by Sean Macdonald of McGill University: *The Shanghai Foxtrot, (a Fragment) by Mu Shiying* available on Project Muse

G.R.G.Worcester, *The Junk Man Smiles,* Chatto and Windus, London 1959

Catherine Vance Yeh, *Shanghai Love,* University of Washington Press 2006

Margaret Blair has enjoyed three careers: as teacher, social marketing researcher, mother of three and grandmother of three.

The author of *Gudao, Lone Islet, The War Years in Shanghai,* Margaret continues her entertaining life in writing. She lives with her husband, an emeritus professor of the University of Toronto, beside a river, among Mennonite farms, in Ontario, Canada.

For more: www.margaretblair.com

CPSIA information can be obtained at www.ICGtesting.com
Printed in the USA
LVOW062322130312

272927LV00001B/7/P